LP FIC REAY

Reay, Katherine

Dear Mr. Knightley

S

⁴/14

W9-AAX-510

White County Regional Library System
113 East Pleasure Avenue
Searcy, Arkansas 72143

Dear Mr. Knightley

Center Point
Large Print

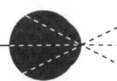

**This Large Print Book carries the
Seal of Approval of N.A.V.H.**

Dear Mr. Knightley

KATHERINE REAY

CENTER POINT LARGE PRINT
THORNDIKE, MAINE

This Center Point Large Print edition is published in the year 2014 by arrangement with Thomas Nelson Publishers.

Copyright © 2013 by Katherine Reay.

All rights reserved.

Quotation from THE VOYAGE OF THE DAWN TREADER by C. S. Lewis © copyright C. S. Lewis Pte Ltd 1952. Used by permission.

Scriptures taken from the Holy Bible, New International Version®, NIV®. Copyright © 1973, 1978, 1984, 2011 by Biblica, Inc.™ Used by permission of Zondervan. All rights reserved worldwide. www.zondervan.com. The "NIV" and "New International Version" are trademarks registered in the United States Patent and Trademark Office by Biblica, Inc.™

This novel is a work of fiction. Names, characters, places, and incidents are either products of the author's imagination or used fictitiously. All characters are fictional, and any similarity to people living or dead is purely coincidental.

The text of this Large Print edition is unabridged. In other aspects, this book may vary from the original edition. Printed in the United States of America on permanent paper. Set in 16-point Times New Roman type.

ISBN: 978-1-61173-973-2

Library of Congress Cataloging-in-Publication Data

Reay, Katherine, 1970–
Dear Mr. Knightley / Katherine Reay. —
    Center Point Large Print edition.
    pages ; cm
    ISBN 978-1-61173-973-2 (library binding : alk. paper)
    1. Women graduate students—Fiction. 2. Self-disclosure—Fiction.
    3. Deception—Fiction. 4. Large type books. I. Title.
PS3618.E23D43 2014
813′.6—dc23
                                                          2013035314

To Matthew, Elizabeth, and Mary Margaret—
for your unfailing love and support.

And to Mason—who gave me the idea
in the first place.

(Much like Sam, the author couldn't help herself—
she "borrowed" this from the movie *Anne of Avonlea*.
Books by L. M. Montgomery)

Dear Sir,

It has been a year since I turned down your generous offer. Father John warned me at the time that I was making a terrible mistake, but I wouldn't listen. He felt that by dismissing that opportunity I was injuring not only myself, but all the foster children helped by your foundation.

I hope any perceived ingratitude on my part didn't harm anyone else's dreams. I wasn't ungrateful; I just wanted to leave Grace House. A group home is a difficult place to live, and I'd been there for eight years. And even though I knew graduate school meant more education and better job prospects, it also meant living at Grace House another two years. At the time I couldn't face that prospect.

My heart has always been in my books and writing, but I couldn't risk losing a paying job to pursue a dream. Now I'm ready to try. Not because I failed, but because this degree gives me the chance to link my passion with my livelihood.

Please let me know if the grant is still available. I will understand if you have selected another candidate.

Sincerely,
Samantha Moore

Dear Ms. Moore,

The grant for full tuition to the master's program at Northwestern University's Medill School of Journalism remains available. At the strong recommendation of Father John, and due to the confidence he has in you, the director of the Dover Foundation has agreed to give you this second chance. There is, however, one stipulation. The director wants to receive personal progress letters from you as reassurance that this decision was the right one. You may write to him as you would to a journal, letting him know how your studies are going. He has opened a post office box for this purpose so you won't feel the added pressure of an immediate connection to him or to the foundation. Additionally, he will not write back, but asks that you write to him regularly about "things that matter."

He recognizes that this is an unusual requirement, but the foundation needs to know that its resources are being used in the best way possible. Given your sudden change of heart, he feels it is not too much to ask. To make this easier for you, he will also remain anonymous. You may write to him at this address under the name George Knightley.

Sincerely,
Laura Temper
Personal Assistant to Mr. G. Knightley

Dear Mr. Knightley,

Thank you so much for giving me this opportunity. I submitted my application to Medill this morning. I had to use a couple papers on Dickens and Austen in place of the journalism samples requested. While that may count against me, I felt the rest of my application was strong.

If you will allow, I want to honor Father John's trust and yours by explaining my "sudden change of heart," as Ms. Temper described it. When I graduated college last spring, I had two opportunities: your grant to fund graduate school or a job at Ernst & Young. In my eagerness to leave Grace House and conquer the world, I chose the job. Six weeks ago I was fired. At the exit meeting my boss claimed I was "unengaged," especially with regard to peer and client interactions. I did good work there, Mr. Knightley. Good solid work. But "relating" in the workplace is important too, I gather. That's where I failed.

I'm guessing from your literary choice of pseudonym that you are very likely acquainted with another admirable character from fiction— Elizabeth Bennet, Jane Austen's complex and enchanting heroine. At Ernst & Young I tried to project Lizzy's boldness and spirit, but clearly she had a confidence and charm that was more than I could sustain on a daily basis. So now here I am, back at Grace House, taking advantage of the state's willingness to provide a home for me till I'm twenty-five if I stay in school.

Nevertheless, Father John still doubts me and couldn't resist a lecture this morning. I tried to listen, but my eyes wandered around his office: photographs of all the children who have passed through Grace House cover every space that isn't taken up with books. He loves murder mysteries: Agatha Christie, James Patterson, Alex Powell, P. D. James, Patricia Cornwell . . . I've read most of them. The first day we met, right before I turned fifteen, he challenged me to stretch beyond the classics.

"Are you listening, Sam?" Father John finally noticed my wandering eyes. "The Medill program is straight up your alley. You're a great reader and writer."

" 'I deserve neither such praise nor such censure. I am not a great reader, and I have pleasure in many things.' " Elizabeth Bennet has a useful reply for every situation.

Father John gave a small smile, and I flinched. "What if I can't do this?" I asked. "Maybe it's a mistake."

He sat back in his chair and took a slow breath. Eyebrows down, mouth in a line.

"Then turn this down—again—and find another job. Pound the pavement quickly, though. I can give you a couple weeks here to get on your feet, then my hands are tied." He leaned forward. "Sam, I'll always help you. But after this, if you're not in school, Grace House is closed to you. This foundation helps a lot of kids here, and I won't jeopardize that support because you can't commit. So decide right now."

A tear rolled down my cheek. Father John never gets charged up, but I deserved it. I should only be grateful to you both, and here I was questioning your help. But help is hard, Mr. Knightley— even when I desperately need it. Every foster placement of my childhood was intended to help me; every new social worker tried to help my case; when I was sent back home at twelve, the judge meant to help my life too . . . I'm so tired of help.

"I'm sorry, Father John, you're right. I want this grant and I asked for it again. I must seem so ungrateful to you, to be questioning again."

"You don't, Sam, and I can understand wanting to stand alone. Even in the best of times and circumstances, it's hard to accept help—"

In the end, Father John believed my commitment. I hope you do too. Here is our agreement: you will pay for graduate school, and I will write you letters that give an honest accounting of my life and school—and you will never write back. That simple, right?

Thank you for that, Mr. Knightley—your

anonymity. Honesty is easier when you have no face and no real name. And honesty, for me, is very easy on paper.

I also want to assure you that while I may not relate well to people in the real world, I shine in school. It's paper-based. I will do your grant justice, Mr. Knightley. I'll shine at Medill.

I know I've said more than was necessary in this letter, but I need you to know who I am. We need to have an honest beginning, even if it's less impressive than Lizzy Bennet's.

Sincerely,
Samantha Moore

Dear Mr. Knightley,

Each and every moment things change. For the most part, I loathe it. Change never works in my favor—as evidenced by so many foster placements, a holdup at a Chicago White Hen, getting fired from Ernst & Young, and so many other changes in my life I'd like to forget. But I needed one more—a change of my own making—so I pursued your grant again.

But it's not of my own making, is it?

Father John told me this morning that he was the one who proposed journalism for me—it was not an original requirement for your grant. I wouldn't have chosen it myself. My professor at Roosevelt College said I produced some of the best work on Austen, Dickens, and the Brontës he'd ever read. I'm *good* at fiction, Mr. Knightley. And I don't think it's right that Father John took away my choice. I'm twenty-three years old; I should be the author of the changes in my life.

I went to Father John and explained all this. I feel he has arbitrarily forced me into journalism —a field I don't know and don't write. "You need to undo that," I pleaded. "They'll listen to you."

Father John closed his eyes. One might think

he'd fallen asleep, but I knew better. He was praying. He does that—a lot.

Minutes passed. He opened his eyes and zeroed in on me. Sometimes I feel his eyes are tired, but not at that moment. They were piercing and direct. I knew his answer before he opened his mouth.

"Sam, I won't . . . but you can. Write the foundation's director and ask." Father John stared into my eyes, measuring his words. "Don't lie. Don't tell them I've changed my mind. I have not. I am wholly against a change in program."

"How can you say that?" My own shrill voice surprised me.

"I've known you for eight years, Sam. I've watched you grow, I've watched you succeed, and I've watched you retreat. I want the best for you, and with every fiber of my being, I am convinced that 'the best' is not more fiction, but finding your way around in the real world and its people."

I opened my mouth to protest, but he held up his hand. "Consider carefully. If the foundation is unwilling to alter your grant, you may accept or you may walk away. You always have a choice."

"That's not fair."

Father John's eyes clouded. "My dear, what in your life has ever come close to fair? That's not how this life works." He leaned forward and stretched his hands out across the desk. "I'm sorry, Sam. If I could protect you from any more pain, I would. But I can only pray and do the very best God calls me to do. If I'm wrong about this, I hope that someday you will forgive me."

" 'My temper would perhaps be called resentful.—My good opinion once lost is lost forever.' " When Elizabeth Bennet doesn't come through, one can always count on Mr. Darcy to provide the right response. I shook my head and, quoting no one, said, "I won't forgive you, Father John. I don't forgive." And I walked out.

I don't care if that was ungenerous, Mr. Knightley. He overstepped, and he's wrong. So now I'm asking you: Will you let me decide?

Sincerely,
Samantha Moore

Dear Ms. Moore,

Please forgive me for violating our agreement already, but I felt your question warranted a personal reply.

I understand your anger. It is hard when others hold power over you. Rest assured, your situation is not unique. There is very little any of us chooses in isolation.

Through my foundation, Father John has helped five young adults from Grace House. One attended junior college; another, trade school; one graduated from cosmetology school; and two successfully completed residential treatment programs. Each individual has grown closer to whole.

Father John not only fulfilled all the grant requirements for your application, but wrote me an additional five pages outlining your writing abilities, your gifts, and your determination. His decision to recommend journalism school was not made lightly, as you well know. Remember that, and remember what he has meant in your life. Don't throw away friends and mentors carelessly. They are rare.

I trust Father John's prayerful counsel and judgment, and stand with his original recommendation. My foundation will only award the grant for Medill's master's program.

The choice to accept it or not is yours, Ms. Moore.

Sincerely,
G. Knightley

Dear Mr. Knightley,

I didn't withdraw my application. I made my choice and now I sit, waiting for Medill to accept or reject me.

In the meantime I've settled into my old ways and my old jobs: I resumed tutoring at Buckhorn Cottage (Grace House's cottage for 8- to 13-year-old boys) and I picked up a few shifts at the public library. I've been working at that library for a decade now, even before I moved to Grace House for the first time.

I was about fifteen when I first arrived at Grace House. Father John took me to his office and invited me to sit. No one had ever done that— invited me to do anything. He chatted for a few minutes, then handed me an Anne Perry novel.

"Detective Huber got your file for me, Sam, and it's full of references to *Pride and Prejudice*, *Jane Eyre*, *Oliver Twist*, and other great classics. I think you must like to read. So until I get some of your favorites, would you like to read one of mine?"

The thick hardback had a picture of a Victorian house on the cover. I slowly turned the pages, hoping if I feigned interest in his book, he'd take me to wherever I'd be staying and leave me alone.

He didn't. "This is one of the first mysteries I ever read. Now I'm hooked. I've got about a hundred titles over there." Father John pointed to his bookcase and waited.

I looked up.

"Come to my office anytime you want a new one. I picked that for you because it takes place in England in the nineteenth century, about the same time as your favorites."

I put the book down, never breaking eye contact. A show of strength, I thought.

He sighed and leaned back in his chair. "Your choice. I'm sure I can get some classics this week. Or you can go to the public library; it's on the corner of State and Van Buren."

I wanted to say I knew exactly where the library was, but that would require speaking to him, so I simply slid the book into my lap. I wasn't going to admit, even to myself, that I liked the man—and still do. In spite of how angry I am with him at the moment, I know that Father John has always been on my side.

He welcomed me at fifteen and again at eighteen, after I tried to move out. And now at twenty-three, despite my heated words, he's opened Grace House's door once more. So while I'm here, I will listen to his lectures and I will try to do what he asks. I owe him that much.

I'll even try to play nice with Morgan, my new roommate in Independence Cottage . . .

"She's had a rough time, Sam. She turned eighteen a couple days ago and her foster family ended the placement."

"She can go on her own. Isn't that a good thing?"

"Not without her GED. You know how important that is. She's testing next month, then joining the army." Father John stared right through me.

"Why are you telling me this?"

"I'm asking you to be kind. Morgan's defense mechanisms are different from yours, and it may be rough going. Please don't make waves."

"I make waves?"

"Like the ocean, kiddo. Then you retreat before they hit the sand."

Ouch.

So I'm being kind, but Morgan isn't making it easy. We were cleaning the kitchen the other day and I told her about your grant. I was trying to be friendly. She was not.

"You're selling yourself for school? I can't believe you'd give it up for tuition. At least get some money or clothes from the deal."

"Morgan, shut up. You're disgusting. It isn't like that. I write letters to an address in New York and I get my tuition paid to graduate school."

"I bet a lot of girls start out that way." Morgan stopped washing her dishes and stared at me. She smiled slowly, almost cruelly. "Letters will

20

be worse for you anyway. Good luck with that."

"What do you mean 'worse for me'? I can write a few letters, Morgan. That's what I do. I write."

"Honesty will kill you. You're a coward, and you'll lie. That makes the whole deal a lie." She put her plate down and walked away.

She's not right. I'm not a coward, and I will be honest in these letters. Simply because I don't blab my business to the world like Mrs. Bennet doesn't mean I'm a coward. I'm prudent when dealing with people. That's smart. Wouldn't you agree?

But Morgan brings up a good point—her only one so far. Have you read *Jane Eyre*? There's a part when Mr. Rochester meets Jane and asks if she expects a present. Adele, his ward, believes everyone should receive presents, daily. Jane isn't so sure. She replies, "They are generally thought pleasant things . . . a present has many faces to it, has it not? And one should consider all before pronouncing an opinion as to its nature."

You've led me to believe your gift has one face, Mr. Knightley. I'll leave it at that.

Sincerely,
Samantha Moore

P.S. Okay, I can't leave it . . .

If you are truly a "Mr. Knightley," I can do this. I can write these letters. I trust you chose that name as a reflection of your own character.

21

George Knightley is a good and honorable man—even better than Fitzwilliam Darcy, and few women put anyone above Mr. Darcy.

Yes, Darcy's got the tempestuous masculinity and brooding looks, but Knightley is a kinder, softer man with no pretense or dissimilation. Yes, he's a gentleman. And I can write with candor to a silent gentleman, and I can believe that he will not violate this trust.

I admit that if you had a face and a real name—or a nefarious name—it might be different. Morgan might be right. But as I sit here and think about this, I feel comfortable. See what power a name holds?

Dear Mr. Knightley,

I thought about you last night and stayed up reading *Emma*. I adore her, though she's out of my reach. Can you imagine such confidence and assurance of your own significance? Do you know anyone who would dare declare that he or she "cannot really change for the better"? I'd like to believe that—even for a moment.

But no, I gravitate toward Fanny Price, morally spot-on, but commonly thought dull. Or Anne Elliot, demure and kind, not one to stand out in a crowd. Or the ever-practical and sensible Charlotte Lucas. Those dear friends I understand. I found my first copy of *Pride and Prejudice* on the 'L' when I was nine. I loved Austen's world. It was safe and I could breathe. By the time I looked up, the book was disintegrating from wear and I had barely registered two foster placement switches. My "inability to relate" caused a few headaches at the Department of Children and Family Services. And that's never changed. I've told you already about my similar failure at Ernst & Young. But trying to relate always seems to end badly for me. My last real attempt was four years ago.

Cara was my roommate at Charing Cottage. She was a lot like Elizabeth Bennet's little sister

Lydia—silly, vivacious, cute, and deceptively street savvy. And as Lydia doggedly pursued Wickham, so Cara was consumed with Ron, a slimy dropout who pushed drugs on middle school kids. And if Cara was Lydia, I'm sure she saw me as a righteous Aunt Gardiner: "And there was my aunt, all the time I was dressing, preaching and talking as if she were reading a sermon . . ." Our differences made us a good team: I helped Cara in school and she shielded me by absorbing all the oxygen in the room.

So at eighteen Cara and I moved out of Grace House together to chase the dream: college, jobs, our own place, no social workers, no tracking . . . I worked out the budget; Cara found the apartment and a third roommate, some girl I'd never met, Jocelyn. Hannah, who is now head girls counselor at Grace House, drove me to the apartment. I knew the moment I stepped from her car that I'd made a mistake.

Hannah grabbed my wrist as we looked up at the building. People were watching us. We both felt it, though we saw no one. I hurried inside, trying to push away my feelings of exposure and vulnerability.

In the lobby, an acrid urine reek assaulted me. That, combined with the clang of the metal doors and the greasy thin walls, made me feel six years old again and back home with Mom. It felt so real. Have you ever confused your senses?

Something tastes like another thing smells? This was one of those moments. I think I swayed, because Hannah shoved me against the wall and pushed me to my knees. The world turned blue.

"You don't have to do this, Sam. Cara makes her own choices and you can't save her. Come back to Grace House with me." She rubbed my back, whispering in my ear.

"I'm fine. I just needed to catch my breath." I pushed against the wall to stand.

"It's more than that."

"No. It's my life now."

"You sound like Cara. Are you going to quit school too?"

Her tone infuriated me. I had worked hard to get into college. "I'm not scared of work, Hannah. Grace House isn't my summer camp."

"But Grace House is free, Sam. How will you pay for this? The 'L,' your food, your rent? And it isn't even safe."

"I'll be fine. I've got my job at the library. I can study there. I've got part-time work at the White Hen near Roosevelt. I'll carry pepper spray." I clenched my jaw and moved around her.

You can only hear so much about options you don't have. This wasn't my dream, but it would do. The idea of going back to Grace House felt like failure . . .

We headed down the hall and into the apartment. It was the size of an old school bus

25

and just as yellow and decrepit. The two bedrooms were no bigger than shoe boxes. The walls held hints of buttercup, but age had soured them. Or maybe it was the yellow light bulbs—everything held a bitter tinge. There were bars on the grimy windows, one tiny moldy bathroom, a kitchenette, and a small central living room. The yellow bulbs in there muddied the gray tones of the walls, carpet, and furniture. Cara and Jocelyn brought in my duffel and tossed around their stuff to make room. I just stood there—lonely and bereft. This was life— this was my future.

Hannah hugged me and left without another word or backward glance. Cara grinned and took over commentary. I didn't hear a word—as usual, I'd already retreated. I figured this was how Nicholas Nickleby felt when he was forced to work at Squeer's squalid Yorkshire School. That was a dark, horrific place, where Mr. Squeer beat life and hope from his students. And those few months beat the life from me too. Hope had died long before.

I don't remember much, to be honest. I worked all the time, studied, and subsisted on granola bars, ramen noodles, and the semi-spoiled half-price fruit at work. My last White Hen shift ended at midnight and I rode the 'L' home to begin again the next day. Until one night . . .

Dickens wrote Nicholas a glorious exit from

Squeer's repulsive school. Young Nickleby beat Squeer with his own cane, freed the boys, and even saved one crippled boy's life by taking him away. My departure was less heroic. I got the beat-down.

I still blush when I think about the names Cara called me as I packed to leave.

"I can't stay here, Cara. I got fired. They said the holdup was my fault. Without the job, I can't pay the rent."

"So get another!"

"Do you know what that's like? A gun held to your head? Your life doesn't flash before your eyes; it stops. Mine stopped, and there was nothing, Cara—nothing in me. I didn't exist."

That's what scared me the most, and the one thing I've never confessed to anyone before, Mr. Knightley. In those few moments, in that White Hen at midnight, I ceased to exist. I was alive, but there was no me. Is that what my boss at Ernst & Young discovered too?

"Grow up, Sam. Get more work." Cara's cold voice shook me.

"I can't. I'd have to quit school," I sobbed. I hated such weakness. Cara despised it too.

"Then quit! You owe us!" She grabbed my book off the counter and tore it to shreds. "You and your stupid books. Eat them, Sam. Live on that. We need your rent!"

"That's all you need! That's why I got my own

room. It isn't even mine. I know Jocelyn sleeps in there when I'm not here, and I bet you do too! I don't live here. No one can call this living!" I'm not used to yelling, but I gave it my best shot. Austen would never approve.

"You're never here! You wanna be here more? Quit school!"

"School's all I've got. It's the only thing that can change all this."

"Ronnie says—"

"No. Don't give me advice from Ronnie. I don't care what he says or even what you think, Cara. Not anymore." My life felt like the torn pages scattered at my feet. I needed to get back to school, get close to my books, and return to a life that made sense—even if that meant living at Grace House. So I grabbed my duffel, shoved a few things into it, and left.

While Cara only wanted freedom from the "system," my dream was for more. I wanted "normal." On the surface it means paying your rent, going to dinner with friends, sipping lattés at Starbucks, and working a good job with benefits. Everything Ernst & Young offered, and everything I lost. But deeper, Mr. Knightley, it's living a life that flows and is not dominated by worry or fear or scarcity. Isn't that the American Dream?

And I still want it. I want it so badly I can taste it. But now I see the hint of more. If I can conquer

Medill and journalism, then maybe I can achieve "normal" and actually like what I do—write for a living. Maybe this is the great leap that will work.

Sincerely,
Sam Moore

Dear Mr. Knightley,

This is my last letter. Thank you for the opportunity, but I didn't get into Medill. I was wait-listed. It means the same as rejected.

Father John can give me a couple weeks while I find more work. He suggested I enroll in Roosevelt's grad school night program in order to stay here, but I refuse to be that pathetic. It's time to go.

I'll keep my library job and find extra work. I filled out five applications today alone. I like the barista position at Starbucks best. It pays well and offers benefits for part-time workers. There are no full-time positions available.

Thank you, Mr. Knightley.

Sincerely,
Sam Moore

Dear Ms. Moore,

Mr. Knightley requests that you continue your letters until you hear definitively from the Medill program. Wait-listed at the nation's best journalism school constitutes an accomplishment rather than a defeat. Should you gain admittance, it would be unfortunate for you to have violated the terms of this grant prematurely.

Sincerely,
Laura Temper
Personal Assistant to
G. Knightley

Dear Mr. Knightley,

Thank you for such optimistic thinking. I will continue to write, for now. I still haven't heard from Starbucks, but I got turned down at Macy's and two legal firms. Desperation claws and chokes a bit more now. On to another topic, any topic . . .

A new kid named Kyle moved into Buckhorn Cottage last week. I hate him. That's not true; he makes me hate myself—and that's worse. Kyle's only thirteen, but he intimidates me. I'm five foot ten, so that's not easy to do. But Kyle's already about five eight, and his features aren't small, cute, and kidlike. He's got a strong nose, his hair is shaved close to his head, and his eyes are the hardest I've ever seen. It took him thirty seconds to pick out the weak and timid boys, and he has spent every moment since torturing each of them. Until yesterday . . .

Hannah dropped by Buckhorn as I was tutoring some boys in math. She noticed Kyle twisting nine-year-old Jaden's arm in the living room and told him to stop. Kyle shoved Jaden against the wall and came after her. He grabbed her shoulder and swung a punch, and I thought she was going to die.

But teeny-tiny Hannah swung her forearm out

to block his punch. He threw another and she blocked it again, slicing her arm in a high arc above her head. Kyle swung again, lunging simultaneously. Hannah blocked his strike with another sweep of her arm as she stepped to the side.

Kyle righted himself and stared at her through narrowed eyes. The moment lengthened, then he backed away, clearly stunned.

"We done now, Kyle?"

He nodded slowly.

"Wise choice." Hannah lowered her arms and sighed. "Don't bully the boys, Kyle, or I'll make sure you get moved outta here."

Kyle stared at her. We all stared.

"Yes, ma'am." Kyle ducked his head and walked away.

Hannah turned to me, completely relaxed. "Sam, I just finished a wonderful book. I'll bring it by after I'm finished in the office. Will you be in your cottage?"

"Umm . . . Hannah? How did you do that?"

"It's not hard. That's first-degree black belt stuff. I'll show you later." And she breezed out. I didn't teach long division coherently after that.

I practically tackled Hannah when she stopped by last night. I'm never eager to chat, but I've known Hannah for years, and everything I knew or assumed had been completely flipped. No pun intended.

"Where'd you learn that? Why'd you never tell me? That was unbelievable!"

"Yeah, I can't believe Kyle walked away like that. He even found me in the office to apologize." Hannah flopped on my couch. "I think I'm going to like that kid."

"No one could like that kid."

Hannah hesitated. "I do, Sam."

"Anyway, tell me how you did it." I knew she thought me harsh, so I pushed her past thinking about Kyle.

"You want me to show you?"

For the next ten minutes I pretended to punch her and she blocked every attempt. Ramp up the power and speed, and I can imagine Kyle's surprise.

"Is that karate?"

"Tae kwon do."

"What's the difference?" *How can it matter?*

"Karate is from Japan. Tae kwon do, Korea."

"How did I not know this about you?"

"That I'm Korean?" Hannah smiled. Then she considered me for a moment. She finally said, "You know, Sam, there's a lot you don't see because you don't choose to. I've studied martial arts since I was nine. It's a big part of who I am. But I doubt Jane Austen would find it ladylike."

"You're probably right, but knock-offs like *Pride and Prejudice and Zombies* make Lizzy Bennet an amazing fighter. I just read one that had demure Anne Elliot from *Persuasion* throwing punches."

Hannah sighed and looked away. Did I say something wrong? She left soon after that. Did I miss something? Those questions kept me up half the night. And the whole conversation irritated me because I suspected she was right: I only see what I want to see.

And then today, I added something else to my pool of self-reflection: I only do what I want to do—even if it costs others dearly.

It all started this morning when I stopped at Buckhorn to return some corrected math work sheets. Kyle was rude, as always, and I got ticked that Hannah got respect and I didn't. Call it jealousy. So when Father John called me later today and asked me to find Kyle, who had missed his anger management session this afternoon, I was already on the offensive.

I started my search at the high school track a few blocks away, where I'd occasionally seen Kyle when I was there running laps myself. Sure enough, he was there. It struck me that racing him might earn me some respect.

"What do you want? You—" He sneered as I approached, and started pacing like a caged tiger, circling me. He acted tough, but a familiar glimmer of vulnerability gave him away.

"Hey! Don't say it!" I reached for tough.

"Say what?"

"You were about to call me something nasty. At Grace House you can't swear without getting detention, but I bet you've got an amazing arsenal. Don't say something you'll regret."

"I don't regret nothin'."

"You might."

He thrust his chin up and glared at me. This boy knows how to hate.

"I know. I don't like you either, but we're both runners. Maybe we have more in common than we realize."

"We ain't friends, you—"

"I said nothing about friends." I looked at the track. "I bet I can whip your butt." Now I had his attention.

"You can't beat me. A skinny white girl like—"

"You scared?" I cut him off with a challenge because that's how you trap a boy, in case you're interested. You dare him. I looked down at his legs. They aren't kid legs. At thirteen, Kyle's legs have enough muscle definition that I questioned my great idea. Yet I refused to back down.

"And stop discriminating. You think because you're a boy or because you're black that you can beat me? You can't." I poked my finger into his chest.

The poke may have been overkill. His eyes flashed to the finger, to my face, and then to the track. "Name it."

"One mile, if you can keep up." I suspected he

was faster than me, but a mile takes more than speed. It takes stamina—my strength. Anything longer, he'd probably refuse.

"Let's go, you—"

"Save the smack and run." I tapped the timer button on my watch and took off. I thought I could do a 6:30, but not much faster. I glanced down as we finished the first lap in ninety seconds. That's a six-minute mile—way too fast for me. But I needed to win, or at least keep up with him. Beating Kyle would get me respect.

As we started the second lap, Kyle surged ahead. I let him go, and within a quarter lap he dropped back. He didn't pace well, and I slowed a touch, hoping he'd fall in line with me. We finished the second pretty tight and I started to break in the third, keeping a few steps ahead.

As we raced, I realized that this kid runs like I used to. All heart and tension with a complete purging of self—no holds barred. Kyle's vulnerability was tangible. I guess my additional ten years have taught me pacing and hiding; because as I watched the emotions play across his face, I missed the abandon I used to feel about running. About anything. When was the last time I felt something? Really felt it?

Right there in the third lap, I knew Kyle should win. I could see it in his pulled-back lips, every muscle tensed and pushed forward. This was more than a race. Kyle was running for his life.

The same run I made many times. Runs I slogged through alone. No one bolstered me or gave me encouragement. I could have done that for Kyle. I should have done that for him. But I hate to lose.

In the fourth he started wheezing, and I pulled ahead. At the first corner I pulled away completely and, despite momentary guilt, kicked up the pace and drove the last half lap in a full sprint. I looked down at my watch as I crossed the line: 6:05! It was the fastest mile of my life. It felt amazing, and I thought I'd die. Kyle came in at 6:39, doubled over, and gagged. If there'd been something in his stomach, it'd have been all over my shoes.

I bent next to him, both of us hanging inches over our shoelaces. "You're my new running partner, Kyle. You got speed, man." I was so elated I forgot about respect. I thought about friendship. My mistake.

"I ain't nothin' to you." He shoved me aside and left. Without a look back, he sped through a hole in the fence and headed to Grace House.

I tried to muster anger and brush off his rejection, but it didn't work. Usually it's a fantastic and safe emotion. But I hurt Kyle, Mr. Knightley, and anger couldn't fix that. I deliberately wounded a kid. He showed me the real Kyle, and I crushed him. Is this the adult I've become?

Sincerely,
Sam

Dear Mr. Knightley,

I took the 'L' to Evanston and wandered around Northwestern University's campus yesterday. Punishment, I think, but I wanted to see it.

Despite it being summer, people were everywhere. I first roamed through the English building. It's gothic and very romantic looking. Full of great literature and ideas, I'm sure. The course listings blew me away: English Literary Traditions, Twentieth-Century American Novel, British Fictional Studies, Shakespearean Tragedies . . . We didn't have offerings like that at Roosevelt. There were only a few in literature at all; plenty in electrical engineering, basic math, and trade, but nothing like this. Hallowed halls of academia and all that, right?

I wandered to Medill next. It's not as architecturally interesting as the other buildings. More straightforward and practical—newsy, I guess. They posted listings too: Ethics of Journalism, Long-Form Reporting, Advanced Public Affairs Reporting. I think I would've focused on magazine and feature writing, half-way between news and a story. I'd have liked that.

And despite Hannah's claim that I don't see the world around me, I paid attention yesterday—to everything. And Northwestern is no Roosevelt.

There's a look there I can't put my finger on. Money? Education? Assurance? The students are a bunch of Emmas. They know they rank in the world, or will someday soon. It's in their walk, their talk, and their clothes. Is it ownership? Confidence? I don't know. But I want it. I don't know when or how, but I do know it's my new "normal."

I also noticed I need to step up my wardrobe. It's not a huge deal, but first impressions matter, and I wouldn't fit in there. I didn't fit in at Ernst & Young either, but I didn't get it then. I do now. They wear jeans and sweatshirts and T-shirts—all the stuff I do—but you can tell Madewell from Goodwill. And it's how they wear them too. There's a casualness about their clothing that belies effort. Then it goes one step further. That detail—a scarf, a necklace, a belt— that one thing that declares you're unique. You matter. So with any extra money I earn, I'll work on wardrobe. Because . . . I got the Starbucks job!

I found out this morning and I'm pleased. I really am. Maybe that was what my trip to NU was about yesterday. Even before hearing from Starbucks, I needed to let go of that dream. Visiting campus closed the chapter.

And Father John helped me find a walk-up about six blocks north. The neighborhood is a bit rough, but I can afford the rent and won't need a car for either the library or Starbucks. I go this afternoon to sign a month-to-month lease. It'll all be good.

> Thanks again, Mr. Knightley,
> for everything . . .
> Sam

I forgot to mail this yesterday, so I'll add a bit more . . .

I put my neck out with Kyle this morning. I know I'm leaving, but his hatred bothers me—probably because it's deserved now. I was so nervous I almost threw up.

"Hey, Kyle. I'm training for the Chicago Marathon this fall and wondered if you'd run with me. I'm heading to the track for a couple miles of warm-up and some speed work. What do you say?"

He drank his juice, completely expressionless. His eyes never left mine—not even to blink. The look was so determined and aggressive that I struggled to keep contact.

"At least think about it. You're good, Kyle—really good. You could run cross-country at school next fall. You'd win a lot of races."

His stare faltered. If I had blinked, I would have missed the longing. I gulped and spoke again. "Listen, Kyle. I'm sorry about the other day. I hope you'll come. I'll be there for about an hour."

I don't apologize easily, Mr. Knightley. I think only Father John has pried a few sorries from me over the years, and he's Father John. Even now, I can't believe those words came out of my mouth. Kyle should've fallen down with shock and gratitude. Instead, he put his glass in the dishwasher and left the room.

So I went to the track, started to run, and hoped . . . That's a lie, I fretted. Wow, did I work up a panic.

But I'm leaving Grace House again, and this time it's permanent. As Father John said, this is my "watershed." There's no turning back. And unlike when I left with Cara or when Ernst & Young fired me, there's no safety net. There's no more Grace House because there's no more school. That chapter has closed. And there are no real friends to catch me either.

I've been thinking about that a lot. That race with Kyle shook me—and not simply because of my cruelty. It shook me because, hanging over our shoes, I suddenly wanted his friendship. I innately understood him and believed he felt the same. Friendship from a thirteen-year-old boy? It still doesn't make sense. I can't explain it. But we're alike, Kyle and I. And I could use a friend.

Outside my books, the only people I talk to are Hannah and you. But Hannah and I aren't true friends. I'm a foster-kid-turned-convenient-acquaintance for her. And you? You're a glorified diary. There . . . my two friends. Thinking about this gave me a new and unsettling sense of isolation. After two laps, the panic almost brought me to my knees.

Then I saw Kyle. He was watching me from the fence line. As I cleared my face of all expression and approached, he joined my pace wordlessly.

"Thanks for coming, Kyle. This'll be my third time running Chicago, and I want to do it better."

"Why you run so far?"

There are always two ways to go here. Normally when asked why I run, I dish out some meaningless lie. To tell the real reason is dangerous. It's too personal.

"It relaxes me," I said.

Kyle stopped. "Forget you." He crossed the inside of the track to get back to the entrance.

I watched him and felt my heart collapse. "Kyle, wait!"

"For crap? I get enough a' that." He turned away.

I didn't think. I yelled.

"I run because it's the only place I'm me. Until I slog out the miles, I can't find myself. But if I do it, if I make one mile more, I find myself. My head clears and sometimes, just sometimes, I see that I'm worth something." I scrubbed tears from my face with the back of my hand.

Kyle had stopped, but he didn't turn around.

I kept going. "I'm sorry about what I did to you. You scared me, you hated me, and I fought."

He turned. "Don't mess with me."

"I won't. I promise." I said it slowly—making the promise to both of us. Without another word or look, he jogged back to the track.

We ran a series of sprints and a cool-down without talking. Maybe he knew I needed space. Maybe he was winded. Regardless, I was reeling with what I'd said and done. Part of me hoped he hadn't processed how much I'd shared with him, while the other part knew that he understood me perfectly. Because he's not dumb. That happens with most foster kids—people underestimate us. They dismiss us—as I had dismissed him.

When we finished I slapped him on the back, expecting that we felt the same. I was wrong.

"Don't touch me."

"I . . ."

"We're running. We ain't friends." And he walked away.

So there it is. We're not friends, but I did my best. And, in this last letter to you, it's important that you know I tried. I am not an adult who purposely ruins kids' identities and dreams.

Now . . . I'm off to find out what kind of adult I am. Thanks for everything. At the very least, your grant let me rest in Grace House's safety for a few months—that helped a lot.

Forgot to mail this again—I'm beginning to think there's something psychological going on here. Attachment issues?

But I'm bored and there's no one here now, so I might as well add more.

The morning started fine. After I recovered from yet another dissing from Kyle, I headed to my library job. Mrs. Grunschovitch, one of my favorite library regulars, was the first through the doors. She's a wonderful, crusty old lady who constantly scolds me for not pulling my hair out of my eyes and not eating enough. Believe me, I eat plenty. I just run more.

Lately she says I need more blush. She says I have beautiful cheekbones. I never noticed. A foster mom once called me a "long drink of water" and I never think much beyond that. When I do look in the mirror, the long brown curly hair and bushy eyebrows stop me way before I get to the cheekbones. Still, it's nice for someone to say something about me is pretty.

A couple weeks ago, Mrs. G helped me put up the Summer Love display. I pulled out Lisa Kleypas, Nora Roberts, and a few other hot, steamy novelists in an effort to appear modern and hip.

"You can't put these out." Mrs. G plucked them from my book pyramid.

"These are summer romances."

"You need the real lovelies. Tales of true love," she sighed.

"Which are?"

"I'm disappointed in you, Sam. I thought you'd know. *The Scarlet Pimpernel, Romeo and Juliet, Persuasion.*"

"*Wuthering Heights? Jane Eyre? Pride and Prejudice?*"

"I knew you understood."

"Some of those didn't work out so well, Mrs. G. *Romeo and Juliet? Wuthering Heights?* The boss likes it a bit lighter."

"The endings don't matter." She waved her bent finger at me. "The love was true. Put them out."

How could I refuse? So I grabbed all my favorites, and she grabbed a few of hers. I also added *Outlander, The Food of Love,* and *Austenland* for a nod to modern tales. I let Mrs. G take home *Austenland.* She wanted *Outlander,* but some scenes would leave her blushing for weeks and then I'd get another kind of lecture.

She came back today and wanted my next pick, because she loved *Austenland.* She's never asked me to suggest titles for her before, so this was high praise and high pressure. I handed her *The Guernsey Literary and Potato Peel Pie Society.* What do you think? I worried a moment about the WWII angle, for I know her family escaped Poland when she was little. But when I hinted at it, she dismissed me.

"The day we forget the horror, Sam, we will repeat it. Never forget your past. It will make you less human, less than human."

I smiled and thought it was unlikely I could forget my past. It presses pretty constantly.

Mr. Clayton came in this morning too. He's one of my all-time favorite patrons, another mystery nut like Father John, and I've been in charge of his recommendations since we first met a few years ago. Everyone else intimidates him, but if we're alone, he'll sit and chat for hours. He needs more action than Mrs. G, but no gore: "Remember the ulcer, Sam. Don't stress me."

I started him awhile back on Patricia Cornwell, but she got too graphic. Alex Powell is his current favorite. Mine too. And today I had a surprise for Mr. Clayton: I pre-ordered Powell's new novel, just for him. Mr. Clayton was thrilled. So was I, because I'll read it next.

I love Powell's books: good writing, solid detective/hero, strong cast of characters, and great plots. Plus all the main gore happens offstage. He gives you enough to keep you riveted but doesn't wallow in the depravity. It's a satisfying brew of old-world charm in gritty, contemporary NYC.

And of course, Powell's hot hero keeps me coming back too. Detective Cole Barker is totally lean, deliciously flawed, smart, loyal, rugged, and, I imagine, gorgeous—a modern Darcy and

Knightley meet Ethan Hunt. *Redemption* comes out as a movie in a couple weeks. We'll see if Hollywood agrees. Oh . . . Gotta go. Someone needs my help.

Later still . . .

Are you beginning to think I'll never go away? I promise I will, but it's hard to let go of lifelines—I mean—friends. Especially when they're dropping like flies all around me.

Dan stopped by the library this afternoon. He's a guy I used to study with at Roosevelt. We've kept in touch over e-mail and texts these past few months, but nothing big.

I texted him that my job fell through and that I'm back at the library. And today in he walked. I was happy to see him. He reminds me of a comfortable sweater that you pull on, knowing it will keep you warm every time. That's a nice metaphor, isn't it? Hannah didn't think so—but more on that later.

Anyway, we chatted a few minutes and then he placed a small black box on the counter. He was so excited and pushed it toward me. I just stared.

"Open it." He poked it again. "What are your plans now?"

"I move into my apartment tomorrow, and I got part-time work at Starbucks. I'll keep my job here too."

"You're so smart. You'll do great."

"Thanks. Not smart enough to get this ribbon off." Still working on the box . . . I finally opened it and looked up. "It's a heart necklace, Dan. It's so nice. But why would you buy me a heart?" Big mistake.

Shutters pulled over his eyes. "I . . . never mind. Wasn't it your birthday awhile back?"

"Yes. Thank you so much." I knew I'd hurt him. I didn't know what to do, so I started gushing. "It's really nice, Dan. I've always wanted a heart necklace. It's so lovely." My words sounded stilted and hollow.

But I wanted his eyes to soften again. I liked that look. This one made me nervous and unsure. How did I go wrong? I know it was awful because he sputtered a few words and left—fast, shoulders down, like Atlas carrying the world. I didn't have the guts to go after him.

Then Hannah blew when I told her about it tonight. Another mistake. See why I don't talk? But she doesn't get it. I'm a twenty-three-year-old woman who has never been with a guy, never really even kissed a guy, and clearly can't speak to one. Who could understand that? My idea of romance comes from Jane Austen—and I was scandalized when Darcy and Lizzy kissed at the end of that BBC movie.

So you see, I'm not trying to be clueless. I simply am. Hannah said I need to get out of my head more, but if that is what happens, why should I? If I hurt people, shouldn't I stay in there permanently?

"How could you do that? He hung around for two years studying with you, asking you out and calling you. And then this past year, the e-mails, the texts—he's put himself out there constantly for you. What were you thinking?" She was yelling, and Hannah never yells.

"I didn't know."

"You didn't know? Sam, you've got to start living in the real world."

"My life hasn't exactly been sheltered, Hannah."

"Yes, it has. You've been knocked around, but you were sheltered all right. You lived in your books."

"That's not true. 'There are just a lot of different sides to me. If there was just one, it would be ever so much more comfortable, but then it wouldn't be half so interesting.' "

"Are you serious?" Hannah stared at me. "Sam, you gave me the book, and that's what you inscribed in the cover."

"Stop pushing me!" I cried. I didn't remember having given her *Anne of Green Gables*.

To her credit, Hannah backed off.

"What color are Dan's eyes?" she asked so softly that I almost missed it.

I stared at her. I couldn't see the point of her

question, and I certainly didn't know the answer.

"Oh, Sam. You never even saw him." She sounded disappointed. I remembered the tone from when she told me about her tae kwon do. It formed a connection between Hannah and Dan—an uncomfortable one.

I did then what I always do when I feel pulled outside myself. I ran. Literally. I grabbed my shoes and left Hannah sitting in my cottage. Kyle was outside Buckhorn as I dashed out, so I invited him to come along. We knocked out five miles. He didn't talk. Maybe he'll never talk. But perhaps that's for the best. I'd only let him down.

After that, I was calm enough to call Dan and apologize—a new and highly uncomfortable habit for me. I tried three times, but he never picked up. I left a message, but I don't expect him to call me back. I blew it. Someone was right in front of me, liked me, and I lost him. I'd like another chance. I'd like more chances with so many people. Do I get more chances?

Well, Mr. Knightley, here ends my chance with you. It's time to mail this. I'm glad you don't have a real name and this isn't a real friendship, because I would just mess it up. Clearly my comfort zone doesn't stretch far, because I've enjoyed these letters more than anything, and I will never know you or the color of your eyes.

Farewell, friend . . .
Sam

Dear Mr. Knightley,

It's been over two months, and I know you never expected to hear from me again. I never expected to write. But Medill's admissions director called—I got in!

Someone backed out and I was next on the wait list. I asked her to hold my spot while I checked on my grant, and she gave me two days. Father John is probably calling your foundation right now, so this will be redundant soon—but I felt it worth a letter regardless.

I want to go to Medill, Mr. Knightley. And if given this chance, I promise I won't fail.

Sincerely,
Samantha Moore

Dear Ms. Moore,

As I am sure Father John has told you—the grant is yours. Mr. Knightley instructed me to wire your tuition directly to Northwestern University. You are enrolled. Medill will contact you directly with all further details.

Sincerely,
Laura Temper
Personal Assistant to
G. Knightley

Dear Mr. Knightley,

Thank you. Thank you. Online registration begins tomorrow at seven a.m. Wish me luck. I don't know how hard it is to get classes. It took me a few semesters to get some at Roosevelt, and I only have four quarters at Medill. Did you know it's a fifteen-month program? I decided to specialize in long feature and magazine writing, so those courses are first on my list. I'll keep you posted.

I should also tell you I'm moving back to Grace House. I don't want to, but I must. I like my little apartment and my sense of freedom, but school will suffer if I work two jobs. I already learned that lesson. This time I will take Hannah's advice immediately and move back to Grace House where I can live for free.

Furthermore (the information doesn't stop, does it?), I gave my notice at Starbucks today. I thought my boss would balk at my short tenure . . . That's not true, I worried she'd be thrilled to see me go. I've been so scared to mess up that I do it daily.

I'm happy to report that she landed nicely in the middle. She said she was very excited for me, but would miss me. She called me an "asset to the team." Never been one of those before. It felt good. And I'll miss working there. Everyone was nice without being nosy. So while the friendships—if you can call them that—weren't deep, at least they weren't uncomfortable.

Everything's falling into place . . . ahhh . . . not everything: I'm safe from becoming too comfortable.

As I left a meeting with Father John today, he asked me to stop by the track and find Kyle.

"Why?"

I want to leave Kyle alone. I haven't seen him since I moved out in June and thought I'd give him a wide berth once I move back . . . He unsettles me.

"He has an appointment with me, and I suspect he'll try to skip it. He runs the track after school. Would you pop over and encourage him to return?"

Encourage Kyle? "He won't listen to me. Send someone else."

"Give it a try." Father John's tone told me this was not a request. He continued, "He's at that track every day."

"He's a good runner. Did he join the cross-country team?"

"No. The coach and I discussed it, but Kyle won't talk about it. Won't talk to anyone. He just runs the track after school." Father John dropped his voice. "I'm worried, Sam."

"This is not about some appointment. You're up to something. What do you want from me?"

"I want you to talk to him. You've been there,

kiddo. And running was your escape. You weren't so different at fourteen."

"I've tried."

Father John lifted his eyebrows.

I sighed. "I did. I tried in June. Just let me leave him alone."

"Don't be that person, Sam—the one who leaves. I'm asking you to try again. As a favor to me, if not for Kyle."

Was he pushing this for Kyle or for me? I'm always the first to leave, figuratively if not literally.

"Fine." I walked out of Father John's office feeling part put out and part called out.

Kyle was easy to spot. The football team was in the center of the field, but he was the only kid circling the track. I watched him for a few minutes. His face was shuttered. There was no joy, no freedom, in his run.

"Hey," I called. "I'm not wearing running shoes. Will you walk with me a minute?"

"Why?"

"Father John sent me to find you. He's worried about you."

"That old—"

"Don't denigrate him."

"Huh?"

"You can hate me, hate anybody, but show Father John respect. He cares about us. Might be the only one who does. And if you are anything like me—which he seems to think you are—he'll

56

get you out of more scrapes and give you more love than you'll ever repay. Remember that."

Kyle said nothing, but he walked with me. As we walked, I realized I didn't want to leave Kyle alone. Suddenly, faced with him, I wanted to reach out. I can't explain it, but the connection is real—even if it's only one-sided.

"I'm moving back to Grace House," I told him. "Do you want to run more?"

"No." He kept by my side. Not ahead or behind.

"I'm not leaving, Kyle. I'm moving back for another year and a half."

"So?" He still didn't leave.

"I'll ask you to run every day then. Eventually I hope you'll say yes." I stopped and stared at him. His eyes were shiny, unsure. He seemed so small at that moment. Granted, his shoulders are getting broad and his feet are huge, but he's fourteen and that's still young.

"Tomorrow I get off at the library at five. I'll meet you here and we'll do some speed work."

"We ain't friends."

"Believe whatever you want. Just be here." I turned and walked away. "And don't miss your appointment with Father John," I called over my shoulder.

Kyle's probably right, Mr. Knightley. We ain't friends, but I don't think he hates me, and that's something.

Sincerely,
Sam

57

Dear Mr. Knightley,

Classes start Monday. I got all my first choices and took the 'L' up to Evanston yesterday to pick up course packets and books. It freaked me out. It was one thing to visit the campus as some strange swan-song farewell, but now I have to fit into that place. I want to fit into that place. I got so worked up I practically hyperventilated on the ride back. A man forced a teenager to give me his seat.

While sitting there, I slapped on a thick layer of Edmond Dantes. He's my go-to guy for any fight. Have you read *The Count of Monte Cristo*? After being framed for murder and imprisoned for years, Edmond finally escapes, finds a huge treasure, and creates the persona of the Count of Monte Cristo. He then returns home to exact revenge—cleverly, coldly, and systematically destroying each man who ruined his life. And he does it with exquisite manners, impeccable style, and an aura of sophistication. Ruthless.

Charlotte Lucas, on the other hand, could never survive at Medill, and Fanny Price wouldn't try. Even Jane Eyre would recognize her limitations, and she's as strong as they come. So I've been trying on small doses of Edmond. By the time I reached Grace House yesterday, I felt strong. Then came Kyle . . .

As we left for our run, he seemed silent, almost sullen.

"What's up, Kyle?"

No answer.

"You know, some conversation will enliven this run."

He stopped and glared at me. "Who are you?"

"I—"

"Forget it." He turned away.

"Fine, run away, Kyle. You coward." Edmond challenges. Edmond never backs down.

"Coward? Me? Why'd you ask me to run? This some charity thing?" Kyle's voice cracked.

And that took care of Edmond. Kyle's a kid— a searching kid—and I had attacked him again.

"No. It's not some charity thing." I deflated, like a balloon with a slow leak, not a pop. I shriveled and floated down. "I'm sorry, Kyle. Don't leave. Just run with me a few minutes. Please."

I think he heard the plea in my voice because he simply turned back and ran. I caught up and neither of us spoke for about thirty minutes. I picked up the tempo until we were running probably 6:50s for the last two miles.

At the end we both hung over our knees. My face felt so hot: sweat, blood, everything pounding in it.

"You okay?" he whispered between gulps of air.

"Yeah." I stood and looked at him. I decided

to go for honesty. Running strips me of my inhibitions. Which is one reason I usually run alone. "I'm sorry, Kyle. It's not that easy for me. Sometimes I get so scared I sort of . . . hide . . . in my books."

He stared blankly at me.

"Come on, you must do something . . . to keep from being afraid?" I was surprised to hear myself ask that question—more surprised that I wanted an answer.

"Beat up Jaden 'cause Nolan dissed me. Jaden didn't do nothin' wrong."

I wanted to pounce. Jaden is a small nine-year-old sweetheart. But a voice deep inside told me to shut up. Let Father John correct his defense mechanisms, not me.

"Hiding in books is like beating up Jaden."

"But you're all grown up."

That struck me as funny and I tried to laugh. "Go figure. All grown up and still hiding." The laughter came out as a pathetic wheeze with a snort at the end. "I guess I don't know how to stop, Kyle."

He stared at me again. What was he supposed to say?

"Hey, you want to see a movie tonight?" I can only take so much personal reflection.

"What?"

"*Redemption* opened last week. I bet your supervisor would let me take you. It's PG-13.

Wait, I heard you just turned fourteen. Wanna go?"

"Yeah!"

So there you go. I took Kyle to the movies. He was pretty good company too. He didn't talk much, but after all my wallowing this afternoon, I didn't want to talk. I just wanted to enjoy the show and sexy Cole Barker.

Sincerely,

Sam

P.S. Okay, I can't help myself. I tried to sign off, but I can't . . .

You're going to think I'm some silly teenage groupie, but I've got to tell you about *Redemption* and you've got to see it. If you haven't read any of Powell's books, start with that one. Then go see the movie. They get Cole Barker perfectly. He is so adorable and handsome and tough, yet vulnerable . . .

I'll stop. Please don't tell anyone I gushed like this. It's embarrassing how much I loved that movie. I think I'll sneak out after my shift at the library this afternoon and see it again. Do you ever see a film twice?

Oh . . . how could I forget? See what Cole did to me? Hannah got engaged last night. I saw her when I dropped off some boxes at Independence Cottage this morning. She lifted her left hand, squealed, pulled me to the bench in the court-yard, and gushed the whole story—without drawing a breath.

The ring is gorgeous, Mr. Knightley. A beautiful diamond set in a circle of gold. I held Hannah's hand up to admire it, then dropped it, a little too forcefully. She shot me a questioning glance, but I think she understood. I felt that little-girl yearning for Prince Charming play across my face. I thought that died long ago. Clearly not—probably Cole's fault.

She started her story in a dreamy voice. "Matt took me to our favorite restaurant, Chicago Pizza and Oven Grinder, last night. There was a two-hour wait, so I told him we should go somewhere else. He was so tense, but he refused to budge. We waited and chatted and drank Chianti. But he kept fidgeting. Finally we got a booth."

"A pizza place? For a proposal?"

"I know it doesn't sound romantic, but it is. The booths have high backs and the lighting is dim. You're alone in a crowded room."

"Did he ask you while you waited?"

"No. When we sat down, he reached for my hand and said the night was perfect. I couldn't quite figure that out. He was so distracted, and his palms were sweaty. I started freaking out and kept asking, 'What's wrong? What are you not telling me?'

"I was sure he was moving or dumping me, but

he kept stroking my hand and saying, 'Everything is perfect.' But it wasn't, and by the end of dinner I was a wreck."

"And?" She was getting long-winded. I needed the proposal.

"After we left, we walked a few blocks to a park and sat on a bench. We searched for stars. Then he got down on one knee in front of me." She paused, and I leaned forward. "And he took my hand and asked me to marry him."

"That's it?" I sat back. "You're worse than Austen. You might as well say that his sentiments had 'undergone so material a change' or that 'his affections and wishes' were unchanged. Anything is better than nothing! She never tells you what's actually said either."

Hannah flushed red. "Don't do that."

At first I thought the red was embarrassment, but her tone hinted at anger.

"What?"

"Compare my proposal from my real fiancé to one of your books. This is my life and I'm inviting you into it. Don't belittle it by quoting fiction."

" 'I wish you all imaginable happiness,' Hannah." I was mad, and I threw that out just to spite her.

"Forget it, Sam. I don't know who you're quoting, but I can tell you are. I thought you'd enjoy my story and I wanted to share it with you,

63

but you aren't even here. I don't know why I bother. I've got work to do." She stood up and walked to the office.

She was right, of course. When she told me about the dinner, I got carried away. I didn't want restaurant details; I wanted emotional details—for me. I desperately wanted some guy's hands to be sweaty because he couldn't live another moment without knowing if I'd marry him. And I lashed out at her because I was jealous. If I couldn't have the reality, I wanted the story. But it was her story and her proposal.

Maybe I shouldn't go see that movie again . . .

Dear Mr. Knightley,

I'm officially learning to be a reporter, so I will report. Here are my classes: Audience Insight, Urban Issues Reporting, Long-Form Nonfiction Narrative, and Magazine Writing. I have the same professor for Urban Issues and Long Form, Dr. Russell Johnson. You may have heard of him. He's won multiple Pulitzers and was a big civil rights guy. He actually marched on Selma with Dr. King when he was thirteen. From what I gather, Johnson *is* Journalism. Capital *J*.

Everyone is in awe. I had both Johnson classes today, and all the students were talking about what an honor it is to work with Johnson, how much Johnson will teach us, what doors a recommendation from Johnson can open, and how impressing Johnson should be the sum of all effort. As if that wasn't intimidating enough, today the man himself loomed over me and bellowed like a drill sergeant. I almost wet my pants. No kidding. He frightened me that much.

But I hope to use it to my advantage: desperation and terror usually bring out my best work, and I already have three assignments. I'll ace these and have it made. Johnson will respect my work, and the rest will be a breeze. At least I can count on that—school always works. Nothing else comes together quite so well. In fact, nothing else works at all. I ran into a girl from my Audience class at Norris, the student center, during lunch. She was with a big group and waved at me to join them. So I took a deep breath and dived in—my first friends on my first day.

"We're just finishing lunch. Grab something and join us."

I quickly bought a sandwich and sat next to her. Her name is Debbie and she went to Duke. I didn't feel so cool with my honors from Roosevelt, so I didn't say much. But I was joining in. It was when Debbie asked about my family that I took the nosedive. I unsuccessfully tried to divert the conversation, but she asked again. I panicked.

"Let's not get personal so quickly." I actually said that.

"Oh . . ." Her jaw dropped and she looked around at the others.

I couldn't stop there. No, I had to say more. I started out as Edmond Dantes and, when I noticed all their weird looks, morphed into a lighter, kinder Jane Bennet. Everyone likes Jane Bennet. Not today. It was humiliating.

After a few minutes Debbie stood up. "I need to head to the bookstore. I'll see you all later." She looked equal parts ticked and confused.

And within three minutes everyone else left the table. I sat alone and finished my sandwich.

I'd be glad to share more of my first day, but those are the highlights. All pretty awful, except the school part. If I can get some good work in, Johnson and Debbie won't bother me so much.

Writing apace,
Sam

~ OCTOBER 20

Dear Mr. Knightley,

I'm sorry it's been more than a month . . . I've been busy. I think you and Father John were wrong about this. The program is too tough. Dr. Johnson handed another of my articles back today and basically called me an idiot. I didn't tell you my first efforts crashed and burned because I thought I could save myself. And this article was better. I was sure of it.

Johnson disagreed. He criticized my topic, my approach, my research, and my tone. I'm "formulaic, pedantic, and prosaic." How can anyone be that bad? I thought I'd specialize in feature writing. I can't now. He's the guru of that, and there's no getting past him. Johnson *is* Journalism.

In fact, I was so certain of success that I pre-registered for his winter class, Journalism Methods: News Writing. I'm dead, and I'm not the only one. One guy already left. He said that Johnson is too powerful and that a bad recommendation can kill a career. He called the *Austin Statesman* and got his old job back. He's headed home to Texas and a good salary with benefits . . . What'll happen to me?

When handing back my assignment, Johnson asked me to stay after the seminar today. Each of

68

my classmates silently ducked out with grimaces and sympathetic glances—even Debbie, who hasn't talked to me since that disastrous lunch. I sat there feeling sick as Johnson crossed the room and sat on the edge of my table.

"Find your voice, Moore, or you're going to have a rough go here." He leaned back and watched me. For a man with an amazing amount of energy and size, he can sit remarkably still.

"Excuse me?"

"I've seen seven exercises from you and four full articles. We move fast here, Moore, and your work isn't cutting it. You're a good writer and I sense real potential, but your topics and approach are sterile. Is this all you've got?"

"I—I need to find more interesting topics?"

"Don't be deliberately obtuse, Moore. That's not the problem; another reporter could make your topics leap from the page. I see no risk in your writing. You need to stretch so that your soul touches each topic. If you fail to connect, you fail the reader."

"I put myself in these articles."

Johnson plucked the paper from my desk and looked it over. "You say here, 'The judge yielded without conviction, which was no compliment to the case's importance.' That voice is stilted, withdrawn, and I can't tell what you mean. Is that you? Because if it is, you stepped away from the subject and created an insurmountable barrier for your reader. You destroyed its relevance. Why?"

"I didn't mean to." I sat there, confused and exposed. "I was trying to be objective." Also, I had loosely borrowed some Austen verbiage to help me out. *Oops.*

"Objective and contrived are two different things." He handed the paper back. "Figure it out, Moore." He dismissed me with a nod and went back to his computer. Discussion over.

What am I to do? If he were wrong, I could dismiss the criticism. But he's right. I chose topics I thought interesting, but ones that wouldn't expose me. Then I hid further because the articles will be judged, graded. I don't know how to be "me" in this kind of writing.

In literature analysis I hid behind the subject, and it made my papers come alive. I had a voice that mirrored, if not emboldened, the subject. When I write to you, I'm safe in your anonymity and your silence. For all I know, you may not even read these letters.

But Johnson? I need to impress him. I need a grade from him. And I need a voice—fast. My characters have always provided that, both in writing and in life—as Darcy said of Lizzy, I too "find great enjoyment in occasionally professing opinions which in fact are not *my* own." But now I need to produce something objective, something original. Is there nothing that's mine alone?

And to top it off, the nightmares are back. I used to get them as a kid, but they've been gone for a couple years. Not anymore—Dr. Johnson and nightmares. Doesn't this sound fun?

Each nightmare begins with bright daylight and gray walls. There's nothing scary as I feel myself falling deeper, but then I start to resist. Fear comes before action. My heart pounds, even before my father enters the scene. He's always larger than life and oddly red. Yelling begins, but I can't hear it. I can only feel the fear and the heat it creates. After that the dreams change: Mom enters some, my father dominates others, or occasionally the Putmans (my sixth or seventh foster family) drive at me. Whoever comes brings a black/red fear with them.

As a small child, Jane Eyre gets locked in her dead uncle's red bedroom for punishment. She grows terrified by the walls, the voices, and his ghost. She bangs on the door, gasping and terrified, as his spirit comes after her, and then passes out. My walls press like Jane's, and I suffocate. That's when I wake up gagging and choking.

Roommates used to shake me awake, but no one's in the cottage now. Morgan moved out last month. So I stay in the nightmares longer and wake drenched in sweat and exhausted.

School and the nightmares are related, Mr. Knightley—even I know that. If I can figure out Johnson, I'm sure the nightmares will go away.

But how? I can't try any harder. If I don't solve this, Johnson will fail me. Then where do I go?

Sincerely,
Sam

P.S. The Chicago Marathon was last Sunday. Kyle and I still run almost daily, but I couldn't get enough long runs in to be ready for a marathon. But on a bright note, Kyle joined the cross-country team. You'll never believe how it happened . . .

We were running laps a couple weeks ago when a large man approached—late fifties, super fit, with gray sideburns and kind, wrinkly eyes.

"Excuse me, miss. Are you a student here?"

"No."

"Do you work here?"

"No." Forget the kind eyes. I grew wary.

"Do you have permission to be on this track?"

"Do I need permission?" I inched toward antagonistic.

"Yes. They aren't my rules and I'm not enforcing them to bust your chops, but we've got a lot of police around here, and if they catch you without permission, they can arrest you."

"Arrest me? For running?"

"It's the drugs, the gangs, and the crime. They can arrest you." He tried to soften it with a smile. Then he stared hard at Kyle. "You're Kyle Baines, aren't you?"

"Yeah."

I got nervous. This man hadn't told us anything about himself, but he knew a lot about us. I started to open my mouth, but he was still talking to Kyle.

"I'm Coach Ridley. I've been talking to Father John about you. He says you're a strong runner. You should join our team."

"I thought—" I started, but Coach Ridley subtly shook his head at me. If I hadn't been so surprised, I might have gotten mad.

He focused on Kyle. "Your friend here can't come back to the track; I don't want her to get in trouble. But her stride's too long. Think you could help her with that?"

Kyle, who hadn't looked the man in the eyes during any portion of this, locked eyes on Coach Ridley. I couldn't believe it. He was listening. But I was listening too, and I felt my face flush with anger. *My stride is not too long!* I remembered the day when I ran Kyle into the ground. I don't like losing. And I don't like criticism.

"Excuse m—" I protested, but that's all I got out as Coach Ridley glanced at me and winked. He winked! I almost laughed as I caught on. The coach was trapping Kyle. It was a dare. And Kyle was eating it up.

"I can run you through some drills with the team, and you can help her shorten that stride. It'll improve her times."

"I can do that."

"Good. I'll see you right here after last period tomorrow." He turned back to me. "And what's your name?"

"Samantha Moore."

"Well, Miss Moore. You'll have a better stride by next week. And the track is open to the public for meets. You can come watch Kyle." Coach Ridley walked away without another word or look back.

Kyle and I turned and walked back to Grace House. I think we were both stunned, probably for different reasons.

"So you're on the cross-country team?" I tried to sound casual. This is good for him. It'd be good for any teenage boy.

"Yeah."

"Are you excited?"

"Dunno."

"You don't know? Why'd you join?"

"You need help."

I shot him a glance, trying to find sarcasm. There wasn't any. I laughed. "Well, Kyle, I'll take all the help I can get." That's irony for you, if nothing else.

It's been almost two weeks now, and Kyle looks lighter. I don't mean his weight—he was already a lanky kid. I mean his eyes. They aren't as cruel, and his mouth isn't compressed so tight. Promising changes, Mr. Knightley.

~ OCTOBER 26

Dear Mr. Knightley,

I turned in another article to Johnson today. It was better. He takes only a couple days to review our work, so I'll know soon enough. I can do this, Mr. Knightley. I hope I didn't worry you last week. I want to assure you that the work is not beyond me. Please don't feel you've wasted your time or your foundation's money.

For a change I should tell you about one of my successes: I think I made a friend. If not, I'm a project . . .

Last Tuesday, I saw Debbie at Norris. She hasn't talked to me all quarter, but I smiled and threw out a hello before I lost my courage. There was some truth to Hannah's criticisms, even if she "never had the smallest idea of them being ever felt in such a way." I know, I'm quoting. But Lizzy expresses things so well. My point is that I've taken Hannah's words to heart and I have been trying to pay attention to people and reach out to them.

So anyway, Debbie looked surprised, and the girl next to her immediately called out to me. "Hey, come join us. I've seen you in here before. Are you in Medill's program?" She looked between Debbie and me. Debbie nodded with that *stop-talking* look in her eyes. I was so humiliated.

I wanted to run, but I forced myself to stand.

The girl smiled at me. "So how do you like it? Debbie says it's impossible."

"I hate the contrast between my ideas and my work. In each article I imagine something which I'm powerless to realize." I cringed.

"That was impressive. Sit down."

I sat, even more nervous. "What was impressive?"

"The way you paraphrased that line from *Jane Eyre* and used it for your own context. I like that."

"You got that?" I was stunned, then caught myself and looked at Debbie, hoping she could understand. Taking a deep breath, I dived in. "I quote when I'm nervous."

"It's brilliant. You should get your master's in English literature like me. You'd have a blast. I'm Ashley, by the way."

Yes, I should. Don't you agree, Mr. Knightley?

I stayed and enjoyed myself. Ashley is unlike anyone I've ever met. She's one of those girls. The kind you see in movies, but you don't believe exist in real life. An Emma. She wears a diamond watch and has blond hair that lies precisely and tosses effortlessly. She has blue eyes and perfect skin. And she's so manicured and polished and perfectly casual that you want to either pinch her to make sure she's real or punch her because you wish she wasn't.

And she says outrageous things. Don't you

agree that spending $900 on a pair of shoes is crazy? I looked up the designer, Jimmy Choo, and found that she was serious. One can actually spend $900 or more on a pair of shoes! I had no idea that shoes could cost nearly as much as a car. After that comment I wanted to dislike her—but she's nice.

Nevertheless I tried to dismiss her. I decided she was superficially amusing and refreshingly knowledgeable about literature, but she had no substance. After all, how much did Emma and Harriet Smith really have in common? Did Ashley regard me as her Harriet? Her poor pet project pursued out of a warped noblesse oblige? Or, worse, boredom?

Then I conceded that Ashley didn't have plans to "improve" me. No reading lists, drawing exercises, or music practice . . . She reached out to make me feel comfortable, declared my literary knowledge "impressive," and included me with all her friends—and there are a ton of them. This girl is rarely alone.

Then last night I learned something new. Ashley called, frantic for Debbie and me to join her for dinner. Her parents are in town and she said her mom was "sucking the life out of her." When Debbie couldn't make it, I almost backed out, but I was too intrigued. I met Ashley and her parents at Davis Street Fish Market after my evening seminar.

Initially I found Mrs. Walker highly entertaining. She's a cross between Lady Catherine de Bourgh and Caroline Bingley. The first brings very strong opinions to the table, while the second adds a bit of insecurity, afraid those opinions aren't well received.

Within the first five minutes Mrs. Walker criticized Ashley's hair (roots showing), her skin (sallow), her boots (scuffed), and her lack of communication (doesn't call home enough—wonder why?). Ashley gave polite, distant replies, but her eyes revealed that each dart hit its mark. The pain and loneliness they conveyed surprised me. While Ashley appears to have everything, something she desperately wants is missing. I know that look.

Then Mrs. Walker turned on me. I quickly yanked out a slightly dusty but diplomatic Jane Bennet and fielded her questions: "Yes, I'm from Chicago. There are lovely homes by the lake. Journalism is very challenging. Yes, feature writing does seem a bit more prestigious than daily news—"

On and on and on. Ashley finally saved me. "No, Mother, Sam doesn't need the name of your personal shopper. Yes, I'm sure one can make a good living as a writer. Mother, don't ask about her love life. Daddy, have you been to an auction lately?"

The last one wasn't an innocent question, but it

was effective. The interrogation stopped. Mrs. Walker's face instantly dropped and her eyes flashed vulnerability and hurt.

A lot of things happen below the surface, don't you think? A jab, a deflection, a hit, then pain—all hidden beneath exquisite manners and an aura of sophistication. There's a little of Edmond Dantes in all of us, I guess.

Mrs. Walker's face closed as she watched her husband and daughter delve into the fall wine auctions. No one else existed for Ashley and her dad. Mrs. Walker slouched in her chair and said it all with a small sigh and a dip of her chin that I alone noticed.

Soon our dinner arrived and I could no longer focus on Ashley's family drama. A large sea creature was deposited in front of me, and I had no clue what to do with it. I've seen ads for Red Lobster, so when Mr. Walker demanded I try one, I agreed. Lobsters look good on TV: all white, red, and buttery. Not this thing. It had a shell, two claws, and a spiky tail, and was delivered with a pair of pliers.

I've struggled with table etiquette lately, and this was way out of my league. No one ever taught me the purpose and propriety behind all the forks, knives, and spoons. And now I was supposed to know how to wield pliers? The waiter tied a plastic bib around my neck, and I almost jumped from my seat.

Ashley and her dad grabbed the lobster with one hand, the pliers with the other, and started cracking the shell. It broke off and they dug out the meat inside with a tiny fork. Holding my pliers likewise, I watched as they'd stab a piece, dip it in butter, and eat it. How hard could this be? So I started in.

The pliers immediately slipped from my hand and the shell cut me. I sat for five minutes with my finger clutched in my napkin to stop the bleeding. That's when I realized that Mrs. Walker hadn't moved a muscle.

"Stanley, call over a boy to help me."

"You can do this yourself, dear. This isn't the club." Mr. Walker sounded exasperated.

"Mother, you can't be serious?" Ashley sounded horrified.

"I am. Call over a boy." Lady Catherine was going to make her presence felt again.

"You could try to crack it, dear." Mr. Walker gave it one more try.

"Do not discuss it further, Stanley. I will not play with my food. Call someone over this instant."

Mr. Walker raised his hand to the waiter and asked him to crack Mrs. Walker's lobster or take it to the kitchen for someone to handle it. The poor guy looked really confused at first, then shrugged his shoulders and carted it away. I sat there clutching my finger in my lap, wishing I had the courage to send mine away too. Her lobster returned a few minutes later beautifully splayed out on her plate. Mine still stared at me. I was so jealous, but determined, once the bleeding stopped. Two bites and I tackled it in earnest. Lobster is yummy.

During the Great Lobster Fight, I simply listened to the conversation. And after a few bites, I identified with Jane Bennet's generous side; she never says a cross word about anyone. I even started a conversation with Mrs. Walker.

"Do you enjoy visiting Chicago? Are the museums to your liking? Have you seen the new exhibit at the Institute?"

Ashley tossed me a wry smile. She knew where I'd gone. Part of me felt exposed, but mostly I felt understood.

That's when I realized how unfair I've been about her. Ashley's not an Emma. Emma would have grabbed her pliers, picked up the dainty fork in her other hand, and widened her eyes at Harriet in a significant manner. Such a look would not only instruct Harriet on what to do, but make Emma's superiority as clear as Harriet's cluelessness. The look, furthermore, would not be skilled enough to hide Emma's delight in the situation and in her role as tutor.

Ashley never did that—any of it. She's as pretty as Gwyneth Paltrow was in the movie, but she isn't Emma. Her assurance and confidence have limits, and I saw them tonight. That makes Ashley approachable—maybe real friend material.

It was good, Mr. Knightley. I'm glad to have my First Impressions reversed. Let's hope I can do the same with Johnson.

Off to revise another
assignment . . .
Sam

P.S. There's more . . . and avoiding it won't make it go away: Kyle fostered out, and I miss him.

I'm happy for him, don't get me wrong. This is no place to grow up. But I've gotten used to Kyle and he's gotten used to me. I don't think either of us would admit we're friends, but we're something. We rely on each other, I think. I went to Buckhorn on his last morning to give him my duffel bag.

"It's yours. I don't want that." He shoved it back into my hands.

"Come on. It's better than trash bags." I started folding his shirts to put them in the duffel, but he kept messing them up. "Stop that. I'm helping you."

"Don't do that." He grabbed another and bunched it up.

I understood. No reminders of help. No reminders of friends lost. I grabbed all the shirts, scrunched them up, and tossed them to him. I thought he'd laugh. He didn't.

"Who you gonna run with now?" Kyle's voice broke, and so did my heart. All this meant something to him too.

"Jaden," I threw out. I couldn't bear to get emotional.

"Jaden? He can't run!"

"I'm just kidding. I'll run alone. No one can replace you, Kyle. But I'm glad you're going. You've got a family now."

"You give me two months?" Kyle refused to look at me. That alone meant the answer mattered. Books are much easier than this real-life vulnerability.

"Don't think that way. You could make all the way to eighteen." I wanted to reassure him and give him that elusive guarantee. "Mr. and Mrs. Hoffman will love you. And I'm always around."

Kyle stood still and blinked a couple times. He whispered, "Thanks, Sam."

I pulled him into a hug and he grabbed on tight. It was the first physical contact we've had since he shoved my hand away on our second run. It lasted a heartbeat before he pushed me away and swiped his eyes.

"Gotta go, Sam. E-mail me. If they don't have a computer, I'll check at school. Every day, you hear?"

"Every day. I promise." *Every day?* I almost made some quip about that being more than we've talked—ever. But I kept silent. You don't make fun of vulnerability. It's too rare.

I was reminded again of Hannah's comments. Maybe all my quips and characters are cowardice—ways to avoid feeling and standing and being me. I didn't want to withdraw at that moment; I owed Kyle more than that. So I forced a pathetically watery smile and watched as he hoisted the duffel, walked out the door, and met the Hoffmans standing in the courtyard with Father John.

So I have a new friend, Mr. Knightley, and I may have lost one too. They couldn't be more different, could they?

"There are just a lot of different sides to me . . ."

~ NOVEMBER 4

Dear Mr. Knightley,

I can't go back to Medill. I'll get my apartment back and I'll work at the library. The library shifts always end in daylight. And Starbucks is only a block from my apartment. They'd probably take me back. Because I won't go back to Medill. I can't take the 'L' again.

At first I didn't think anything of the commute. I ride the 'L' late at night all the time. Evanston is safe, and Grace House is only a few blocks from the stop downtown. There are always people milling around. I've never felt the slightest bit afraid. These are my neighborhoods. I've lived in Chicago all my life.

I heard the footsteps. But there are always footsteps. People are everywhere. It wasn't until the first hit that I knew I was in danger.

I don't know what he wanted. He didn't take my bag. He didn't ask for money. He just kept hitting me—and hitting me. I tried to get up, twice, but he looped back. He went about ten feet away then circled back to hit me again. He was swinging a bar or a bat or something—over and over.

Then I heard yelling. Someone must have scared him away, because the hitting stopped. Not the pain.

Father John came to the hospital. So did the police. They kept asking the same questions: "What did he look like? What did he say? What did he do? What did he say? What was he wearing? What did he do? What did he look like?" Again and again . . . and again.

He was short. About my height, but that's not tall for a man. Where I am thin, he was stocky. He wore a dark hoodie and had stubble. I remember his stubble. And I remember his hands around the bar. Mine are long. He had small hands with short fingers. Isn't that odd? I noticed every detail about his hands. His thumbs were stumpy, and three fingernails were beaten black on his left hand. The right hand was scraped up, but the nails were intact. And they were dirty. Both hands were dirty. I remember the hands.

They kept me at the hospital overnight to watch me. I have a concussion and thirteen stitches along my right eyebrow. There's some pretty good bruising too. My right forearm is pretty bad. I used it to shield my head, I guess. They also took X-rays to see if he fractured my jaw. He didn't.

I've been trying to work up the courage to go back to class tomorrow, but I can't do it. I barely made it to the library today, and it's only a few blocks away. Ten in the morning, and the footsteps behind me paralyzed me. I couldn't move until there was no one behind me. I ended up walking almost sideways, pressing my back against the buildings. It took me over an hour to walk six blocks.

And they didn't find him, Mr. Knightley. He's still out there. Was he behind me today? Is he near the 'L'? Is he near Grace House? Does he wander the streets? I don't have any answers. I don't even remember his face.

Please get as much of your tuition back as you can. Again, I'm so sorry.

Sincerely,
Sam

Dear Ms. Moore,

Father John and Mr. Knightley agree that no time should be lost to make you feel safe. Nor should you sacrifice your program. As you know, Father John has secured an above-garage apartment for you at the home of Mr. and Mrs. David Conley on Lake Avenue, two blocks south of campus and within easy walking distance of downtown Evanston.

Mr. Knightley has extended your grant to cover the additional expenses such a move entails. You will not need to seek further employment during your tenure at Medill. Additionally, please find the enclosed check for $300. This money is to be used for cab fare to and from Northwestern University until your move this weekend.

Father John can provide further details. Additionally, please contact me if any of these arrangements fail to meet your expectations.

> Sincerely,
> Laura Temper
> Personal Assistant to
> Mr. G. Knightley

Dear Mr. Knightley,

Thank you. I don't understand this kind of generosity, but I thank you—you and Father John. It's a little overwhelming, to be honest. I questioned Father John about it.

"This doesn't make sense. I don't need to get a job? This is costing that foundation a fortune. What's the catch?"

"There isn't one. Consider it grace—a gift unwarranted and undeserved."

"Everything comes with a price, Father John."

"Not everything, Sam. Not always. The foundation's director has never extracted a price before, never even accepted thanks. Your personal letters are the most he's ever become involved."

"You don't know him?"

"I feel I do, but, no, I've never met him."

"Then I'm coming after you if this turns weird." I raised my eyebrows. I was both making a joke and letting Father John glimpse my skepticism. It didn't work—moving the right eyebrow made me flinch and simply reminded me why you and Father John are doing this—and how much I need it.

Father John caught it all and smiled at me. "Don't fret. I'll be right behind you."

"Thank you."

That was a couple days ago, and now I'm packed, just some clothes and a whole bunch of books. I move tomorrow morning. And I attended classes these last three days. Thank you for the cab money. I have savings and could have paid for it myself, but I didn't think of it. Your foundation's check reminded me that I have options. I'm not a total victim, despite how I feel. Thank you for that too.

I said good-bye to my Buckhorn Boys this after-noon. I think most felt relief that I won't tutor anymore. I've been a more regular academic influence than most of their teachers. Only Jaden, I think, might miss me.

"Sam, I only got to division. There's lots of math left."

"You'll be fine, Jaden. You've got a sharp mind. Keep at it." I hugged him. I hugged all of them, whether they wanted it or not.

Hannah laughed at me. "Is that more hugging than you've ever done in your life?"

She meant it as a joke, but it stopped me cold. I don't like hugs. I don't like physical contact much. I have few childhood memories of it being gentle.

Hannah looked horrified by her comment. "Sam, I'm sorry. I didn't mean to be insensitive. I didn't think."

"No. It's okay. I guess it's a disadvantage to be so guarded. You miss out, don't you?" Maybe

I'm more like Jane Bennet than I thought . . .

Hannah pulled me back. "Wait here, I've got something for you." She ran to the office. When she returned, I plastered on a quick smile.

"I hope you like it." She handed me a small, wrapped package.

I tore the paper and found a soft blue leather journal with beautiful, thickly-lined pages. At the top of every few pages was a quote by Jane Austen. I flipped through and found my all-time favorite: *I cannot fix on the hour, or the spot, or the look, or the words, which laid the foundation. It is too long ago. I was in the middle before I knew that I had begun.* Mr. Darcy spoke those immortal words in answer to Lizzy's question about falling in love with her. I sighed and showed Hannah the page.

"I don't know the book like you do, but those are the best words ever." She sighed too.

"Does Matt say such things to you?"

"He's not that eloquent, Sam. But I can tell he feels them. Someday you'll have that. And knowing you, you'll hold out for that one guy who not only feels them, but can say them." She gave me a tight hug. And I didn't pull away.

I didn't think it'd be so hard to leave, Mr. Knightley. Maybe the Great Beat-down (humor keeps fear at bay) made me more emotional, I don't know. Maybe it's because this time I know it's permanent. There's no turning back. Grace

House has been good to me: "I have lived in it a full and delightful life, momentarily at least. I have not been trampled on. I have not been petrified . . ." Lately Jane Eyre's melancholy and complex emotions resonate strongly within me.

It's my last night here and, in many ways, I feel the same apprehension Jane felt before her marriage to Mr. Rochester. She had nothing to fear—she didn't yet know about the crazy wife in the attic. But like Jane, I too "look with foreboding to my dread, but adored, type of my unknown future day."

> Always ready for dread,
> but hoping for adored . . .
> Sam

Dear Mr. Knightley,

You must know what I'm typing on. Thank you so much. I'm still trying to process all this. I am completely stunned and need to start at the beginning. You may need to write me a letter, Mr. Knightley. Why did you do all this? And that's only my first question . . .

I arrived here late this morning. I thought I'd feel so free and independent embarking on this journey, but I felt small and scared. More mouse than lion. By the time I reached the Conleys' house, I was bug-eyed.

Have you ever seen the homes along the lake north of Chicago? They are huge and lovely. The lawns are deep green and manicured like golf courses. The Conleys' house is no exception. Mrs. Conley met me at her door and walked me around to the garage. She said they built the apartment last year for her husband's mother, but she's not ready to move in yet.

"This is an adventure for us. We hadn't thought to rent it until Father John called. I hope you like it."

"I'm sure it's lovely. I'm so appreciative." I felt stiff, and my words came out stilted. Everything is more formal when you're nervous—at least for me.

She left me at the stairs to see it alone. "Call me up when you're ready. That way you can see it for the first time without feeling like you have to compliment it. You may not like it."

I loved it at first sight. It has hardwood floors, a bedroom and bathroom and a tiny kitchen that opens onto the living room. Huge windows let in the dappled sunlight and made a dance of light and shadow across the floors. It's perfect and it's mine. And it's yellow. The way pale yellow should look, like sunshine and butter, mixed with hope and cream. I watched the light shine through the bright clean windows and my mind flashed back to that first apartment with Cara. That place scared me, made me feel hopeless; this one invited me in, soothed and healed—all with light and super-clean white trim.

And the furnishings are comfortable with a hint at bold. Exactly how I want to be. The bedroom has a queen bed with a wooden frame and headboard, a huge dresser, and two wooden bedside tables. And there's a big fluffy armchair with flowers embroidered in the fabric. The living room has a red- and white-striped couch with huge pillows featuring embroidered sunflowers. I've also got a big desk in front of the bay window and a small table with two chairs over by the kitchenette. And there's a huge television on the wall—my very own TV.

I called to Mrs. Conley, and she came up and

started going through everything with me, as if I had the power to complain.

"Father John wanted you to have everything you need, so the apartment now has wireless, and I got you digital cable with DVR. I don't know if you watch much TV, but I figured that was good. There are fresh sheets on the bed and towels and spare sheets in the bathroom closet. The washer and dryer are stacked in the kitchen pantry." She walked around the living room pointing to different doors and areas.

"And your foundation sent a computer and printer. They're on the bookshelf over there. The printer is wireless. I've been begging David for one of those, so you'll have to tell me if it works. Is there anything I forgot?"

Dazed, I stumbled on the only detail that stuck. "Did you say computer?"

"It's this laptop." She pulled down a sleek laptop from the bookshelf. "Are you sure I haven't forgotten anything?"

"I'm sure I'll be quite comfortable." My brain felt fuzzy.

I think I seemed eerily calm and uninterested. Really it was shock. I wanted to know more, so I probed a little.

"Who arranged all this?" I asked.

"Well, Father John contacted us first, but then a Ms. Temper handled the details. Does she manage your foundation?"

95

"They gave me a grant and they pay the rent, but I don't know them. Do you know anything about them?"

"No, but we've known Father John for years. How do you know him?"

This is why you don't probe, Mr. Knightley. The turn-around can bite you.

"I've known him for years too," I answered vaguely. Fearing more questions, I floundered for a distraction. Through the window I saw a swing set in the yard. "Do you have kids?"

Mrs. Conley smiled. "Four, and they're dying to meet you. Parker is oldest at fifteen. Then comes Henry. He's thirteen. Isabella's almost twelve, and James is four. They'll be home later and will probably run straight this way. This is very exciting for them. Do you have siblings?"

"I'm an only child, but I've been around kids my whole life. Please tell them they are welcome to visit."

She glanced at me again. I was screwing up. I felt a little like Catherine Morland arriving at Northanger Abbey, though this splendid apartment is anything but gothic.

Mrs. Conley took my pause in stride. I must have appeared to be struggling, because she tilted her head to one side and said, "I'll leave you to settle in. You know, Sam, please don't feel pressured to spend time with the kids or with us. You're simply renting this apartment.

You have no obligations." She turned back at the door. "These UPS boxes arrived this morning."

"For me?"

"Yes. Enjoy settling in." She carefully shut the door and walked down the steps.

Of course, the first thing I did was tear open the boxes. Thank you. I know you read my letters now—I remember complaining about my wardrobe. That was more of a life-direction-desire moment, not a please-fix-purchase-need-now moment. And you are fixing so much. Thank you for moving me up here. And thank you for this gift.

I don't know who actually chose all these things; perhaps your assistant, Ms. Temper? It's hard to imagine "Mr. Knightley" poring over a J. Crew catalog! But if you'll indulge me further, I'm going to be a girl for a moment and really gush. I love the jeans. Two pairs plus the brown pair was extravagant. It's not like I have no clothing. I also love the white blouse. It's so crisp and pristine that it looks almost blue in the light. I've never seen anything that bright. And the black one? I love black. You can take jeans and a black top anywhere. For me, it's usually jeans and a black T-shirt, but I still feel sleeker. It's a girl thing.

The sweaters are gorgeous too. Cashmere. Lovely stuff—so soft. I could go on . . . The skirt, the boots, the belt, the flats, and the coat . . . Everything's magnificent.

I'm completely overwhelmed and I thank you. It was incredibly generous of you. I also appreciated your note: *A true voyager is outfitted for every journey.* You pegged it.

But I have even more questions now. How is it that everything fits? Do you know me? Do I know you or Ms. Temper? Have you seen me?

Lately I feel watched, stalked. Rationally, I know it's not true. But since the Great Beatdown, I feel exposed and fragile. They never found the guy, but that hardly matters. Even if they had, I would still walk around wary. Because now I know—I know what can happen. So I look over my shoulder . . . and into my letters. You don't deserve such distrust. Father John trusts you, and I trust him. But there it is. I hope you won't take my insecurity as an insult.

I can't think, thank, or write any more now. I'm somewhere I never imagined. I'm also tired, and I haven't handled all this or Mrs. Conley well. I probably offended her. I was too remote.

I need to do better here, Mr. Knightley— moving up here requires more commitment. I was invested in Medill before, but I kept one foot in my old world. Now there is no Grace House Escape Hatch. It's slipping away, and I'm packed with equal parts of gratitude, unworthiness, and fear. Topped with a fierce determination to succeed. With deep breaths, I can do this.

And to think, I almost let that small-handed mean man steal this from me.

Thank you for giving it back,
Sam

P.S. I've been sitting in my living room organizing my books. It's so quiet and dark, but I don't feel lonely. I feel safe. How could I not? All my friends are here. You should see them lined up. I almost broke my back hauling them here, but now they are all arranged: Austen, Dickens, Webster, Gaskell, the Brontë sisters, Christie, Powell, Perry, Peters, Cooper . . . They're safe and sound and standing proud. I hung my Georgia O'Keeffe lily poster above my bed and pinned my photographs on the bulletin board near the kitchen. It looks like the home I never dared imagine.

As I was making dinner, the Conley children knocked on the door. I've never met kids like them. No wariness. No anger. No reserve that I can tell—all curiosity and unbounded enthusiasm.

Little James ran in first. "Have you jumped on the bed? It bounces really high."

"Jamie, get off her bed! I'm sorry. He knows better." That was eleven-year-old Isabella. "Do you like it here? I sometimes dream I live up here and that I can't hear all of them." She motioned to her three brothers.

Parker grabbed her in a hug and knuckle-rubbed her head. She feigned anger, but a giggle gave her away.

Then they showered me with helpful hints: stick my trash in the bins on the other side of the garage; their mom makes them clean the bathroom weekly, but she probably won't check on me; the DVR cuts one hour of television down to forty-two minutes once you skip commercials.

They stayed for about forty-five minutes, until Mrs. Conley called them for dinner and homework. I like them. Just thinking about them makes me smile. I hope they liked me too.

One a.m.

I can't sleep. Georgia O'Keeffe is keeping me awake.

Ashley came over last night to return a book I lent her and to see my new digs.

She walked in and *ooohhh*-ed and *aaahhh*-ed perfectly. Then she noticed the O'Keeffe poster. "That's nice, but you should hang something real there. A watercolor or an oil. You need more substance for the room's focal point. The lilies are a bit cliché, don't you think?"

Then she flopped on the couch and pulled out her phone and started playing on it. I stood there stunned. First about the poster comment, then because she sat texting or whatever for a full five minutes.

"What are you doing?" I finally asked.

"Updating my wall."

"Why?"

"Sam, I've got over a thousand friends on Facebook. Do you know how much maintaining that takes? There's an art to doing it well. Not that you'd care." She waved her hand airily at me.

" 'There's a meanness in all the arts. Whatever bears affinity to cunning is despicable.' "

"Nicely done."

I knew she'd recognize Mr. Darcy.

She looked up and shrugged. "Don't be so sensitive. I wasn't being mean. I simply meant you should put more thought into the space above your bed."

"You were being a snob."

"Forget it. I thought we could have a conversation."

"A conversation? As far as I can tell, you came to my apartment, insulted me, and are playing on your phone. What are you even doing here?" I was mad. I had thought we were friends, had hoped we were friends, but now I felt taken in— by an Emma.

Ashley tossed her phone across the couch. "You've got this wall around you. Figuratively speaking. Or is it literal?" Ashley tried to laugh, but tears came out instead. She quickly swiped them and glanced at me.

Did she hope I wouldn't notice? She dropped her gaze and mumbled, "What does it matter?" Then the tears started to fall—really plop down her cheeks.

I didn't know what to do. Part of me wanted to be all Elinor Dashwood—and Ashley did seem a bit Marianne-ish. Another part of me just wanted to kick her out. I was still angry, but I stayed quiet. I sat on the couch next to her.

Ashley blubbered on. "It's like you're the only one who's clever and the only one who's been hurt. I don't even know who hurt you. I don't know anything about you. You don't let me in. Like when that guy hit you? Where'd you go?" She paused and then, thankfully, continued without waiting for a reply. "You don't act like a friend, Sam. I could use a friend. A real one."

I could too, Ashley.

"You don't take me seriously," she said. "No one does. My parents don't. Will doesn't." She rolled against the pillows and swiped the back of her hand across her nose.

"Will?"

"Never mind. He's just a silly boy. He's not the point. Can't we be friends, Sam? Real friends?"

The moment felt like my tae kwon do conversation with Hannah. I don't mean to make people feel distant and unseen, but I do. And I do want friends—that's new for me. They never mattered before. Life was a job. But now I think friendships make it more worthwhile. What's the cost of real friendship?

Ashley sucked in a deep breath. "I have a wall too, Sam. The clothes, the shoes, the hair products. I'm not proud of it, but it's a good, strong wall." More tears dripped from her nose. "And tonight my mother placed another brick in it."

"What do you mean?"

"Mother sent me a blouse. I texted a picture of me in it to thank her, and here's what I got in reply." Ashley picked up her phone and read the text. " 'Clearly you need an appointment at Sania's. Go there straight from the airport Wednesday.' " Ashley looked up. "I can't even go home for Thanksgiving without a cleanup."

"Who's Sania?"

"It's a brow bar on 56th and 5th." Ashley sniffed. I laughed. "A brow bar?"

She frowned at me, so I rushed on. "No, that's what you don't get, Ashley. I'm serious. What's a brow bar?"

"Eyebrows. Shaping, waxing, threading. Not that you need it." She squinted at me. "You just need tweezing."

And there she hit it: my biggest insecurity. Eyebrows like Oscar the Grouch. I reached up to cover them. She pushed my hand away.

"They're pretty, Sam. I'm sorry. I shouldn't have said that."

"They're horrible."

"Get me tweezers."

"What?"

"Just do it. It'll give me something to do. And trust me, I know how to do this. Maybe it's all I'm good for." She rubbed her nose with the back of her hand again and sat up.

Speechless, I started for the bathroom to grab both tweezers and Kleenex, questioning my sanity. First I let Coach Ridley insult my stride to help Kyle, and now . . . Was I really going to let Ashley yank out my eyebrows to boost her self-esteem? Was she helping me? Or was I helping her? Then I had to concede, Kyle is doing better and I'm running faster. We both won.

So I got the tweezers. But that didn't mean I wasn't nervous. "What do you plan to do with these?"

"Sit at the table."

I sat in front of her. Ashley reached up and plucked a hair between my eyes.

"Ouch! You can't do that!" I jerked my head away.

"Stop it and sit still."

"Watch the scar, it's super tender."

"I won't go near it. Sit still or I'll miss and land right on it."

I froze. I didn't even breathe. Clearly she needed this. Maybe I did too.

"I'm sorry I criticized your room, Sam. I was angry. I know you hide, but at least you do it somewhere intellectual. Most people don't think I have a real thought in my brain."

"Of course you do. You're smart, Ashley. You're just amazingly pretty too, and that can be intimidating—ouch." I tried not to cry out each time, but it hurt.

"Really?"

"Sure. You're the classic kind of pretty: petite, blond, blue-eyed. And you have that great accent. It's intimidating. And I think you know it."

"Sometimes." She had the grace to smile.

"Then you can't blame me for throwing out a few quotes here and there. Sometimes I use them to hide and sometimes just to even the score."

"Even the score? But you're so smart."

"And tall and gangly and clueless. Like the other day—you were laughing about rhino-plasties. I thought you were talking about some kind of rhinoceros."

"Rhinoplasty means my mother hauled me and my big nose to a plastic surgeon when I was six-teen to make it into a cute little button." She tapped her nose in staccato with the last three words.

"She did?"

"Yeah." She pulled extra hard on the tweezers.

"Ouch! Maybe we shouldn't talk about your mother."

She grimaced. "Probably not the best topic right now . . . I'm almost done. You look like Anne Hathaway, you know."

"Yeah, right."

"It's true, whether you believe it or not. So tuck it away and pull it out when you need it." Her voice drifted. "You know the best compliment I ever got?"

"Hmmm?"

"I was in seventh grade and a friend was over. We were flipping through magazines, yapping about something, and she turned to me and said, 'Ashley, you always make me feel so good about myself.' " Ashley paused, tasting the compliment in her mind. "That's nice, isn't it?"

"Very nice."

We were silent for a few moments.

"I pull that out sometimes. I'd like to be that person." Ashley sat back and examined her work. "Go look."

I went to the bathroom and looked into the mirror, and was shocked. I'm not saying I was instantly gorgeous. No Anne Hathaway. But I looked pretty. My eyes looked bigger, browner somehow. Everything looked neat and refined. I didn't even feel so tall. That probably makes no sense to a man, but it felt good—really good.

I returned to the living room with a huge grin on my face. Ashley laughed. "My work here is done." She grabbed her bag off the couch and headed to the door.

"Thanks, Ash. You can stay, you know? Do you want some popcorn?"

"No, but thanks. I've got some work to do." She looked through the door to my bedroom. "I'm sorry about earlier. None of this was about your poster. I love the O'Keeffe."

"I get it. And I'm sorry I push back at you sometimes. Just call me out when my quoting is obnoxious."

"Yeah. And tell me when I go all Park Ave on you, okay? I don't mean to sound like such a snob." She hugged me. "Ugh . . . so much to improve. See you tomorrow."

Now I sit here thinking about Ashley, and about that stupid poster, and about my characters. It's time to lay them down, isn't it? They've gone from helping me to trapping me to hurting others. That can't be good.

Good night, Mr. Knightley. Thanks for reading. Sleep well . . .

Dear Samantha,

Mr. Knightley asked me to write to you. He didn't dictate this letter, only asked me to alleviate your worries about the clothing. I hope I didn't overstep. He told me what Father John arranged and asked me to "purchase some nice articles of clothing." I may have gotten carried away.

I visited Grace House last fall and passed you outside Father John's office. You had just turned down the foundation's offer for graduate school and accepted the position at Ernst & Young. In fact, you were moving out of Grace House that very afternoon. You were a few inches taller than me and I noted your warm complexion, brown eyes, and beautiful brown hair. The several photos that Father John attached to your application confirmed my memories and added further insights into your size and stature.

Armed with my gathered information, I hit the stores. I thought the cream sweater, orange scarf, and brown coat would look perfect on you. Except for the one blouse, I stayed away from black, as I imagine your coloring more suited to warm tones. I think my favorite item is the pair of suede boots. I almost bought a pair for myself and still might.

Mr. Knightley did not know the details of a single item purchased. He didn't ask, and he has never met you. Nor will he attach strings to this gift. This I know: he is a good man and would never cross the line with any woman. Please don't hold my exuberance against him or his foundation.

I hope this note assuages your concerns and that you enjoy the clothes. One more thing—I know you are busy at Medill, but your new laptop has amazing resolution. Great for movies. *Downton Abbey* and the new *Sherlock* are available online, if you've never seen them.

Sincerely,
Laura

Dear Mr. Knightley,

Thank you for allowing Laura to write to me. I can't tell you how much her letter helped. Will you please thank her?

On to life here . . . I feel I've been looking over my shoulder so much lately, I haven't moved forward. Well, last night I moved forward—full speed ahead.

How, you ask? I had a date. Twenty-three years old, and it finally happened. You're the only one who knows that little detail, so please keep it to yourself. I'm a full decade behind the curve. But no longer—and I figure if you've been on one date, you can make it a verb. "I date" or "I'm dating." I love verbs!

You need the whole story. Well, I need to tell the whole story, and telling Debbie and Ashley was awful because I had to act so blasé. Dates happen to them all the time: Ashley went out with four different guys last month alone, and Debbie has a boyfriend in Minneapolis. So I pretended last night was no big deal. But you? You get all the details—so I can relive them.

It started a couple weeks ago, when Ashley, Debbie, and I went to a Kellogg Halloween party. Kellogg is the business school at Northwestern, and those folks host the best parties. Anyway, we each dressed in black with sunglasses and walking sticks. Get it? We were the Three Blind Mice and a huge hit. The party was down on Davis Street and spanned three floors of an old walk-up apartment building. It was warm and noisy—everyone trying to make first impressions, second impressions, any impressions. Me, I was trying to sneak home to a good book and hot cocoa. There were simply too many people. I was almost out the door of the top floor's apartment when he stepped in front of me.

"Are you trying to get a drink?" He was not much taller than me, stocky with black hair and equally dark eyes.

"Trying to make a getaway," I shouted.

He touched my shoulder to corral me toward the hallway stairs, where the music wasn't blaring. "How can I convince you to stay?"

That melted me a little. I thought about saying, *What do you have in mind?* but even thinking such a flirty reply made me blush.

"Tell me who you are," I replied. He was dressed like a pirate.

"I'm Captain Jack Sparrow. Can't you tell?"

"I thought Black Beard."

"Really I'm Josh Duncan. I graduated last year, but I still hang with these guys. Are you at Kellogg?" Marilyn Monroe and Joe DiMaggio pushed him closer to me. He smelled like pretzels.

"No, I'm in Medill's journalism program. I'm Sam."

"Undergrad or grad?"

"Grad. Do I look that young?"

"You look great." I melted a bit more and my heart started fluttering. Josh looked pleased, and all my thoughts of escape fled.

After a few minutes, he took both my hands. "Sam, I want to get us some drinks, but you have to promise not to leave. I'm placing your hands on this banister. Don't go downstairs. Don't move at all until I get back."

"I promise." So there I stood, with my hands on the banister, until Debbie found me.

"I've been watching. You need to flirt more."

"I was flirting."

"That's you flirting?"

How do I answer that?

"He's gone to get me a drink. He told me to wait here."

"Oh . . . Sam. He's so cute. Can I have one?" Ashley joined us.

"She's not flirting enough." Debbie turned to her, dismayed by my performance.

"She's got a point, Sam. He won't make a move unless he thinks you're interested."

"Yes, Charlotte." I knew I could count on Ashley catching the allusion. It was Charlotte Lucas's belief that a woman had better show more affection than she feels.

Ashley smiled. "He's definitely into you, Sam. Just look at those eyes."

"They're brown." Yes, Mr. Knightley, I notice the color of everyone's eyes now. Ever since Dan, that's a big deal with me. It's my litmus test to prove I'm in the moment.

Ashley rolled hers. "Not the color, dimwit. The look. It's like Colonel Brandon watching Marianne Dashwood."

Aha, so we weren't in *P&P*, we were in *Sense and Sensibility*, and I apparently had discovered a Colonel Brandon. My eyes widened at the thought.

Ashley grinned. "I find it sometimes best to speak your language."

"I will never doubt you again," I said and hugged her.

Then they both started dishing out the advice: "Toss your hair, lick your bottom lip, tilt your head, smile, smile smaller, laugh softly, make him lean in . . ." Ninety seconds of pure torture before I replaced my hands on the banister and the girls took the stairs down to the apartment below.

But it worked! Josh asked for my number. I thought he'd call the next day, and I got surly when he didn't, but Ashley and Debbie said that was normal. I like normal. So I waited. And a few days later, he called several times—right after the Great Beat-down. I never picked up.

I thought he'd given up, but yesterday he called again—for a date last night. A whole menagerie of butterflies took residence in my stomach. I only had an hour to get ready.

I jumped in the shower, forming a plan, and accidentally shaved across hundreds of goose bumps on my legs. I know, that's more information than you need, but OUCH! Then I panicked. I called Ashley for advice, and within minutes she and Debbie were at my door. The room got so giddy you'd think no one had been on a date ever. The two of them dived into my closet.

"She should wear black with the jeans. It's casual and sexy." Ashley held the blouse to her face.

"Of course it looks good against you, Ash. You're blond. Look at all her gorgeous dark hair. She'll be better in this." Debbie held up the cream sweater.

"Sure, at a study session. It's a date, Deb. She needs to make a statement."

"Hello? I'm in the room. I vote cream and brown. I like study sessions."

Ashley rolled her eyes. "Please, Sam, put a little Marianne in your Elinor." I smiled. It was a lovely idea.

How would it feel to get carried away on emotion like Marianne? To be so recklessly entranced? So passionately in love? I never thought Marianne's devotion to Willoughby was prudent, and it wasn't, but I bet it was fun. And later, I'm sure all that passion enveloped Colonel Brandon.

In the end we decided on jeans, brown high-heeled boots, the cream sweater, and a cream-and-brown patterned scarf around my neck. We had just finished adding the scarf when Josh knocked on the door. Ashley and Debbie ducked into my bedroom, which made for a weird first moment. Then I almost forgot them as Josh walked me down my apartment steps. He looked so good in a black sweater and jeans.

"You look great tonight, Sam. Thanks for saying yes on such short notice. A meeting fell through and I thought I'd take a chance."

"I'm glad you called. Where are we going?"

"To my favorite Indian restaurant on Devon. Do you like Indian food?"

"I'm not very familiar with it."

"You'll love it. If you want, I'll order for us."

Is that how it always is? It felt lovely to have someone take such good care of me. Brandon took care of Marianne like that, I'm sure. Josh opened the car door and practically settled me into the passenger seat. We chatted while I floated along in my plush, beige leather seat with built-in warmer.

At the restaurant, I was out of my league again. Where is a burger joint when you need one? I couldn't understand a word on the menu and finally put it down. Josh looked pleased when I asked him to order. He did a good job: chicken tikka masala, tandoori prawns, some vegetable samosas, and naan. I looked them all up so I could spell them for you. See what care I take with your letters?

It was delicious: hot and spicy, deep and earthy. Dinner, time travel, and sunbathing rolled into one culinary experience. While we ate, Josh asked a lot of questions, some twice. I felt reluctant to answer. One—concentrating on my inner Marianne and feeling the moment took energy. Two—I hate talking about myself. So I opted for a few well-timed deflections. Most of the evening went like this:

Josh: "Where did you grow up?"

Sam: "Right here in Chicago, but I've never been here. Could you pass the chicken dish? It's wonderful . . . Thanks. Are you pleased you stayed here after business school?"

Josh: "Of course, you can't do better than Leo Burnett for advertising. I interviewed in New York, but found more innovative work coming out of Chicago."

Sam: "Tell me about it. What are you working on?"

And off he went. I didn't manipulate him, I promise. I genuinely loved hearing about his life and work. I learned he is the youngest of three boys, grew up in Cincinnati, graduated from the

Miami University of Ohio before Kellogg, likes to play basketball and run, only reads magazines, and doesn't like milk. See, lots of stuff.

And he has the neatest hands. He uses them when he talks, and I like the way they move. Is that weird? There must be something about hands from my childhood. I notice them—best not dig too deep into that one.

This is what I told Ashley and Debbie this morning: "We had a nice time. I hope he calls, but I gather he's really busy." I was ready to share all the silly details, but it was too mundane and normal for them. They didn't ask for more.

Only Debbie replied, "Don't worry, you're too cute for him not to call. Let's go grab a coffee."

So we went for lattés and discussed finals. Back to the real world. Oh, by the way . . . I got a real kiss too.

Sam

P.S. Okay, that was unfair. So while it's very tacky to "kiss and tell," I'll share some of the scene. Granted, thirteen-year-olds probably do this, but you'll have to cut me some slack. I'd like to relive that moment too, and who am I going to tell, Isabella?

I had almost gotten sick as Debbie and Ashley raced around my living room cleaning while I dressed. They believed I would "invite him up"

117

after our date. That hadn't occurred to me, but it worried me throughout dinner. And as we turned into the Conleys' driveway, my stomach dropped and my skin grew clammy. Panic is not just an emotion. It's a very physical phenomenon. The butterflies fled my gut—crickets overtook them.

Josh parked right in front of the garage, and his previously quiet Lexus Hybrid sounded louder than a jet engine. Everyone could hear. Everyone knew what was about to happen—everyone but me. *Does he open my door? Does he walk me up? Does he expect to come in? Do I kiss him? Does he kiss me? Enough!*

"I had a wonderful time tonight, Josh. Thank you very much." I reached for the door handle.

"Me too. I'd like to do this again."

"Sure. Give me a call."

"Sam?" He gently pulled my arm, turning me back and slightly across the center console. Before I had time to think, he kissed me. Not quick, but slow and soft. First it was a question, then he seemed to find an answer and he deepened it. I've heard all sorts of things about a kiss (melting, fireworks, music), but no one ever told me it's a conversation: asking, accepting, deciding, inviting, giving . . . Questions posed and answered. After a few moments, my head spun and the car felt steamy. I pulled away to catch my breath.

"Shall I come up?" He brushed my hair back,

and I couldn't help but lean into his hand. His eyes seemed black in the dark car as they rested on my lips.

"I don't think so. I don't want Mrs. Conley to see your car here too late. Another night?"

"Do you care what they think? Are you related?"

"No, but they have four kids. They're a nice family. You'd like them." I reached for the handle and climbed out. I got halfway up the stairs when he called out the window.

"Sam, I've got meetings for the next few nights. Can I see you Friday?"

"I'd like that."

"Great. I'll call you." He waited for a moment, then backed out as I entered my apartment.

So that was it. I once heard a wonderful line in a movie that the first kiss is not the one you judge. Instead all the meaning is in the second . . .

Dear Mr. Knightley,

I've got even more exciting news than my last letter. But before I get to it, I need to tell you about school. I feel I haven't been completely honest by avoiding the topic. Clearly I'm still here, but my last several Johnson assignments received Ds. I know that's not great, but—

Who am I kidding? It's horrible. I've never gotten grades like this. I've never seen so many red markings. It's pathetic. I keep trying, though, and I submitted an article to the *Tribune*. Publication can't help but impress Johnson, right? I figure he'll commend my drive, if not my writing. So you see, I have a plan and I'm still kicking . . .

Now on to the fun: I met Alex Powell today. *The* Alex Powell! I'm sure you've read his books. They've all topped the best-seller lists and rightfully so. You should read them if you haven't. Anyway, one of Ashley's professors announced yesterday that he was coming to her class this morning, so Ash snuck me in the back.

Mr. Powell was such a surprise. At first I thought he was the TA. The guy looks about twenty. He talked for half an hour, then answered questions on his writing methodology, research, and favorite authors. He then thanked Professor

Thomas and walked out. The whole class was in chaos, so I slipped out too. And banged right into him.

"Whoa. Isn't there more to the class period?"

"I am so sorry. Did I hurt your foot? No, I'm not in that class."

He hiked his eyebrow.

"I came to see you." *Did I say that out loud?*

"And?" Powell smiled.

"You were great. I mean I like your approach. I mean I like your books. I mean I'm going to stop talking now." I sounded like an idiot.

"Did you miss class for this?" He chuckled.

"Today's light for me. I'm in Medill's grad journalism program." *Please don't think I'm a high school groupie.*

"Journalism? You aren't going to write about me, are you? I'd rather you didn't." It was his turn to sound uncomfortable.

I laughed—a skittish giggle really. "I wasn't there for a story. I actually know that about you. There are no pictures on your book jackets and you rarely give interviews. You don't even have a photo on your website." *Stop talking, Stalker.*

But I kept on. "I expected you to look different, older—gray hair, black glasses. You're surprisingly young."

Eyebrow hike again.

"I'm Samantha Moore." After all my lunacy, I thought introductions were in order. I reached out my hand and for a second he simply stared at it— so I blabbed on. "I'm sorry I ran into you and I'm not a stalker, I promise."

"I didn't think that." He took my hand and forced a thin smile. "No worries."

I didn't scare him too much, because a minute later he asked me to grab a coffee with him. Once outside, I stopped and took a deep gulp of air. I thought I might hyperventilate. I know he heard me, but he didn't say anything. As I led him toward the Starbucks in Norris, we got side-tracked and wandered around campus for about fifteen minutes. He went to school here, but I gather new buildings have popped up in the last few years.

Did you get that? He graduated from NU and is only about thirty years old. My image of him was definitely older, but after that it was vague. I was always more entranced by the hero than the author. His detective, Cole Barker, is my Darcy, Wentworth, Rochester, Bond, and Hunt—all the great men, dressed in jeans and a black jacket.

Alex is very different from that. Cole, in my mind, has dark hair and wire-rimmed glasses and is super-fit. Hollywood followed that idea in the movie. Alex embodies all that, but differently. He's got the firm jaw and he's tall (like six foot four tall), but his eyes aren't dark and they're not hidden behind glasses. They're deep blue and actually snap. When he looks at you, it feels like he's studying you, focusing energy on you, and all this connects in his eyes. It was intimidating at first, and I got self-conscious. I stammered and resorted to my fallback friends: a quick amalgam of Lizzy Bennet and Edmond Dantes gave me my voice back. Then I was able to laugh. Talking to him became easy, and soon I quit thinking about my characters at all. After we bought a couple coffees, we wandered back outside and he turned toward town.

"I'm meeting an old professor at Barnes and Noble in a few minutes. Are you heading that way?"

"No."

"Then it was nice to meet you, Samantha." He put out his hand to shake mine.

I looked at it a moment and realized I didn't want to say good-bye. How often do you get to meet one of your literary heroes? And most of mine are dead. "I'll walk with you. I can get some work done at the Starbucks across the street."

"You have a coffee in your hand."

"Oh . . ." I wanted to run. I had clearly used up all my social skills. But I also felt more myself than I had felt in months, and I didn't want it to end. Alex hadn't asked me lots of personal questions, so I hadn't lied to him. He hadn't treated me as insignificant, so I let my guard down. And Lizzy and Edmond and all the rest had silently slipped away. No one was yelling in my head. No one even whispered. My processing all this must have played across my face.

"Are you okay?" he said.

"I am." I was completely amazed, exhilarated, and alarmed. So you can see why I wanted to run and why I wanted to stay. "Just realized that two coffees would be a bit much."

"Buy a decaf. Come on." And he started walking toward town. I followed.

When Alex discovered how much I loved to read, he suggested a game. He proposed we quote from a book, no movies allowed, and the first one stumped, lost.

And I won! It took about ten quotes, but I foiled him with "Wait and hope." He smugly shot out *Wuthering Heights*—as if Heathcliff or Cathy knew anything of either.

I struggled to keep a straight face. "*The Count of Monte Cristo*. Edmond Dantes writes that in closing his letter to Maximilian."

I forgot to cross the street once I saw Barnes and Noble—it's like a homing beacon to me. I automatically walked through the doors, forgetting that Alex and I were to part ways. Alex bumped into me when I stopped in the lobby. His face had the same kid-in-a-candy-store expression I imagine my own wore. This is a particularly potent store. We stood in a two-story lobby with a huge chandelier bouncing light off the thousands upon thousands of books lining the walls.

I pulled at Alex's arm and raced to the escalator. When he laughed I realized what I'd done and dropped it like a stone. Then I felt silly and tried to shake my schoolgirl reaction.

"I'm sorry. You go meet your professor. I'm going to find a table in the back to study. It was great to meet you." I started to walk away.

"I've still got a few minutes." He turned in the aisle. "Look here—mysteries. Do you read mysteries?"

I smiled. "A few." I ran my fingers along the books, tapping some of my favorites. I stopped at Perry, traveled to Peters, and landed on Powell. "And here you are."

"I am. They've got a good selection."

I pulled out a book and grabbed a pen from my bag. "You need to sign some. Can you imagine how thrilled people will be to see your signature?"

"That's called vandalism," he quipped, but I could tell he was intrigued.

"Only if *I* sign your name. If *you* do, it's called winning a golden ticket."

"Fine."

We picked out a few of his books and he signed them—real notes too. In a copy of *Salvation Bound* he wrote: *Enjoy my favorite passage on p. 187. It really happened. All the best, Alex Powell.*

I flipped to page 187 and started reading from the top. It's a defining moment for Cole. A break in his father's murder investigation rocks him to his core, and we find him inside a church, bereft and questioning everything he's done and is. A pastor approaches from behind and asks to join him. Cole nods to the pew, but continues to look forward, uncommunicative and sullen.

The pastor sat for a few moments, then turned to Cole. "You're going to be okay. Trust your heart."

Cole turned, angry at the intrusion, angry with himself. "What?"

"You have to stop questioning and fighting so much."

"Who are you? You know nothing about me."

"I don't need to."

"But you're giving advice, or worse, assurances?"

"I must be right or it wouldn't anger you so much."

"Go away." Cole turned forward, unwilling to give the intruder his time or energy.

"I will, but listen to your heart. That's where He speaks."

The pastor leaves the pew and Cole sits there, stunned. I knew that was the scene Alex meant.

He had revealed himself and some conflict that had impacted him deeply. I looked up at him; my eyes asked, *What happened?*

"My father wasn't murdered in a police-mob conspiracy, but yes, at a very dark time, a young pastor took me on. Just like this. He's now one of my best friends. He got a kick out of being in my book."

"Can you tell me more?" I sensed that this was fragile ground.

"Maybe another time." His crooked, sad smile ended the probing.

He grabbed another book, *Three Days Found,* and lightened the mood. *Enjoy the story,* he wrote. *It's my favorite. And if you're in NY, eat at Patsy's and bring this. They'll love it. The description starts on p. 206. Joyfully, Alex Powell.*

"Patsy's?"

"It's the most amazing Italian restaurant in New York. It was Frank Sinatra's favorite place and still has that authentic Rat Pack vibe. The food's amazing and the portions will feed a starving writer or fuel a marathon runner."

"Which are you?"

"I'm occasionally hungry as both, but I've never run a marathon. A few friends like to go there each year before New York."

"I'd love to run New York someday."

"You should. They say it's the best. The crowds

are amazing, and you run through all five boroughs."

I looked down at the book in my hands and was reminded of my mental image of him. "Why do you never put your photo on the back cover? You aren't ugly."

"That's good to know." He laid his hand on top of the book. Not really talking to me, he continued, "I don't, because however people imagine me is always better than I am. And I don't want to be defined by these."

"I thought fame was the icing on the cake."

"It should be avoided. It limits you and hurts you. Besides, if I was shackled by too much of it, you and I couldn't spend even this time together. Too many people already know what I do and where I go. People forget your face after a book tour or an infrequent interview on Letterman, but put your face on your books and you're handing them your life. They presume to know what you think or who you are. Not like a movie star or anything, but you definitely give yourself away."

Alex leaned against the shelves. "No more spontaneity. No more first impressions. All of that gets tainted by the fame and the money, and even by Cole Barker himself."

"I never thought of it like that. I used to believe all those externals meant happiness. I'm beginning to see they don't." Ashley and her mother came to mind.

"Often they lead to pain." It was a cryptic answer, but one I couldn't question.

We wandered a bit more. I confessed my obsession with Jane Austen. We agreed that Barnes and Noble could devote an entire section to Austen's sequels, prequels, mimics, knock-offs, and add-ons . . .

Last year I got the flu and went through about forty titles: *The Darcys Give a Ball*, *The Watsons and Emma Watson*, *The Darcys and the Bingleys*, *George Knightley's Diary*, *Captain Wentworth's Diary*, *Fitzwilliam Darcy's Diary*, *Austenland* . . . I emerged with no aches and pains, but with a stilted language pattern that took a month to purge. My new favorite title is *How Jane Austen Ruined My Life*. I don't have the courage to read it, though. I'm afraid to discover she's ruined mine too.

We were talking next to a display table when a booming voice startled us.

"About time you came home, young man!"

I looked up to see a blur of white bounding toward us. Professor Muir is tall, thin, and intense like a lightning bolt, with the bushiest white eyebrows imaginable. Without Ashley and those tweezers, mine may look like that someday.

The professor grabbed Alex into a quick hug and, after much backslapping, started rapid-firing questions. Alex jumped right in, and I faded into the background. It was like watching puppies play in a pet shop window, all unbridled affection and enthusiasm.

"You carrying your books around with you now?" Professor Muir joked to Alex.

"I signed these." Alex threw me a glance. "Couldn't help myself. I'll take them down to the customer service desk on my way out."

"Not yet, we've got a few minutes." He took Alex's arm to lead him toward the café.

I inched away.

"Don't leave." Professor Muir looked straight at me. "Come sit for a few minutes."

"No, thank you. I just met Al—Mr. Powell today. You two catch up." I turned to Alex. "Good-bye."

He studied me for a moment. "Sam, I've only got about fifteen minutes before I'm needed downtown for some PR work. Come sit. You should know this old guy." He poked the professor in the ribs. "He's good to have in your back pocket."

To be honest, it was time to leave. I was intruding and I knew it, but I didn't know how to politely decline. And it was fine for a few moments. Then I opened my mouth and humiliated myself. I should have left when I had the chance.

Alex clearly got that "quote from a book" game from the professor, because that's what got me into trouble. I corrected an English professor and America's best writer—who does that? They were talking about another writer they both knew and disliked.

"I saw him last week and couldn't help but think 'How tartly that gentleman looks! I never can see him but I am heartburned an hour after.' " Professor Muir laughed as he delivered the line in a high falsetto.

"Katherine to Bianca, *Taming of the Shrew*. Bravo, Pops. Very appropriate. I feel the same way."

"No, no! It's from *A Midsummer Night's Dream*. You've forgotten the Bard." The professor sounded pleased.

"I have not. You're confused. Katherine says it about Bianca's suitor in act 1," Alex replied.

"I beg—"

"You're both wrong," I announced. Their heads swiveled so fast I thought they'd twist off. Alex hiked his eyebrow at me, questioning.

"Beatrice said it to Antonio in *Much Ado About Nothing*."

Both men stared at me. My face burned.

"Are you sure?" Alex said.

"Yes. It happens in the scene right after—" I clamped my hand over my mouth. No more talking! They didn't seem angry, but I'm not sure . . . Alex left moments later.

I sat with the professor for a few minutes while he drank his coffee. I didn't know how to leave without being even more insulting.

"You should meet my wife."

"Excuse me?"

"You should come to dinner. Here, write down your number and she'll call you."

"You don't need to—"

"Nonsense. I like you. And a friend of Alex's is always worth knowing."

There was no point protesting again that I'd just met Alex, so I wrote my number down, thanked him, and left.

It was a great day, Mr. Knightley, and I'll never forget it. And though I tarnished it at the end, I am determined to revel in what began as a most spectacular day. I'll never see him again, so what does it matter? Besides, can you believe that, for a brief shining moment, I was on a first-name basis with *the* Alex Powell?

I called Ashley to recount the morning; she chewed and savored every detail. I'm meeting Debbie after class tomorrow, so I'll get to enjoy the whole story again. Now it's late and I need to sleep.

Lovely dreams,
Sam

Dear Mr. Knightley,

I know I just wrote yesterday—but I need to sort this out, and writing you is always good for that. I shot an e-mail off to Kyle yesterday just to see how he's doing and got a horrid reply. I've been on the phone with Kyle and Father John all afternoon trying to understand.

Kyle's e-mails have been nonexistent the past couple weeks, and I just thought he was busy. I hoped cross-country, studies, and his new family filled his time. Perhaps I saw only what I wanted to see. Or had time to see. Life's been busy and school's a struggle. Maybe I shut him out too—I don't know.

Anyway, Coach Ridley saw marks on Kyle's neck and refused to send him home a few days ago. Ridley called the police, who took Kyle to a holding house and brought Mr. Hoffman in for questioning. Father John says DCFS believes there's no wrongdoing and that Kyle is self-sabotaging. It's a term used to describe when kids push new families away to test their loyalty. Kyle didn't talk and he's going back to the Hoffmans' this afternoon.

I asked him myself and he didn't deny it—so maybe DCFS is right. Maybe he was just testing them. He sure tested me long enough. No, that's not fair—we tested each other.

"Did you do it, Kyle?"

"Do what?"

"Hurt yourself? To see if they cared? You know you can talk to me."

No reply.

"Heck, we've been through a lot. If we can't be honest with each other, who can we trust?"

"Dunno. You okay?" *Nice deflection, Kyle.*

"Your e-mail said you were flunking out."

"I'm doing better. I'm getting the hang of it." *Counterattack.* "Let's talk about you."

Kyle paused. At the time, I thought he was thinking. Now I wonder, was his deflection a test of my honesty? A test of my loyalty? And I failed?

It was—I know it. Darn it! I really like that kid and for some reason feel he's an indelible part of me. I've tried to call him a couple times, but he won't answer. It's so clear to me now that I let him down.

I need to give him space to work out his life without me pestering him. And I've got to remember this is about him, not me. But I have that sinking feeling I had when I beat him on the track—that he needed something and I deliberately withheld it to protect myself. I was wrong and I will apologize . . . again. But for now I think I need to let Kyle enjoy Thanksgiving with the Hoffmans.

I've got other stuff on my plate anyway—which leads me to you. Loyalty and honesty, right?

Yesterday, after my once-in-a-lifetime hour with Alex Powell, I ran into Dr. Johnson. He, of course, remembered that I submitted an article to the *Tribune*. Why did I ever tell him? And I couldn't lie when he asked . . . They refused it with a very succinct *Not suitable for publication at this time.*

"It was my first try, Dr. Johnson. I'll refine the next one and submit again."

"You can try as often as you like, Moore. It won't help. You need to decide if you're right for this program. You're way behind where you should be by now."

My heart stopped. "What are you saying?"

"Simply this. Medill is expensive. If you have the funds and can afford a low-paying newspaper job, let's keep at this. If you're on loans, you might want to consider more lucrative work. Graduate school takes serious commitment and, given that, can yield serious results. Careers are made within these walls, but students are broken as well."

"I've given everything to be here."

"You have? Tell me what you've sacrificed, because I've never seen a student give so little."

"What?"

"I see no passion in your writing. Only technique. It's good, but it's empty."

" 'I certainly have not the talent which some people possess . . . ,' but I am working hard." I grimaced. Spewing forth a hackneyed Darcy line confirmed, not refuted, Johnson's point.

"There you go, Moore—a perfect example. Can't you feel yourself step away from the subject? Right here in this conversation." He studied me a moment. "If you don't commit, consider yourself warned. You'll be one the faculty cuts. We don't keep students who hold the others back."

How did he know? He studied me again and, I think, pitied my fallen expression. I blinked hard to clear my eyes as he continued. "You must press deeper, stretch farther, dig. Give up on the *Trib* for now. Try the *Evanston Review* and some township papers. Get some publishing credits, grab a bit of encouragement, and drive harder. You've got two months, Moore. Don't waste them."

So here I sit, trying to stretch and dig. A writer is revealed through her work, journalism or fiction. I know that now. I learned it from Alex. Last night, I pulled a few of his books from the shelves and reread my favorites. And I found him, the real Alex, on every page. Not him directly, but I found his passion. That's what Johnson is talking about. In journalism, you can take an objective subject and infuse it with life by your commitment to it, your passion for it.

I learned something else while perusing Alex's books: Fiction is great to read, but it's not for me to write. There are stories in me—hard-hitting stories, factual stories, life stories, news stories. I see them in front of me, and now I see them slipping away.

This has been plaguing me, especially since lying to Kyle about school this afternoon. I know that avoiding the bad doesn't make it go away, and escaping into a good book or character doesn't help either. I must deal with reality and all the mess I've pushed away for so long. Please know I'm working. This program, this work, has come to mean the world to me. I won't/can't fail.

Thanks for listening,
Sam

Dear Mr. Knightley,

I'm flooding your mailbox. Sorry about that. There is so much happening right now and you're the best place to send this—the good and the bad. Mrs. Muir called today, and I took the Metra up to Winnetka for dinner. I'm still shocked both that she called and that I accepted. To make it more dramatic, Alex Powell showed up during dessert—and none too pleased to see me.

When I rang their doorbell, Professor Muir immediately opened it and bounded onto the front walk.

"You're here. I was sure you wouldn't come . . . Don't just stand there. Come in." He led me into the front hall. The walls were light brown and there was a patterned rug on the wood floor. The front stairs arched around the entrance hall. Not grand, like in the movies, but large enough and strong enough to contain Professor Muir. It looked like "home."

"I have something you should read. I think you'll love it."

"Let her settle a moment, Robert." A quiet voice came from beside me. I jumped, for I hadn't noticed anyone standing there. "Would you rather help me in the kitchen, Sam? It's Sam, right?"

Mrs. Muir was tall like her husband, but exuded

serenity, not fireworks. Can someone personify peace? It's the best way to describe her.

I looked back at the professor, who nodded at me. "Go ahead. We can talk after dinner."

I followed Mrs. Muir into the kitchen.

"I'm Frances Muir. I'm so glad you came tonight."

"Thank you for inviting me. And yes, it's Sam—short for Samantha."

"Robert always loved inviting students to dinner, and Alex was and is his most favorite. It's wonderful to have one of his friends join us for dinner."

"I just met him briefly a couple days ago. He gave a talk on campus and I snuck in; then I stepped on him and walked downtown with him. I don't really know him." I pressed my lips together. *Stop babbling.*

"Well, Robert liked you, my dear, and he's a good judge of character." Mrs. Muir smiled. "And as for Alex, he may drop by later, so perhaps you can get to know him better."

"Alex?" *Gulp.*

"He has some signings and a couple events downtown this evening, but he hopes to drop by. He's got a flight back to New York tomorrow morning."

"Oh." I never expected to run into Alex again, and now I felt that I was intruding into his private world.

"Why don't you wash that for me, and I'll finish the sauce." Mrs. Muir pointed to a head of lettuce.

I grabbed it, happy to contribute. There was something about the Muirs—the professor's intensity and Mrs. Muir's serenity—that intrigued me and made me feel safe. I wanted to be there. That in itself was highly unusual. Most of the time I want to be anywhere other than where I am.

As I washed the lettuce, I looked around. It was clearly a working kitchen. Some, you can tell, are just for show. You might get a snack out of them, but they're not fortified to put out great meals every day. This one was the real deal. Cookbooks lined the shelves, spices stood at attention in a rack, knives rested in a huge block next to a massive Viking stove. And the aura of tomatoes, anchovies, and garlic dominated the landscape. I worked in silence for a moment and then decided to ask about Alex and the professor.

"They seemed very close at the café. Have they always been like that?"

"From the moment Alex stepped into Robert's class. We never had children, and in many ways we regard Alex as a son."

"Does he come here often?"

"He used to schedule a lot of media work in Chicago so he could stay with us for a few weeks, but with the last book he never left New York.

We've been out there a few times, but he's had a hard time the past few years." She paused for a moment, then added wistfully, "He's worked nonstop for years now."

I learned that Alex's parents are alive and well and living in Washington state—but they don't mind the time Alex spends with the Muirs. Can you imagine? Another set of parents looking out for you, loving you? Then Mrs. Muir asked if I missed my family. I was tempted to tell her the truth. The kitchen felt warm and safe, and I think Mrs. Muir is trustworthy. I came so close.

"I don't miss them too much. I'm so busy. Would you like me to chop this as well?" The dodge worked and the moment passed.

We soon sat down to *Bistecca alla Pizzaiola*, the Steak of the Pizza Maker's Wife. Basically it's a steak, pan-seared then slow cooked in a thick tomato, garlic, and anchovy sauce. The food was rich, comforting, and delicious, and the conversation felt the same. We talked about literature, writing, movies—all sorts of stuff. I even confessed some of my problems with Johnson.

"Russell's as tough as they come." Professor Muir leaned back in his chair.

"Too tough for me. He's going to fail me."

"Have you talked to him about how to improve?"

"A little." The idea of willingly pursuing Johnson for a "talk" was unimaginable.

"Keep at it. I say he's tough, but he's also one of the best men I know—a man of incredible skill and incomparable integrity. You keep at it. You're in good hands."

I sat there stunned. I knew Johnson was powerful, but this was a peer, not a student or even a journalist, singing his praises. I saw Johnson in a different light, and it didn't make him any less intimidating.

I let these thoughts dance in my mind while we cleared the table and began washing the dishes. Then Alex arrived . . .

He walked straight in the front door as Mrs. Muir was putting a plate of cookies on the kitchen table. She said it was our reward for a kitchen well cleaned. I turned around to comment and there he was, staring at me.

"Sam? What are you doing here?"

I froze. I thought I might be intruding before; now I knew I was.

"Alex," Mrs. Muir gently reprimanded him. "We invited Sam for dinner. We're having a lovely time."

Alex shook his head as if clearing a thought or rustling up some good manners. "I'm surprised, that's all. I didn't expect to see you here."

"Professor Muir took my number at the café. Then Mrs. Muir called me."

He waved his hand. "Don't explain. I told you they were good people. Glad you're here." But he didn't sound glad. He turned away from me, crossed the kitchen, and kissed Mrs. Muir on the cheek. "Where's Pops?"

"He went to get Sam a book from the study."

"Great." Alex grabbed a cookie and left in search of the professor.

Mrs. Muir studied the empty doorway for a moment. "That was abrupt." She turned to me and smiled. "Don't let him rattle you, Sam. We're so delighted you came."

"I'm intruding on his time with you. You said he's like your son, and now a stranger is mucking up his last night here."

"Not at all. When Robert was teaching we had lots of 'sons' and 'daughters' coming for dinners. It was great fun. But since his retirement, Alex has been the only one around. Perhaps he's grown a bit spoiled." She grinned and handed me a cookie. "Let's sit."

Alex and the professor came back to the kitchen and we sat around the table, chatting and eating cookies for another hour. Then the conversation dwindled, and I knew Alex needed time alone with them.

"Thank you so much. I need to get home and finish some work."

"Remember what I said about talking to Johnson." The professor smiled at me.

"What are you working on?" Alex looked across the table at me—directly for the first time.

"I have an article due, and I'm reading *The Merchant of Venice*. It's showing downtown and I thought I'd see it and write a review for one of my classes."

"Good for you. That's very thorough of you, Sam, to read the play first. I'm impressed." The professor cut into the conversation.

"Ah, Portia and her secret identity . . . I love that one." Alex nodded and chomped a cookie.

"I do too." I paused and looked at him for a moment. It was a surreal experience. It's not like I have a crush on him; I don't. Alex wasn't that nice tonight, and I'm seeing Josh—we went out again last Friday. But sitting across a table from Alex Powell, eating cookies, was unique.

"Let me drive you back to campus." Alex slid his chair back.

"No, I'll be fine." I didn't want to take the Metra at night, but I was not about to take Alex from the Muirs.

"You're not taking the Metra. I'll drive you if Alex won't." Professor Muir stood as well.

"Take a seat, Pops. I'll drive Sam and be right back. While I'm gone, you can read my plot points for the next book."

"Excellent." The professor rubbed his hands together in anticipation.

Alex stalked to the front hall without another word and grabbed his coat. I felt like the Ugly Duckling—obtrusive and unwanted.

As he opened the door, the professor rushed into the hall. "You're staying here for Thanksgiving, Sam? On campus?"

"Yes, how did you . . . know that?" I stammered.

"Students usually babble about home this time of year. You never mentioned it."

"Ahh . . ." I let it hang. There was nothing to say.

"You'll come here."

"No, I . . ." I fumbled for an excuse. Any excuse.

"Franny will call you. I make stuffing. It's the only thing I make all year, and I have a talent. You'll love it." He winked at me and leaned down for a bear hug, and I couldn't pull away—he's too big—so I surrendered. I'm unused to hugs, so at the time I couldn't enjoy it. Several hours later, I loved that hug.

Alex and I got into his rental and headed south. He didn't speak. I thought a fifteen-minute silent ride with Alex Powell might kill me, so I started asking questions.

"You've got an outline for your next book?"

He turned his head and looked straight at me for a moment, studying me. I guess I passed some test, because he visibly relaxed.

"I do. This one's been hard. All the publicity I'm doing for *Salvation Bound* hasn't helped, but they've got me on a yearly release now, so I keep chugging."

"That's a lot of writing."

"It's a much different pace than I kept for my first two. I wrote *Redemption* while getting my MFA at Columbia and worked in a coffee shop while finishing it. It was easy, I guess, because I didn't have any expectations. Now there are expectations."

"Do you get any breaks?"

He laughed this self-deprecating chuckle that sounded tinged with regret. "This week was supposed to be that. I decided to visit Mom and Pops Muir at the last minute and look what happened—PR events, signings, interviews. I told my publisher my plans, and 'vacation' went out the window."

"Your talk at Northwestern?"

"That? No, I set that up on my own. Megan and I were at Columbia together, and she's been begging me to talk to her class. But the dog-and-pony show downtown? Not my favorite." He looked at me again. "I'm sorry I'm complaining, Sam. I sound pathetic. 'Poor me, too many people love me.' "

I laughed. "I was not thinking that."

"I wouldn't blame you." He paused. "Let me tell you something else. Something good, that's not a complaint."

Alex then shared that he comes from eastern Washington and has three siblings; he thinks Mrs. Muir's chocolate chip cookies are straight from heaven; he loves to watch baseball; and he gets his hair cut only at places with a traditional barber pole outside. Don't ask how that last detail came up. I can't remember, but it didn't sound odd at the time.

We were in the Conleys' driveway before I knew it.

"Thanks for putting up with me, Sam. I was rude tonight."

"Not at all. I intruded on your family. I'm sorry about that. I didn't mean to."

I started to get out of the car, but he called me back. "Sam?"

I leaned into the open door.

"Please go to their house for Thanksgiving. They never had kids and always wanted them. I think retirement has been harder on Pops than he'll admit. He misses his students."

"If they call, I'll go. He was right. I don't have any plans."

Alex nodded. "Good then. Thank you." He reached out to shake my hand.

> I'll keep you posted
> on Thanksgiving,
> Sam

Dear Mr. Knightley,

I hope you had a wonderful Thanksgiving—filled with turkey, green beans, potatoes, fall leaves, pumpkin pie, family walks, movies. Mine was packed with all that and more. It was one of the most warm-feeling, broad-smile, deep-belly-sigh days ever.

I anticipated a lonely day: Josh went home to Cincinnati, Ashley to New York, and Debbie to Minneapolis; Kyle was with the Hoffmans, and everyone else was gone as well. I couldn't bear to call Father John and ask if I could come to Grace House, so I planned on heating a frozen turkey dinner here and watching the old BBC *Pride and Prejudice*. I didn't expect Mrs. Muir to call. But she did.

She invited me to spend the whole day with them. But, unlike the professor, she invited me so softly and with such care that I didn't even try to refuse.

I was so anxious and excited that I couldn't sleep past five and went for a run. Ten miles definitely calms one's nerves. It was perfect: dark, cold, and silent. It was my first time out in the dark alone since the Great Beat-down, so I stuck to the main streets and felt safe. I loved each step and felt myself settle with each mile.

The sun came up over the lake in a spectacular series of blazing oranges, pinks, and yellows. At the end, I knew I could handle the day—all by myself.

I then worked on a few articles until it was time to grab an apple pie at Foodstuffs on Central Avenue and hop the Metra north.

Mrs. Muir welcomed me with a huge smile and an equally warm hug. "You didn't need to bring pie, dear. We just wanted you. Come in."

I walked in to the most amazing smells of garlic, turkey, potatoes, and something citrus . . . It was tangible and delicious.

"You're finally here. I've been waiting for you," the professor started with little preamble. "I want to see what you think of this." He handed me a couple printed pages.

"No work today." Mrs. Muir gently took the pages from me and handed them back to him. "Right now we cook."

"But I think young Sam here will have good insights."

"I'm sure she will. Another day."

"Very well." He winked at me and slid the pages into my bag as he followed his wife to the kitchen. "Another day, Sam."

We cooked, chopped, tasted, and laughed throughout the day. We didn't talk about anything specific, just stuff that meant nothing and everything: books, movies, weather, trees, politics, school, personalities, Chicago, art . . .

After an amazing meal, during which I did not embarrass myself or insult anyone else, we grabbed seats on the couch for their annual Thanksgiving Day tradition of watching George C. Scott as Scrooge in *A Christmas Carol*. I've read the book about six times, but I'd never seen the movie. At each reading I struggle with Scrooge's turnabout. It seems too fast, too complete. I mean, he resists goodness with the third ghost, and then flips almost instantly into the embodiment of St. Nicholas. It never made sense to me.

But post movie I feel differently about Scrooge. I watched the transformation play across the screen, and I saw his longing for love and community earlier in the story than I'd noticed in the book. From the beginning, I now suspect his isolation hurt him deeply. I watched as he painfully built each wall in his life and, even more dramatically, how he tore them down. It was both wonderful and unsettling.

Afterward the professor offered to drive me home, but Mrs. Muir invited me to spend the night.

"It's so late to go home, dear. Why don't you stay? There are clean sheets on the guest room bed and fresh toiletries in the bathroom."

"I don't want to impose."

"Not at all. I want to try a new French toast

recipe tomorrow, and Robert is hardly helpful. He says everything tastes good."

"Everything does," the professor protested.

"Stay, and then I'll know the truth." Mrs. Muir smiled at me.

"Samantha will be just as polite as I am, my dear. She won't be objective at all . . . No, wait! She corrected my Shakespeare. Maybe she will give you an honest opinion. Let's keep her."

The professor laughed as I felt the color rise to my face.

He caught my arm. "Samantha, I value your little blunder, as you might regard it, and hope you take my teasing lightly."

I simply nodded. Mrs. Muir took that as a yes to stay and led me to the guest room. My mind remained muddled as I brushed my teeth and turned out the lights. Then panic hit—the nightmares. *What was I thinking? What if I wake up my hosts?* I lay there for hours listening to the house settle and the clock tick. The room smelled like starch and lavender, and eventually I fell asleep. No dreams.

And that is how I know what one should eat and what one should do on Thanksgiving Day. The whole day played out like every movie and story I've ever seen or read.

But now school's back in session and I've been researching, writing, and editing all day. I'm going bowling with the Conleys this evening, so that should be a good break. Josh is joining us—that was like pulling teeth.

"I don't want to bowl, Sam. Come down here. We'll go to dinner."

"I've already accepted. Besides, I'd like them to meet you. They see your car in their driveway, they should know who drives it."

"So if they meet me, and know it's my car, you won't kick me out so early?"

I thought about this and couldn't see the link. "I guess."

"Okay, bowling it is. I'll be there by six."

Maybe his point was that no one likes an unknown car in their driveway, but one accepts, even welcomes, the car of a friend. I still don't get it. At least he's coming. I think Isabella will like him. Every time we watch a movie, she asks if I think the actor is cute. And Josh is cute.

So I have a break coming in two hours—which is good because my head is about to explode. I'm sure most of my classmates are resting before the storm of exams in a couple weeks, but work presses me. I'm still at the bottom, Mr. Knightley. The *Evanston Review* rejected my last submission, by the way—so much for Johnson's advice about getting encouragement from smaller papers. I can't even get published there. I hate the bottom.

Back to work,
Sam

Dear Mr. Knightley,

Do we ever get a break? Can't we thrive? Why work to make our lot in life better if we keep getting beat down?

Kyle called Coach Ridley a couple days ago and asked him to take him to Grace House. Ridley did. Within hours Mr. Hoffman demanded Father John release Kyle and pressed kidnapping charges against the coach. Kidnapping? Can you believe it?

It won't stick. Kyle started talking. Mr. Hoffman did hit Kyle. Father John called the police, and they took Kyle to DCFS. He recounted all kinds of abuse, to him and to the Hoffmans' son, Brian. It sounded so awful that the police sought former kids placed with the Hoffmans to confirm. Four corroborated Kyle's testimony.

The stories make you want to cry: standing in the corner for hours; beatings around the lower abdomen and butt, where marks wouldn't be seen; getting chained to the kitchen table or to the bed at night. Horrid stuff. And things that wouldn't leave visible marks once Kyle put on clothes. They were careful, which is even more disgusting. Kyle did actually give himself the bruises on his neck that Coach Ridley saw a few weeks ago, by falling out of a hiding place. That's why he wouldn't talk then. He was afraid no one would believe him.

So Kyle's back at Grace House. He thinks he failed. I went down and had dinner with him tonight. I had plans with Josh, but canceled them. I lied and said I had a seminar.

"I forgot," I told him. "It's a makeup from when Professor Feinberg was sick last month."

"All right. We'll be at Twin Anchors on Sedgwick. Just come after. I'll text you if we move on."

"It'll be late. I don't want to take the 'L' at night."

"Then take a cab. You take a cab home all the time when you come down." He paused.

I know my fears frustrate him, but some are legitimate. Aren't they?

"Forget it, Sam. I'll call you tomorrow, and maybe you can come down this weekend. Downtown isn't that far, you know?"

"I know." I started to feel small and defensive. "I'm sorry, Josh. Listen, I gotta go. Have fun tonight."

"Fine." He then relented a little. "Work hard, okay? I'll talk to you tomorrow."

And that was it.

I like Josh, I really do. He's a great kisser. Is that too much information? But he is. I love his arms around me. I love his smell. I love that when he walks next to me, I don't fear steps behind me. But I don't always feel he understands me, though that's probably my fault. I haven't always been honest with him. Like when we went bowling last week. Josh made the effort to come north and meet the Conleys, but I wasn't honest at the end of the evening.

"Thank you so much for coming."

"You're making me leave? It's only ten. Why meet them if I get kicked out early like always?"

"I've got a ton of work tonight. You remember exams."

Josh relented. "I do." He kissed me lightly. "No big deal. I'm busy tomorrow, but I'll text you about this weekend." And he left.

While I did need to study, I didn't kick him out because of exams. I'd been watching Isabella study Josh the whole evening. She absorbed everything we said and every romantic gesture he made. Back at Grace House, when Father John told us to set an example for the younger kids, I couldn't have cared less. *Let them figure it out on their own.* But Isabella matters to me. I want to set a good example for her. And with her bedroom window facing the garage and my apartment, I felt certain she'd be looking for Josh's car long after her bedtime. Maybe I should have told Josh. Explained that girls have active imaginations . . . I don't know.

But with that in mind—the importance of

honest communication and setting a good example—I took a cab downtown to see Kyle after my last class this afternoon. And, boy, did we start out rough. We're two peas in a pod, Kyle and I. At first he refused to talk and I couldn't say anything meaningful. He was as low as I've ever seen him—no anger, only sorrow. I wished for a bit of his old fight.

I finally stopped my inane chatter and told him the truth about school and all my other struggles. It helped us both—shared failure is always a comfort. I don't mean that flippantly. I mean that sharing my dismal grades, poorly written articles, limited friends, horrific nightmares, and even all the details from the Great Beat-down and its aftermath made me relatable to Kyle. We could talk. We were alike.

By dessert Kyle was sharing as well. And it helped. I could see it in his eyes. They started the night tight and predatory, rounded and softened during pizza, and showed flashes of laughter during ice cream. It made me smile.

And so tomorrow we begin a new day. Can we make it better, Mr. Knightley? Can we make life "normal"? I want that more for Kyle than I want it for myself.

Sincerely,
Sam

Dear Mr. Knightley,

Kyle and I talked for a long time this afternoon. He's doing much better. I suspect he'll be at Grace House permanently now. He said Dr. Wieland wants to up his meds, but agreed to hold off if Kyle promised to make all his counseling sessions. I'm proud of him, Mr. Knightley. If Kyle needs medication, great, but the fact that he's trying to take ownership for his actions and emotions is good too. And he's writing again! I get e-mails daily now. They're more like laundry lists:

Ran 6 x 800s @ 3:20s with 3-minute rests. You can't beat me now.
Got invite to Coach's house for Christmas dinner.
Jaden fostered out. Miss him.
Hannah flipped me, 'cause she can. Gettin' better at falling without breaking my butt. She says she'll teach me.
Later, Kyle.

Some are chattier. I sent him some of my writing with the hopes he'd be proud of me. I don't know if he even read them. I want someone to. To read them and say they've got merit. Say I have what it takes to be at Medill, to be a journalist.

Look, I'll be honest here, Mr. Knightley. I'm rattled. I know I'm changing subjects, but this plays in the background of my every waking moment. Graduating college, I had a job and a life picked out. I earned it and it was mine. And I lost it—all of it. Now I'm on to my second dream. What if I lose that too? There's no landing pad now. I can't return to Grace House, and I don't know where I'll go or what I'll do. And I can't give up. But how long do I have before Johnson takes this from me? This is the only place in the world I want to be.

I tried explaining all this to Josh last night, but I think it went over his head. He has this enviable and somewhat simple view of how the world works. My striving and angst don't register with him.

"Sam, why do you get so worked up? Just get it done and move on. How hard can it be?"

"Johnson's recommendation means a ton, but so does his respect. I want him to believe in me." I felt like I was pleading simultaneously with both of them.

"Do the job and move on. You'll graduate next January and never see the man again. Get through the class and get your degree."

"Of course, you're right. I should 'keep my breath to cool my porridge'," I said archly.

"What?"

"Nothing. It means I need to stop thinking and get the job done."

"That's my girl." Josh sounded pleased, finally.

I ended the conversation feeling totally misunderstood. Maybe it would have been better if I could've seen Josh's face, felt his arms around me. Sometimes I wonder if he even hears me. I haven't seen him in a week, and we do better with closer contact. I guess I just miss him.

Thanks for listening,
Sam

~ DECEMBER 20

Dear Mr. Knightley,

Christmas break has started, and I'm shredded. I'm killing myself fixing articles and working on the January feature, but it's all crap. I handed in that review of *The Merchant of Venice*, but I couldn't find an objective yet warm tone for the article. I liked the production, but I couldn't get perspective. And between work for all my classes and Josh, there was no time to think it through.

Josh wants to go out practically every night and calls for me to meet him downtown with his friends, and then it's late and hard to get home on the Metra. I feel wasteful paying for so many cabs, but the 'L' still scares me. Night still scares me. I can't decide if I'm exhausted from the late nights or the stress.

Josh also seems put out with my worrying and early departures. He says I should just stay at his place, and I guess he's right. We've been dating for a couple months now and it's expected. I don't know why I don't agree, and I think he's losing patience. Last night it almost came to a fight.

"Do you have to leave before even ordering dessert? You missed drinks out with Scott and Jessica last night, and it's rude. I feel like a third wheel. What's up with you?"

Ashley says I'm acting prudish. Debbie refuses

to weigh in. There's something very sensible and Midwestern about Debbie that I really appreciate. She's like Jane Eyre; she doesn't lose her way. She says I have good instincts and should trust them. I think that's why she's top in our class—she listens. No one absorbs the most important points and then draws them out as well as she does. Ninety-nine times out of a hundred, that's brilliant. But doesn't she know that I have no instincts? That it's impossible for me to draw my own conclusions?

I shouldn't canvass my friends on this, but I don't know what's normal. That's what I can't tell Debbie or anyone. None of them know I haven't slept with a guy. I gather everyone has. My reticence seems strange, even to myself. And I love Josh. At least I think I do. He loves me. At least I think he does. He's never said the words, but it's in his look and actions. Goodness, I sound exactly like Marianne Dashwood. She felt the same about Willoughby, and look where it got her—the poor girl almost died. Thank goodness, Josh is an honorable Colonel Brandon and not a villainous Willoughby.

But I have to admit that, while he makes me feel very attractive and cherished, I also feel uncomfortable with some of his ideas. I suspect that's my issue, not his, and that I really am "two steps behind reality." I try to share my reality with him, but he doesn't hear me. Our conversation while running this morning is a perfect example.

"You can't be that naive, Sam. It's the way the world works. Everyone is like that."

"Not everyone."

"You've got the brains and certainly the determination, but it takes more than that to cut it at Medill and certainly in the newspaper biz. You have to take the next guy out, even if it's Debbie or another friend. They'd do it to you. Get out of your head and your books, Sam."

I ran silently a few minutes. Is that really how I need to think? Is that what living "normal" looks and feels like?

"I probably do spend too much time in my books. They saved me, you know?" I wanted to share my life and let him know how little I understand these new arenas. *Ask about the real me. Can I trust you?*

"Saved you from what? The mall?" He laughed.

"My childhood wasn't like yours, Josh. I didn't have a bunch of brothers playing football in the front yard."

"Whatever, Sam."

"And Debbie and the others are my friends. I'm not going to 'take them out,' as you say."

"Listen, Sam, I get that you love to stand out by acting clueless, but don't pretend it's not an act and that you're not as cutthroat as the rest of us."

Love to stand out? Cutthroat? How could anyone think that's me? I spend every moment of every day painfully working to fit in. I work to *not* stand out in any way, to *not* get noticed. At least not in a negative way—I'd love it if my classmates and Johnson thought I occasionally brought something good to the table.

Of course, I didn't say all that. I never do. But I did subtly pick up the pace. Josh could barely breathe by the end—not that he'd ever admit it. And I felt a little better. Maybe I am cutthroat, Mr. Knightley. I wanted a little of my own back, and I purposefully ran Josh into the ground to get it. And unlike that first race with Kyle, this time I felt no regret.

We had plans to spend the day together, but they evaporated. Josh suddenly had a meeting, on a Saturday, and I needed to study.

Isn't your boyfriend supposed to want the real you? I mean I know I've hidden stuff, most everything, I grant, but I've tried to let truth slip out too. And today I was ready for honesty.

Sincerely,
Sam

P.S. Mr. Knightley, thanks for this—these letters. At first I questioned them, even though I found them oddly easy. And now I trust our one-sided, soul-purging relationship. I depend on it. It's got to be more therapeutic than all those psychologists people pay in the movies. It's certainly more helpful than all that chatting I had to do with Dr. Wieland at Grace House. So again, thank you.

Oh . . .

I just got a text from Alex Powell:

Mom M gave me your number. Saw *Hamlet* off Broadway. Thought Much Of You. How's school? A. Powell

I wrote back: LOL. Heard *Three Days Found* is coming out as a movie. Congrats. Will see it opening night.

Alex: It's fun. Flying to LA to consult storyboard and set. Am getting so Hollywood.

Me: Careful. Next you'll put your picture on your books.

Alex: Never! Thanks for staying @ Muirs over turkey day. They get lonely.

Me: Me too. Loved it. Can see why they're your 2nd parents.

Alex: No fear. I share well. Gotta go.

I promptly deleted his number. You might call me ridiculous, but it was necessary. What if I couldn't help myself and started texting, pestering, stalking? It wouldn't be my fault! I'm already following him on Twitter. He really shouldn't guard his privacy so much. Other than the upcoming movie, very little leaks out. And I refuse to pepper the Muirs. But I did find an interview with Conan on YouTube. Now do you understand why I got rid of his number?

Dear Mr. Knightley,

It's Christmas Eve and all I can do is sit here and cry. Why is it so hard? I need to quit. Everyone knows I can't cut it. Johnson will kick me out in January anyway. I should go—on my own terms—just like he advised.

The nightmares are back full-force and I can't sleep. They've been around for months, but the past few nights they've been relentless. I haven't slept a wink in three days. I can't look in the mirror. The circles under my eyes tell of too little sleep and too much pain. I can't talk to my friends. Most have gone home, and Josh is in Cincinnati for Christmas. I don't want to talk to him anyway.

Johnson yelled at me the last day before break—so much for honesty. He asked me to stay after class and then started yelling. He'd probably say he talked loudly, but it felt like yelling.

"Moore, what are you doing? You picked a fine subject, one with meat, bones, and questions; yet you breezed through it. That production is provoking discussions, debate. You addressed none of it. Stop wasting my time."

He'd printed out my *Merchant* review—I'm sure just to emphasize his point with all the red slashes. Hard copy is much more devastating.

"I thought it was better, Dr. Johnson. I put myself in there."

"If that's the best you've got, don't bother with the January feature. Stop by the office and withdraw on your way out the door."

"Are you serious? You're kicking me out?"

"I'm letting you go on your own terms. Come January, I won't give you that privilege." He sat on the edge of his desk. "Look, Moore, a newspaper will assign you subjects; I'm letting you pick them. Already that's a leg up. If you can't handle subjects you select, how do you expect to handle the rigors of daily assignments and deadlines?"

"I thought I could handle this. I know a lot about literature. I reread the play and saw the production for this review. It's thorough."

"I never said it wasn't thorough. It's too thorough. It's a review, Moore, not a dissertation."

I slumped in my chair.

He leaned forward. "Find a topic in which you can express your voice, your own voice, Moore. I get a new take on you with each exercise, and each is more distant and shadowed than the one before. What interests you? What gets your heart beating? Tell me, where do you find yourself?"

"This is it. This is what I know best." I shook my review.

"That's a shame. There's no more of your voice

in that than was in your article on water rights. I don't know what else to do with you."

Right then I recognized what Professor Muir was referring to that night. Dr. Johnson *is* a good man. He's tough, but he wanted to help me. He was ready to do all he could to make success possible, but I didn't know what to say. Finally he got up and withdrew behind his desk. I was dismissed.

I said with such bravado that Dr. Johnson would have to kick me out—and I think he did. He told me to go on my own terms. I should've taken his advice and dropped out as I exited his office—because he's right, there's nothing more to be done with me. I've been working for five days on the January feature in an attempt to find something powerful and compelling in me, and I've come up empty.

If I could just sleep, maybe I'd think more clearly and write better. But I can't. I go downtown to join Josh and to have fun for a few hours in the hope that I'll forget all this. Then I come home, crawl into bed, and get pounded every night by a different horror. I awoke last night unable to move—finally I convinced myself that my arms and legs still worked and I was safe. And then today . . . It was a nightmare and I was fully awake.

I took a break this afternoon and walked into town to do some Christmas shopping for the

Conley kids. They're so sweet and constantly leave pictures and cookies at my door. Anyway, as I crossed Clark Street I ran into Sienna, one of Ashley's English lit friends. I don't like her, but I accepted her invitation to Starbucks to warm up.

As we walked the block, a teenager with dirty-blond hair and the most haunted gray eyes asked us for money. I recognized the look; I'd seen it in the mirrors of a dozen bus stops and store windows. And like me once upon a time, she had no coat. In December.

Sienna turned to me and said in a mock whisper, "There are places for these people. We shouldn't have to see them." She sounded like Ebenezer Scrooge defending workhouses and prisons.

"Those places are hard to get into," I said. "This may be the best she can do."

I pushed some bills into the girl's hand, but Sienna never paused. She threw back such a condescending sneer, I stopped again. If she were literate enough to have known the line, I swear she would have said, "If they would rather die, they had better do it, and decrease the surplus population."

Instead she tossed her red hair and called in her southern snobby twang, "Don't you have a marvelous social conscience? Why don't you invite her for coffee with us?"

She tapped her Prada-booted foot. "You've given her money, now let's go. It's cold out here." Then she flounced, yes, flounced, away.

I'm so embarrassed that I noticed her boots and even more humiliated to admit that I followed her. I don't even remember what I said in Starbucks. I guzzled my latté, mumbled some excuse, and ran out as my life played before my eyes.

What do you know about me, Mr. Knightley? Really know? No matter what Father John told you or sent you, you can't know it all. No one does. I alone carry it each and every day. And no matter how many characters I hide behind, how much work I bury myself beneath, my past still pushes me every day and haunts me every night.

Before the police took me to Grace House, I spent two months living on the streets. I spent most nights sleeping under Wacker Drive, hiding in sewage tunnels from men and gangs, crouching in dark doorways, eating from garbage cans and handouts, and constantly moving. Walking, shifting, drifting—anything to keep warm, stay safe, and avoid the cops. I remember an old woman gave me a hat from her grocery cart to cover my hair. She said I'd be safer as a boy. I never let my imagination go there.

I didn't have energy to think past the simple actions for survival. I didn't know where to go or whom to trust. I couldn't risk a shelter—it would lead to a state home, a juvenile detention center, or my social worker, Mr. Petrusky. And he had already failed me.

I should go back farther . . .

I'm about six in my earliest memory. It took me five years to remember that day, and now it won't leave. In my mind, I see myself look up as my father runs across a dim room. I feel weightless, soaring through the air until I hit the wall. Then I see my father follow me. I feel his steps shake the floor as I try to get small and still. That's the start of many dreams.

In reality, my father hoisted me up to a mirror and gripped my neck so I could watch myself choke. My legs danced like a rag doll. I watched them as I tried to shut out the gasping, gargling noises. I also watched his hands. They grew red as the sounds grew louder. They were horrible sounds and I didn't know until much later that they came from me. I don't know why he stopped; maybe he thought he'd killed me. I only remember being carried away as the police grilled my mom. She didn't speak or look up. She sat at the kitchen table, tracing a crack with her finger.

I didn't speak of this. In fact, I said nothing for over a year. After a stint in the hospital, I was fostered out to the Chapmans. Mrs. Chapman takes on the glow of an angel in my memories. I can't recall her features, but I spent hours in her lap listening to her read. She smelled sweet like gardenias, and her voice was deep and cheerful. I felt so safe in their care. Of course, I didn't stay long. Mr. Chapman got a job in Wisconsin, and I couldn't cross state lines. That's when I learned what a commodity my life was.

The Desouza family came next, the Gibbons after that. I only spent a few months at each. It was during my stay with the Gibbons that I found *Pride and Prejudice*. Mrs. Gibbons would get so mad at my obsession with it that I hid myself to read. I have little memory of the homes after that. I think there were two or three before the Putmans.

Mr. Putman was burly, smelly, and mean. He started hitting me soon after I arrived, and Mrs. Putman would make up lies, expecting me to rewrite each incident in my memory.

"Oh, Sam. You were so silly to leave your shoes scattered across the floor. I'm so sorry you tripped and hit your head." Her voice was saccharine sweet.

"I didn't hit my head. You saw him."

"Don't tell tales, Sam. Messiness can be such a danger. I'd hate to tell Daddy that you fibbed to me. I'm so good to you, Sam."

That's when I found *Jane Eyre*. How could we not have an instant bond? *I dislike Mrs. Reed; for it was her nature to wound me cruelly; never was I happy in her presence; however carefully I obeyed, however strenuously I strove to please her . . .* Jane endured Mrs. Reed and Brocklehurst School, and I endured Mr. and Mrs. Putman. I was only taken away when my social worker quit and a new one, with fresh energy and clear eyesight, demanded my removal.

There were about three other homes after that, but I was barely present. I had learned to hide well. I don't mean to sound breezy about all this, but I actually don't recall much outside the deep aloneness I felt when I was apart from my books. I tore pages out of some of my favorites and carried them around in my pockets.

Maybe that's why there were so many homes. I assumed no one could ever love me, but I didn't give anyone much of a chance, did I? I would arrive, everyone hoping for the best, and then a few months later DCFS would get the call. "Sam has failed to connect again. Sam has failed again . . ."

Then one day another call came. My mother had passed the reinstatement tests, and I was going home. *Home?* In the seven years we'd been apart, she had never contacted me, not once. Yet she worked to pass her tests and now wanted me back? I didn't even recognize her when she came to pick me up. Nothing about her touched any feeling inside me.

How did she fool them? That's one question that still plagues me. Within weeks of my moving home, my mother was drugged out and incapable of caring for me. I played parent and went to school when I could. That's when I found the library. I volunteered to shelve books one day, and the staff sort of adopted me and "paid" me with food and gifts of clothing. I loved it there.

Then, about a year later, my father got released from prison. He'd been arrested that fateful day for armed robbery and assault, but with good behavior and early parole, he was back.

My mother was happy. She hadn't been alone—a line of men passed through our apartment weekly—but once he walked in the door, it was all about him. I called Mr. Petrusky over and over and begged to be moved.

The last time we spoke he said, "Sam, you've got a mom and a dad and a roof over your head. That's better than many."

But I couldn't be in the same room with my father without fear choking me and sweat dripping down my back. I couldn't breathe—physically couldn't breathe. I learned to avoid the apartment, but when he expected me and I was late, he hit me.

"Just a reminder, Sammy-girl," he would whisper. "I'm boss here. You think you're so smart, but I'm the boss here. Aren't I, Sammy-girl?" Just writing that nickname, Sammy-girl, makes me want to vomit.

The end came a month before my fifteenth birthday. My father came home and grabbed me by the arm. Without a word, he pulled me down the stairs and around to the alley. He shoved me into a group of greasy men. They were small and had hard eyes; they scared me more than all my father's size and brawn.

"Here she is. We square?"

The tallest of the three grabbed me with one hand and felt me up and down with the other.

"She ain't worth a nickel."

Another sneered, "You owe me a dime, Joe."

"She's worth more than a grand. She cooks, cleans . . . ," my father begged the leader, who stepped back to appraise me. "She's old enough, Fish. You can use her."

I knew "use her" had only one meaning, no matter when or where it's said. I looked at him, but he avoided my eyes.

"You'll make at least a hundred a pop. We good now?" He nodded like it was done. Fish nodded back.

The first guy was still holding me with only one hand. I twisted with all my might and wrenched his wrist backwards and I ran. I heard shouting and footsteps behind me, but I was fast. Within two blocks, I lost them. Within twenty, I lost me.

I lived on the streets for a couple months before a cop found me. I was too tired and hungry to run, so I bit him. Detective Huber hoisted me over his shoulder and took me to Father John at Grace House without even processing me into the system. And there I remained—excluding my three-month venture with Cara and my few months at Ernst & Young—living without really living. Even the news of my parents' deaths didn't faze me: my father got shot somehow and my mother overdosed. Father John thought I'd feel safer knowing the truth about them, especially my father. But he didn't realize they couldn't hurt me anymore. Nothing could touch me.

Only people in books had any appeal for me, and it's been like that ever since. Dr. Wieland had me on an intense talk-therapy routine for a couple years, and I'll admit it helped. He's a good man, and talking eased some of the pain. But the characters remained. I needed them.

Not anymore.

They can't save me. They certainly can't write for me. Heck, they don't even show up like they used to. And when they do, they don't fit inside comfortably. They jar me and leave me feeling even more disconnected and alone. But without them, who am I?

Did you think you were helping someone worthy? Mrs. Conley might kick me out if she knew. Wouldn't you? Her children are so innocent and trusting. And I'm a mess. I can't be good for them. And that girl today . . . I wasn't good for her. Seven bucks isn't going to help her, and I, of all people, should have done more.

I looked for her after I came out of Starbucks. I did that, at least. As I searched, I wondered about what I've become. I feel like Dorian Gray. He sold his soul for external beauty, and his face remained young, unlined and perfect. Only his portrait, hidden in an attic, displayed the horror and depravity of his life. I'm no better than he. My insides feel so horrid. But that's not what I want or who I want to be.

Isabella Conley gave me a book a few weeks ago with the most haunting and beautiful passage I've ever read. I found a character in it that offered me, not just understanding, but hope. But I don't know what to do with it.

The book is *The Voyage of the Dawn Treader* by C. S. Lewis. There's this boy, Eustace, a perfectly pugnacious little twerp, who turns into a dragon while thinking greedy, dragonish thoughts. But once Eustace recognizes his true state, as a real dragon, he starts to behave more kindly. He strives to change. But it's too late and he's too far gone. He can't do it. He can't tear off the dragon skin.

Only Aslan, this amazingly huge and glorious lion, holds that power. *The very first tear he made was so deep that I thought it had gone right into my heart. And when he began pulling the skin off, it hurt worse than anything I've ever felt. The only thing that made me able to bear it was just the pleasure of feeling the stuff peel off.*

But I'm still under that skin. It suffocates me, chokes me, and is killing me. There's no Aslan in the real world, so there's no hope. Mrs. Muir would say I'm wrong. She says there is hope in God and hope in Christ. They've invited me to dinner weekly since Thanksgiving and, during each meal, she drops hints and hope like bread crumbs for me to follow. But I can't see it. I just feel swallowed by darkness.

I promise to write at least once more when I figure out what to do. This isn't your problem though, Mr. Knightley. Even a lovely apartment and new clothes can't dress this up. Thank you for everything. You gave me my best shot. I'm the one who failed.

I hate to do it, but I need to call Father John. He always has good advice, and I need some of that right now.

Sincerely,
Sam

Dear Mr. Knightley,

I'm still here. After my last letter, I should have written sooner. I'm sorry if I worried you. Father John said it was disrespectful not to contact you immediately when I got to Grace House, but I was pretty hurt and depressed. I'm better now.

First of all, belated Merry Christmas. I forgot that detail in my last wallow. Thank you so much for the beautiful book. I love *North and South*, but have never owned a copy. I inhaled it this weekend. Margaret Hale and John Thornton. Working class vs. gentry. Hopes and dreams. And the idea of one last fight—a final go at all that matters. It had me crying. It resonates more deeply now, which is part of my second point . . .

It's been a packed two weeks. Poor Henry Conley found me in my apartment Christmas morning, doubled over on the floor, sweating and moaning. I don't remember that part. I do remember waking up in the hospital following an emergency appendectomy.

After surgery, the doctors refused to release me to my apartment alone, so I called Father John and went to Grace House. He thought I was coming to simply recover. But I was back for good—at least for as long as he'd let me stay.

Kyle knew. I don't know how, but he knew.

"You ain't comin' back here." He stormed into Independence Cottage within minutes of my arrival.

"My options are limited, Kyle. Let me figure it out." I unpacked my small duffel, feeling defeated and still in pain.

"Your options are endless if you fight."

"It's not that simple."

"Yeah, it is. What are you scared of? This ain't the girl who whipped me 'round the track and you ain't the girl who don't let me quit."

"It's 'isn't,' 'aren't,' and 'doesn't.' At least use correct grammar." I had a small spark left.

"Make me. Show me what you're made of."

"I'm not made of much, Kyle. Haven't you figured that out?" Spark gone.

He sat down, deflated. "So all that crap you told me was just that, huh? Crap. We don't deserve no better. We can't break through and find someplace to thrive? That's what you keep saying, isn't it, that we can 'thrive'? It means more than grow. I thought it meant happiness."

"I still believe that . . . for you." I started crying. *Will I ever stop crying?*

"But not for you?" he asked.

My jaw dropped. It was true. Not for me. I'd never felt such loss, as I realized that all my dreams were gone. I couldn't pick up the pieces of a single one.

His voice softened as he continued, "What does it take to get you there?"

"I don't know," I cried. "Kyle, I don't know. There's all this inside me: shame, lies, and fear. It has filled me up and there's no room for anything good and bright. I used to bury it and hide it away. It doesn't work anymore and I can't sleep. I can't eat . . ."

"Get it out."

"How?" I looked at him as if he held all the answers, and I sincerely hoped he did.

"Write it. No lies. Only truth." He crossed the room and tossed me my laptop. "I want to tell you about the Hoffmans."

I held the computer. "Am I to write something?"

"Type what I say."

He sat on the bed as I moved to the desk and opened the laptop. He started talking, not to me, just talking. I typed.

"The first night I arrived at their house, Mrs. Hoffman made a huge spaghetti dinner and told Brian to clean the kitchen. I was the guest that night. When he came up 'round midnight, I was still awake. He looked hard at me and said, 'I'm sorry you're here.' I thought he was a jerk. It took me a couple days to get it . . ."

Kyle talked and I typed. Later that night, something he said struck me, and I shared a nugget from my past.

"Mr. Putman used to do that to me. He'd pull my hair to drag me across a room. It hurt, but never left a mark."

"Lots of stuff don't leave marks."

"And did you know . . ." Soon there was no form or structure. We shared tidbits, whole horrors, and food Hannah brought from Grace House's kitchen. She was wise enough to never say a word.

I kept typing and recorded almost every line of our two-day conversation. There was no hiding, no pretending. At the end, he looked at me exhausted and wide-eyed—we'd stopped only for a little sleep in over thirty hours.

"I'm done with that, Sam."

"Me too. I can't live there anymore. Where do we go now?"

"I don't know." Kyle looked so young. It was like his childhood came back to him. He's just a fourteen-year-old kid and now he looked it.

Kyle didn't know where to go next, but I did. I had the beginnings of an article that needed to be edited into my final project for Johnson: the 5,000-word feature due January 14.

Kyle and I had gotten all this out and, to start our road to freedom, we needed to fling it far. If Johnson wanted passion, this was it. If I wanted to stretch, here was my chance. If I wanted to live, here was my lifeline. And, without doubt, here was my voice.

"Can I use it? For school?"

"You want to hand this in for a grade?" Kyle's eyes rounded with shock.

I understood. This is not what anyone would submit to a high school English teacher.

"Something like that. It'd be a newspaper article. Like the features we read in the *Tribune* on the weekends, but this won't get published. It's for my professor."

"You need it?"

"I do."

He was silent for a moment. Emotions played across his face. And rather than beg, I stayed silent too. It was a big decision. His decision. This was raw stuff—this was his life. Kyle took a deep breath and caught my eyes. "You can have it."

Rather than think about it, and let fear stop us, Kyle and I committed. We started editing our lives and thoughts down to the essentials: what we survived, what we feared most and loved best, what we felt others needed to see, and what we knew we could no longer carry. It took us a week of nonstop work. I couldn't even stop to write and tell you what we were doing. If I had left that place of purging, I might have quit.

Not Kyle. Once he committed, he was all in. He hounded me constantly. "No, Sam, that's not how that feels and you know it. Tell it right or stop."

The honesty he demanded scared me. I don't know what drove him, but I think he did it for me. Maybe that's what love is—sacrificing yourself to save another, taking the insult or taking the hit. Kyle did that. His story was so raw in places that I stopped typing. He heard the silence and glared at me. "Can't take it, Sam? That's why we're here. Keep going." And he was the same with my story. "Keep typing what happened. The Putmans locked you in a closet. You gotta feel something."

"Of course I felt something. It was horrible. I felt subhuman, you know? I mattered less than their dog."

"I know . . ."

I don't think that either of us has ever cried so much in our lives. We gave up on day two trying to hide tears from each other. And eight days later we had it: our lives compressed and edited into 5,000 words that I prayed would push us forward. It wasn't the Christmas break either of us anticipated, but maybe it was the best we've ever had.

And I'm proud of it. I'm proud of us. This is the first honest and powerful thing I've ever done. And to share that with Kyle was amazing. Neither of us could have done this without the other. I felt us change during the week. Kyle's shadows drifted a bit, and his whole demeanor took on more boldness and confidence.

And me? I feel stronger and lighter. The tight dragon skin is thinner. Perhaps even peeled back in places. Peace is creeping into my thoughts. And I'm sleeping. The nightmares come with less urgency and force, and I'm able to wake myself up. I can't tell you how good that feels.

I took the Metra north to the Muirs' yesterday afternoon. They'd left for Florida before Christmas and didn't know about my appendix. Mrs. Muir was devastated she hadn't been here to help. She insisted I come to them for the weekend, and I knew it was time to come clean.

I started my story as we sat around the kitchen table eating chocolate cake. Mrs. Muir got up (still listening) to get us milk. She does that. When the professor and I start on something serious, she gets up and makes tea or cookies or putters nearby. At first, during Thanksgiving, I thought she did it to avoid our discussions, but now I think she does it to give space. It diverts attention, thereby freeing the conversation. Or maybe it's to offset the professor. He never gives space.

At one point last night he leaned across the table—fork paused in front of his mouth—and focused his hawkish eyes on mine for about two minutes. He didn't breathe and the fork didn't move. I looked at my plate and pushed cake bits around while my mouth blabbed on. I was too scared to look up. Until you and Kyle, I've never shared my story. It's not the world's "normal," and I still fear judgment. Most days I feel cast off, dirty, and not worthy. Won't others feel the same about me?

I found that sticking to the facts was the easiest approach. I could have been reciting a grocery list for all the emotion I revealed. The professor caught that and responded in kind. He wanted to know everything and demanded new facts, new details.

"Why did they return you to your mother? Why didn't she lose rights to you?"

"I had a social worker, Ms. Saunders, who said just that. She vehemently protested my return, but Mom passed the tests, and the state believes that the maternal bond should be upheld. And she seemed stable."

"What did Ms. Saunders do?"

"She was removed from my case. She said they wouldn't let her stay because her opinions were 'counterproductive.' That's when Mr. Petrusky took over."

"They stole your single advocate? What did Petrusky do?" The professor leaned so far forward that Mrs. Muir put a hand on his arm. Chagrined, he settled awkwardly back in his chair. He looked like a tiger forbidden to pounce.

The professor can be critical at times, and his wit is so sharp that it startles me, but I was wrong to believe that any of that comes from a judgmental place. He was very kind and wanted to know everything, not to dissect it, but to share it. Once I understood that, my fear vanished, and we talked long and comfortably into the night and finished off the cake, a roasted chicken, and tons of salad.

As we headed to bed, Mrs. Muir prayed for me. No one has ever done that before. Sure, the Muirs made references while saying grace during my weekly dinners, but this prayer was only for me. As we got up from the table she, came over and hugged me. She then prayed that I would feel safe and loved forever, and that God would take away my pain and leave strength and compassion. Sometime during the prayer, I felt the professor's hand rest on my other shoulder.

Part of me wanted to back away at the end and quip, "That was nice, but He doesn't pay attention to me." But I couldn't. I couldn't because I want so badly to believe that God cares, that all this matters to Him, that all this pain has a purpose and that none of it tarnishes me forever. That longing is there, and a single word last night might have blown it away.

I barely held in my tears as I walked to the guest room. Then I bawled. It felt good somehow, almost hopeful. The tears felt like they were welcoming the new rather than clearing out the old.

We started this morning in a lighter mood—

pancakes and belated Christmas gifts. A box from Alex was first. He sent Mrs. Muir beautiful linen stationery; the professor, a gorgeous edition of *The Old Man and the Sea*; and me, a beautiful deep green scarf and winter hat. I can't believe he remembered me. Should I have sent a gift to him? Too late now. I penned him a note, and Mrs. Muir will include it with her letter.

I also exchanged some texts with him a few days after Christmas. It was right during my work with Kyle. I still have them on my phone. I couldn't delete them.

Alex: Merry Christmas. Mom M & Pops had it right to go to FL. NY freezing. Chicago?
I replied: Brrrrr . . . Keeping warm with work.
Alex: Going well?
Me: No. Got 1 chance to make it good.
Alex: ??????
Me: Can't. Like your p. 187. But if I get through this, I'll be OK.
Alex: Thoughts and prayers with you. :) Keep me posted.

I was touched, Mr. Knightley. I didn't tell him anything, yet I felt he understood. Is that possible? Maybe he doesn't understand or even care, but I like to believe he does. The gifts suggest he might, right? Not like a boyfriend, but like a real friend.

So there is my Christmas. School resumes in three days, and I'll go back to my apartment tomorrow. The professor sits next to me reading the book Alex sent him, and Mrs. Muir is writing letters. This feels nice.

That said, this whole experience has been too exhausting for me to want to repeat it. Kyle said he slept for three days straight, and I believe him. But I wouldn't trade all this either. Through it, I found a new character. Me. She's bold and fairly feisty, with serious timidity issues at times. Every step she takes forward, she glances back and even retreats. But she's got courage. I think she'll make it. I don't know when she'll be free to run— figuratively, that is. Physically she runs plenty, and that's where she gets her courage. I hope to like this new character.

I hope Josh does too. He came by my apartment when he got back from Cincinnati and brought me a beautiful bouquet of flowers. He's on a business trip now. We talk every night, and it's going well. I feel like he is more accepting of me. Or perhaps I am simply more honest with him. Either way, it's good. I'm going downtown Friday for dinner with him and his friends, and I think that I should stay at his place. He keeps asking, and I don't know why I don't.

Mrs. Muir asked me to bring him up here for dinner sometime, but Josh says it's too far and that he's already met the Conleys. No big deal, I guess, but I'd like him to meet the Muirs. They're important to me. Do you think Alex would mind if I considered them surrogate parents too?

All the best,
Sam

P.S. Is it odd that I keep asking you questions? On some level, I believe you'll write back and answer them. I know I said I rely on this one-way relationship, but should I put that away? I'm trying to stand on my own. Should this be a part of that? Would you consider writing?

Dear Samantha,

Please consider carefully. You have lauded our "soul-purging-one-sided-relationship" many times. If I reply to your letters, that will change. Everything will change. The decision is yours.

Sincerely,

G. Knightley

Dear Mr. Knightley,

What's wrong with me?

I paced this apartment for two hours and I have no answers. No sleep and no answers. I planned to stay downtown tonight. I did. I told Josh as soon as I met him at the restaurant. I convinced myself it was right.

"That's perfect, sweetheart. It's about time." He leaned over and gently kissed me, lingering too long with all his friends watching, but they do that too—so I guess it's not a big deal.

The evening went great. Josh spent most of the night with his arm around my chair, acting more affectionate than I've ever seen him. It was wonderful. I've worried about telling him my past, but I felt so loved all night that the worries dissolved. It couldn't have been a better evening.

Then Josh's friend Logan stepped in. There's a nastiness about him that repels me. I think if Logan ever decided to go after someone, there would be no end to his depravity. He may actually be a Dorian Gray. While looking over the dessert menu, Logan made a big show of yawning and checking his watch—a slick gold and silver thing he's inordinately obsessed with.

"How'd it get so late? Sam, you'd better head to the Metra or catch a cab. Josh, I know you get tired of always walking her, but a lady shouldn't go alone. I'll stretch my legs and provide a proper escort. Ready, Sam?" He stood up and leaned over the girl next to him. "Lucy, be a love and keep Josh company."

Josh's arm tightened around my shoulder. "Sam's staying with me tonight."

"Is she?" Logan sat and let the question linger until he'd gotten everyone's attention. He draped his arm across Lucy's shoulders, squeezing gently. "This is a big night. Perhaps we shouldn't have dessert. Wouldn't want to get too full." He stared straight at me. No blinking, just a hard smile.

"Let's order. My treat." Josh called over the waiter.

Logan hiked one corner of his mouth and continued to stare. He was challenging me, undressing me, and dismissing me simultaneously—right across the table, while holding Lucy tight. She looked equally uncomfortable. Josh caught none of it as he continued to jostle with his other friends, talking about their ad campaigns and trashing the competition's upcoming Super Bowl commercials.

We sat for another half hour, then as we grabbed our coats, Josh's hand brushed under my arm. He whispered in my ear, "Are you ready?" He wasn't talking about hailing a cab. The hair on the back of my neck stood up.

Logan followed us out the door and waited with us, even though he lives only a few blocks from Café Ba-Ba-Reeba. He waited and watched. As I climbed into the cab, Logan elbowed Josh. "Have a great night, big man. See you at the office. I'll bring the cigarettes—I mean doughnuts."

Josh laughed and climbed in behind me. I didn't know if he was offended and laughed to cover his embarrassment or he thought Logan was funny. We all laugh at inappropriate things—I get that. You don't want to feel left out. But this was too far. I felt like a piece of meat. It wasn't Josh's fault, but he didn't stop it.

I told the cabdriver Josh's address and sat silent. Josh took my hand. I didn't pull away. I waited. When the cab pulled to a stop, Josh moved to get out.

"Josh, I'm heading back north tonight. I'll call you tomorrow."

He dropped back into the car. "Sam, that's just Logan. You know him. He doesn't mean any-thing."

You knew Logan was out of line. "Yes, he does. He made me feel cheap, and you didn't call him on it."

"You're overreacting, honey. Just forget about him and come inside. It's cold." He leaned in and kissed my neck. Then he pushed himself out of the car as if all was settled.

"Not tonight, Josh." I reached for his door.

"You're kidding. Right?" He was irritated now.

"No. Good night." I tried to shut the door, but he held it open.

"You can't keep doing this, Sam."

"What?"

"This. Whatever *this* is to you." And he slammed the door.

I turned to the cabdriver. "Sorry about that." I gave him my address. "Do you mind driving all the way to Evanston?"

"Not at all, miss. Let's get you home." He sounded like he was glad to be rid of Josh too. He didn't say another word, and I was grateful for that. My thoughts were loud enough. Was Josh right? Had I overreacted? Was I a prude? Or worse, a tease? Was Josh a jerk? We know what Logan was.

Now that I've cooled down, I admit that I took my anger with Logan out on Josh. Or should Josh have shut him up? That's where I'm still confused. And there's something else—something hard to explain. Logan's comment tonight saved me from a tough decision—and part of me is grateful for that. His insult made it easy for me to leave. It gave me courage. Next time, I'll need to decide where I stand—on my own.

I tried to call Josh to explain, but he wouldn't answer. He says he sleeps with his cell phone next to his bed, so I assume he's mad at me. Any insights, Mr. Knightley? (That's rhetorical, by the way. I'll explain after I finish this thought.) As I said, I don't have enough experience for this, and I don't want to ask my friends. It's tiresome to always be clueless, and this one's a little more personal and embarrassing than my usual blunders. I will let it rest for now. I'm sure I'll have to pick this up again tomorrow and talk to Josh.

I'm sorry I launched into tonight's events without addressing your letter. It arrived today and made one thing very clear: I need these letters—as they are, with no changes to our agreement. Thank you for the final chance to come to my senses. Don't write me. Never write me. I can't believe I asked you. The moment I opened your letter and saw your signature, I panicked. I recalled all I'd told you, all you knew, and all I feared. I felt more exposed than in the article Kyle and I wrote. You know my heart.

And tonight confirmed it. When I got home, I paced for a while, then knew I'd find comfort if I turned to you. I'm not ready to give you up— just the way you are—a safe place in which to share my life and my dreams. Thank you for this. I may keep asking questions—I can't seem to help myself—but please, never supply the answers.

Time to sleep,
Sam

Dear Mr. Knightley,

I handed in my 5,000-word feature to Johnson yesterday. Now I wait . . .

And during my free Saturday—after all, this piece will either save me or get me kicked out, so there's no sense stressing about classes until I hear—I went in search of Cara. Does that surprise you? It did me.

I discovered the need to find her while writing with Kyle. It was right of me to leave her at eighteen, but I did things wrong too. They were relying on me and my rent money; I shouldn't have walked out. Maybe it was reading that Lewis book, maybe it's talking to the Muirs; for some reason I felt the need to make things right with Cara—as best I could.

I started my search at our old apartment, which is as wretched as I remembered. No one there remembered her, so I canvassed her old work-places and followed the trail until I found her five hours later. Her new apartment is worse than the one we shared. It's on the west edge of Hyde Park abutting the highway, near the site of the old Robert Taylor Homes. Many of those have been torn down or abandoned now, but some remain and are shockingly scary places. I clutched my pepper spray and jumped at every noise. In spite of it being about ten below today, I was sweating under my coat.

The lobby was vacant, and the stagnant air brought back painful memories. Gunfire or a car backfiring—I didn't dwell on which it was—sent my pulse soaring. And the clanging of the metal doors on each floor didn't help. I'm lucky nothing happened, Mr. Knightley. It was probably pretty stupid of me to go there alone. But I'm safe now, so I can tell the story . . .

I knocked on the door to 3B and got no reply. I'd come all this way, so I decided to wait. I slid down the wall outside the door and pulled *The Life of Pi* from my bag—a Mrs. Conley recommendation. It's about a young boy and a tiger in a lifeboat, in the middle of the Pacific. That's as far as I've gotten, but I feel a connection to young Pi, trying to survive alongside the very thing that can kill him. Is a tiger easier than your own past? I was thinking about all this so hard that I didn't hear anyone coming until the metal door slammed on the stairway.

I jumped to my feet and shoved the book in my bag. A huge Hispanic guy with long hair rounded the corner and rattled off some harsh-sounding Spanish. He looked me up and down—slowly. He made my skin crawl.

He switched to English. "Who are you?" He stopped inches from my face.

I wanted to cower, but forced myself to stand

tall and straight. "Is this your door? I'm sorry. I thought Cara Sanchez lived here."

"What you want with her?" He glanced around.

"I'm a friend."

"She's comin' up." He turned the metal knob and shoulder-butted his way into the apartment. I remained in the hall and again heard the screech of the door. Cara rounded the corner and saw me.

"Hi." My voice sounded high and oddly perky.

"What do you want?"

No hello? "I just wanted to see you."

"How'd you find me?"

"I asked around. All those detective novels served me well. First your old place, some job sites, friends . . ." I rushed to help her with her bags. "How are you?"

"Like you care." She shuffled on, but I stopped.

Do I care?

Kyle and I worked hard to pull out our pasts and loosen their grips on us. Fixing things with Cara was another step in that process, but faced with her, I wondered if there was more to it. Our pasts were linked. Are our futures?

"Cara, I need to apologize for how I left our apartment."

"Don't just stand there. Ric's ice cream'll melt. Come on." She opened the door, using three shoulder-butts, and there sat Ric, sprawled on the couch with the TV blaring. Cara didn't even look at him as she passed into a dirty gray kitchen.

"Bring a spoon," he called.

Cara didn't miss a beat. As I put the bag on the counter, she grabbed a spoon next to the sink, snatched the ice cream, and carried it to the living room. I stood awkwardly and calculated the difference between this and my warm apartment and the difference between Ric and Josh.

I sat down in a metal chair to give the impression I was staying as she came back to the kitchen. She narrowed her eyes and leaned against the counter.

"When did you move?" I pretended this was an afternoon chat with a friend.

"I stayed a couple years, but Ric and I are together, so I moved here a couple years ago. Rent's cheaper and we're good."

"I can see that." *Oops, bad sarcasm!*

"What?"

"Nothing. Where'd you two meet?"

"He's a friend of Ron's. Ron got sent up on charges. Loser. Ric keeps tabs on him, but I don't care. Don't need that."

I didn't know what to say to her. Her defenses were up, and why wouldn't they be? I was intruding. I could see it in her body language: neck pulled back, jaw pushed forward, arms crossed.

"You don't look good, Cara. Are you okay?" That was exactly the wrong thing to say.

"What?"

"You just look tired. I'm sorry. I'm not doing this right."

Tired was an understatement. Cara was always rounded and boy crazy—think Lydia Bennet or Harriet Smith. Now she looked wizened, haggard, thin, and defeated—think any Hollywood celebrity you want, during dieting and before her next rehab. And I was screwing it up.

"You talk different. You dress rich." She assessed me, and I didn't make the grade.

"I'm wearing jeans just like you." I cringed as I glanced at my sweater and boots. They looked too polished, too refined.

"You think I'm trash, but you're no—" She interrupted herself with a coughing fit.

"You're ill, Cara. Do you have the flu?"

"It's nothing. I got some bug at the Shell. There's cold medicine somewhere 'round here."

We talked a little while longer. Short sentences with no real meaning. I told her about life on campus, but left out a lot of details. "I wanted to come and apologize for the way I left."

"You're sorry?" Cara sounded shocked.

"Yes."

"You sound like Father John," Cara sneered.

Why does everyone disrespect Father John? I caught myself. *I did the same thing over the grant. That's another apology I'll need to make someday.*

"I've hung around him enough, and he does

make some sense. After I left you, I lived in Independence Cottage until a couple months ago. I'm up in Evanston now, but I went back to Grace House over Christmas."

"Why?"

"I got sick, and it was the only place I could go."

She opened her mouth as Ric's yell cut across the room. "I'm goin' out. Get me dinner, and none o' those ramen noodles."

Cara pushed off the counter and fidgeted with her hands. I knew that gesture. She needed me to leave.

"Thanks for seeing me, Cara. I'm sorry. That's all I wanted to say." I tried to hug her, but she didn't lift her arms. I walked through the living room. " 'Bye, Ric. Nice meeting you." He didn't look up.

It had turned dark outside. There were no cabs around, so I ran to the 'L' fast enough that I don't think an attacker could have caught me if he'd tried. Luckily it was so cold no one was outside or interested in coming out. I hopped the train and gulped in air. Each breath took me north . . . and forward.

When I got home I took a hot bath and invited Isabella up for a movie. We chatted, ate popcorn, and drank hot chocolate. It was just what I needed to settle my thoughts and memories. She's a cute kid. I gave her a copy of *Emma* for her twelfth birthday last week. I thought you'd appreciate that.

And now I should tell you about my classes this quarter—assuming I stay. You know about my Johnson class, the features one. I'm also taking Distribution Statistics and Audience Variance, as well as Quarterly Reviews. I know, statistics is a math class, and you might question the relevance. But Johnson always talks about the importance of connecting with the reader, and I figure I can do it better if I understand my readers, where they live and what they think. Hmm . . . I sound like a kiss-up. Still, it's a solid topic and it makes good sense. Quarterly Reviews covers academic writing and, although I doubt I'll do much of that, many such articles are written by free-lancers because there's good money in it.

So there you go. Either it's going to be a good quarter, Mr. Knightley, or I pack my bags. No halfway.

Sitting and waiting . . .
Sam

P.S. Just got a text—while brushing my teeth. I sincerely hope we never have instantaneous and unknowing video access to people.

Alex: Mom M said you had a rough go at Christmas. Here's to happy healthy spring. Still working hard?

Me: Much better, school and health. Thanks for the scarf and hat. How's movie?

Alex: Stop thanking me. Movie great. Better than last but keeping me from my book. Thinking _____ for a title. Thoughts? But don't tell.

Me: Very intriguing. Lips are sealed.

I sat speechless, toothpaste dribbling off my chin. Alex told me the book title. I feel like an insider, a trusted friend. What do you think *ET* would pay for that title? Just kidding. I wouldn't even tell you. After all, I'm a woman of integrity —an insider with integrity.

Dear Mr. Knightley,

You're the first—second—to hear the news: Johnson loved my article. He was stunned. I'm stunned. You have no idea what this means, Mr. Knightley. Maybe you do.

He called my cell this afternoon and demanded I come to his office. I dropped my tuna fish sandwich and left Debbie and Ashley at Jimmy John's, worried for my survival.

He stood as I entered and pointed to the chair across from him. "Sit down and tell me about your feature." He sat and bounced back and forth in his office chair, tapping the armrest with his fingers.

"It's my story, in my voice. It's a beginning if I have any hope of writing or staying here."

"Hope of writing? This is it, Moore. I see you. And even though you say it's your story, you've approached it with astounding objectivity and subtlety—very impressive. Where's it been hiding?"

I sat there a minute. *How to explain?*

"Sometimes it was too hard to be me. Eventually I forgot how." I looked toward the window to calm my breathing. "I literally broke over Christmas. My appendix burst, and I don't think it was a coincidence. And I was sure you were going to kick me out, so I went back to Grace House. I thought I'd move back in and find work, but Kyle got me talking, and . . . this is what came out of us."

"I added a lot of pressure, didn't I?" His voice was quiet and concerned.

"You were right. I've been picking subjects that couldn't touch me or ones that I could hide behind—until this. Kyle started us, and then we couldn't stop. We needed to get it out."

"Tell me about Kyle. Tell me about everything." He bounced forward and leaned over the desk—getting closer to the story.

And that's what I gave him. My story. I told him everything. It was another one of those cathartic afternoons: I talked, he asked questions, he pulled out a ham sandwich to share, and three hours later he stretched and said, "You're going to be fine, Moore. This is good work. I'm sending it to the *Trib*."

"Really?"

"It's that good. What'd you think? You can't use this simply for a grade. I told you, Moore, we make careers here. The *Tribune* awards a couple internships each summer—not errand-boy jobs, but the real deal, writing and investigating. This may be strong enough to land you a spot."

He noticed my fallen expression. "What is it? Your mouth turned down."

"Sir, as I said, I've hidden my past for a while

now. And there's Kyle to consider. He may not want this published."

"Tell you what, talk to Kyle. While I like my writers to stand behind their work, pseudonyms might be appropriate here."

"Thank you."

"E-mail me the piece with the names changed tonight, and I'll send it in."

"Thank you. I'm completely honored." I stood to leave.

"Don't be. You deserve it, Moore. And if you get that internship, it'll push you harder than I do. You're green, but I suspect you need challenge to keep you going." He reached out to shake my hand. "Well done, Moore. I'm proud of you."

I grasped his hand in a daze and turned to leave.

"And, Moore?" Johnson's tone told me that I wasn't out of the woods yet.

"Yes, sir?"

"This is outstanding, but it's only a quarter of my assessment for a concentration in feature writing. I don't grade on potential. Unless you want to switch specialties, all your work must come up to scratch."

"It will." There was nothing more to say, so I bounced out on little puffs of joy. I know the last comment was a downer, but it was also very hopeful. Johnson is proud of me and, I think, believes my work can improve. He wouldn't send me as a possible candidate to the *Tribune* otherwise. So I'm not going to talk myself out of being pleased and extremely relieved.

As I sat on a bench to call Kyle, I got scared. *Published? I'll be exposed to the world. Am I ready for that?*

Kyle wouldn't hear of pseudonyms. "We use our own names or nothing. We did this to be free. Fake names ain't free."

"Kyle, you can't stop me." I felt backed into a corner.

He didn't answer for an eternity. "I can't." He took a deep breath. I could hear it shudder over the line. "Sam, I'm fifteen next summer; guys I know have babies or they're dyin' on the streets. I'm past being a kid and I got choices to make. To be the kinda man I see in Coach, the kind Father John talks about . . . I won't hide anymore, Sam. Don't make me ashamed of my life. Do what you want, but I got no part in it." He hung up.

I sat stunned. I've replayed his words in my mind, Mr. Knightley, and I'm so ashamed. I thought only of me, and I made Kyle feel like *less*. I can't have it both ways, can I? It's that moment. We go forward or we're done, trapped forever. I will never hold Kyle back.

I e-mailed a note to Dr. Johnson:

Thank you so much for this opportunity. Please submit the article with no changes and use our real names.

I sent it an hour ago and I still feel shaky. There are so many people I need to warn—so much to say. What if the *Tribune* actually prints it? I'm going running . . .

Sincerely,
Sam

Dear Mr. Knightley,

School is moving along well. My favorite class is actually statistics. It's a nice mental break for me—crunching numbers is far easier than figuring out how to reveal yourself in print while still "maintaining objectivity and perspective." It's a fine line I haven't learned to walk, but I'm getting better help now. Johnson is more constructive in his criticism, like he believes I'm worth his time. It's a good feeling and makes me work harder. Debbie noticed it and congratulated me on getting out of the doghouse.

I haven't told anyone about the article yet. Even if the *Trib* doesn't publish it, I need to be honest with my friends. And I need to talk to Josh. He came to my apartment last night. I cooked him dinner before we watched a movie. Afterward I thought I'd tell him, but he seemed interested in other things . . . so I never said a word. Part of me thinks it should affect nothing. Another part knows it changes everything. I called Hannah this morning in a panic.

"You'll be fine, Sam. I've never seen you so free. Don't step back now."

"It's too hard, Hannah. I already feel raw. What if I retreat into my books?"

"You won't. Besides, how could you ever want to be Fanny Price?"

I laughed. "You're reading *Mansfield Park*? Fanny's dull at times, but she has her uses. She's very capable of fading into the background, and she's a perfect moral compass."

"Are you channeling her lately?"

I was confused. "I'm trying not to project anyone, remember?"

"I don't mean that. I mean the moral compass thing. Josh?"

"What about him?" I said, although I knew what she meant.

"Intimacy isn't always about love. You've got to talk to him."

"We're not sleeping together! I—" I clamped my mouth shut. I never blurt that out, because no one would understand why we aren't.

"That's good."

Now Hannah shocked me. No one else has said that.

"You think so?" I tried to act casual, but I desperately wanted to know her thoughts.

"Absolutely. It complicates everything, changes everything. I believe if you're not married to the guy, that shouldn't be happening."

"That's not very forward thinking of you, Hannah." I wanted to push her. I wanted answers.

"Put it in your terms. Take all those Austen and Brontë characters who went astray. They

211

weren't villains, but they paid a price. Natural consequences for making poor choices. Those consequences still exist today. You're always saying that's what makes Austen so good, right? That she portrayed human nature accurately, and that human nature hasn't changed."

"Yes?"

"Then look at Lydia Bennet, Maria Bertram, Marianne Dashwood—"

"Marianne?" I never told her about my musings that Josh and I are a modern Colonel Brandon and Marianne.

"Yes, Marianne. She lost her sense of right and wrong. She thought that because loving Willoughby felt good, it had to be right. Later she knew her mistake and she regretted it."

We didn't talk much after that. I was too confused. Hannah knew she had dropped a bomb on me.

"Sam, I'm thrilled about the article. Call if you need me. I'm always here." She paused again. "Sam, I love you. You know that, right?"

My eyes teared. "Thanks, Hannah." I hung up the phone. Hannah's known the real me and stood by me for five years. I think she does love me. And although I have only recently come to see her clearly, I trust her. I haven't given her enough credit.

Now I don't know what to think, Mr. Knightley. I thought I was backward about this whole intimacy thing, and now I wonder. Every time Josh pushes, I back away. I want to talk to him about it, but I know it's not a discussion he'll like, and I don't know what to say. He still gets silent when I leave dinners to head north. Maybe I'm making this too complicated. Maybe I should address it head on. The new me is supposed to be filled with courage, right?

And I'd better get some because between this and my article . . . there's a lot of talking to do.

Love,
Sam

Dear Mr. Knightley,

The *Tribune* bought my piece. I can't decide if I should jump for joy or throw up. They will publish it as a Sunday feature next month. There are so many people to talk to now—and there's a deadline. What have I gotten myself into?

There is one person I won't have to tell, though, and I thought I'd feel good about that—now I'm not so sure. As I told the Muirs about the article and the internship interview (Susan Ellis, the *Trib*'s Deputy Editor, called to schedule it), Alex came to mind, and my heart jumped to my throat. I don't want him to know my past. Call me a coward, but in this case I don't care. He doesn't need to know. So I extracted a promise from the Muirs not to tell him.

The professor wasn't pleased. "Why? Do you think he'll use it against you? Put it in a book?"

"Of course not." Those thoughts hadn't even occurred to me.

"Then why the subterfuge?"

Subterfuge? "He doesn't need to know. It's not important to him, and I don't want any more drama." I hoped the professor might believe my oh-so-casual approach. He didn't.

He leaned forward and templed his fingers in front of his chin. He looked remarkably like

Father John at that moment, and I fully expected a lecture. But it didn't come—only a few sentences that carried more power than any of Father John's speeches.

"I won't tell, Sam. It's your past—your story to share. But remember: it doesn't define you." His words hung above us. "Never let something so unworthy define you."

I got my promise of secrecy, but now it doesn't feel good.

I'm going running,
Sam

Dear Mr. Knightley,

Happy Valentine's Day! I know it was yesterday, but still . . . Happy Valentine's Day. I thought about the library yesterday. I bet they have a great LOVE display up. I need to visit there soon. Mr. Clayton and Mrs. G and the staff feel so far away. I e-mail occasionally, but that feels empty and impersonal. Everything feels that way—I barely have time to keep in touch with Kyle.

He was proud of me about our names in the article and we're good now. He's doing great and still at Grace House. Coach Ridley put together a winter running plan for him, and he's going to tackle the track team next month. His e-mails are full of Ridley, which is nice because I know from his tone that Ridley is good for him. Father John confirms that the coach is a solid man. Kyle needs that. And Kyle has a new girlfriend. Not sure if he needs that. I'm kidding. She sounds cute.

Alex sounds good too. He texted me yesterday.

Alex: Happy Valentine's Day. Hallmark holiday, but still fun. Plans?
Me: Dinner with boyfriend then back to work. :)
Alex: Poor boyfriend. Have more fun.

Me: Come visit and I will. Muirs miss you.
Alex: Soon. Gotta go.

I can't believe I wrote that. It sounded flirty. I meant to express a simple truth, but was so embarrassed when I read it over. Yet it's true; I get electric whenever I receive a text and I hang on every word the Muirs relay from him. I hope I haven't crossed some line—one I don't even know exists. But it was Valentine's Day, and everyone gets to be flirty on Valentine's Day, right? Besides, that silly text was the best fun of the day. Dinner with Josh wasn't so rewarding . . .

It started well. Josh took me to Spago, which is very romantic. I had asked to go to Chicago Pizza and Oven Grinder. After Hannah's engagement story, I imagine it to be dark, cozy, and perfect. But Josh says the lines are always too long and he doesn't trust a host who claims he can remember your face rather than write down your name. So, no go there.

But Spago was lovely; I'm not complaining. Josh pulled out all the stops: he held my hand, opened the car door for me, took my coat . . . everything. I felt cherished, adored, and beautiful. But, as is my way, I put my foot in it during dessert and the evening banked south.

Over a wonderful crème caramel, Josh started talking about the future and seemed to include me in his plans, so I felt it was time for honesty. I owed him that.

I pulled my article out of my bag and asked him to read it.

He pushed it aside. "Sam, I want to be with you tonight, not read your classwork."

"It's more than that. Read it, please?"

He sighed and flattened the pages on the table. As he read, I told him that the *Tribune* would be publishing it in a couple weeks. His eyes widened with excitement. Then his expression changed. He stopped after the first two pages and pushed it back.

"This is pretty disturbing, Sam. What were you thinking? Where'd you get all this?"

"That's me, Josh. I'm this girl. Kyle and I wrote this over Christmas break while you were in Cincinnati."

"This is what you were doing? I thought you were resting."

"I was. I was healing in many ways."

"Who's Kyle? Did he stay with you in your apartment?"

"Kyle's fourteen. He's a foster kid who lives at Grace House Settlement Home. I went there after the hospital. It's where I lived from about age fifteen until I came to Medill. Kyle and I worked on this for over a week, and then I went to the Muirs' house. I told you that."

"You told me about the Muirs. You never

mentioned this." He took back the paper and read more. "This is you . . . ," he mumbled.

I sat silent. The article told him everything, and that was easier than talking. And this way, his eyes were looking down, focused on the pages. There are first moments when the eyes tell one's real emotions, before the brain reminds them to bank and hide. Finally he looked up.

"Everyone reads the *Trib*, Sam. All Chicago will read this—all your friends, my friends, my co-workers. You should've given me a heads-up."

I stared at him.

"Don't give me that, Sam. You hand me this paper and expect me to be happy for you. I need time to digest this. And, by the way, Valentine's Day was supposed to be fun."

"I wanted to tell you the truth."

"You did that." He shook his head. We stared at each other. It was hard, but I refused to be the first to look away. He shifted his eyes and relented—a touch. "This my copy?"

I nodded, completely deflated.

"Sam, listen." Josh reached over and lifted my chin. "I'm sorry. You've really caught me off guard. I'll take this and read it again. Let's enjoy tonight, okay?"

We made inane chatter and ate our dessert. He was mildly affectionate the rest of the evening, but distracted. I felt like he was going through the motions of being a boyfriend without feeling them.

He didn't ask me to stay. He waited while I hailed a cab, and when it arrived he put his hands on both sides of my face and kissed me, long and slow. Kisses have meanings, I have learned: some are light and playful, others search, and others promise . . . This one? I pondered it and came to no decision—decidedly undetermined.

I feel the same way,
Sam

Dear Mr. Knightley,

The *Tribune* interview was ten days ago. I didn't write you because I didn't know what to say. I do now; but I'll keep this in order.

I met with Susan Ellis and Kevin McDermott downtown at the Tribune Tower. It was very exciting, which never works in my favor. I got nervous. I didn't fall on my face, but I certainly didn't blow them away. It was a mediocre interview—because, let's face it, I'm mediocre. And while I worked hard not to retreat into well-worn fictional friends, making myself appear stellar was beyond my reach.

A few days after the interview, my article came out. The timing was good for me; this way, I entered the interview with a shot at a good first impression. The other way around? Game over.

I'm enclosing a copy for you. Can you believe the layout? No one told me it'd be a four-page spread, complete with pictures, bold type, inserts, the works. I almost regret sending them some of the photos. I assumed they wanted them for context, not content.

Kyle called, and I burst into tears when I heard his voice.

"We did it, Sam. We're in print! Did you see my picture? We look great."

"We sure do, Kyle." And as soon as we hung up, there was a knock on my door. Mrs. Conley stood there with the paper in her hand.

"Sam, is this you?"

"I'm sorry, Mrs. Conley. I wanted to tell you. I hope you don't think I'm a bad influence—" I couldn't breathe.

"Stop, Sam. This doesn't matter to us. Though it does explain a few things." She smiled.

"It does?"

"My children fascinated you. The way you watched them, watched all of us. I felt like we were in a petri dish. And the way you talked."

"Yeah, you probably met a lot of sides of me."

"I only wish you'd told us. I'm sorry if we made you uncomfortable."

"Please don't say that." My issues are not her responsibility.

My cell rang and startled us both. She quickly added, "I don't want to keep you, but I want you to tell the kids. I won't show them the article. How about dinner this week?"

"I'd like that."

"Good. I'll cook that lasagna you love. Thursday night?"

"It's great. Thanks, Mrs. Conley." She quickly hugged me and left, and I dashed to my phone.

"What's this?" Debbie screamed.

"Are you mad?"

"It's amazing, Sam." She let out a low whistle. "Girl, you can write."

"That's all you can say?"

"You haven't been very open with your friends. Is that what you want me to say?"

"Yeah."

"We're okay, Sam." Debbie paused. "Coffee later? My treat, if you talk."

"Sure. Grab Ashley so I won't have to tell it all twice."

"Ashley's in New York all week for the Sotheby's interview. Tell her over spring break. I can't wait."

"Sure. Let me make some calls and I'll meet you in an hour."

Then I called Josh. I opened with "The article came out today." No hello. We've gone to dinner a couple times since Valentine's Day, but there's a distance now. I suspected he was deciding if I was worth his effort. And frankly, it ticked me off. Now I don't know what to think.

"Yeah, Sam, I've seen it. In fact, Logan and Steve already called. You're the talk of the town, sweetheart."

"I am?" His endearment surprised me.

"They thought you were smart and pretty before, but now you've got grit. You know, guys find that very appealing."

"They do?"

"Of course we do." He dropped his voice just

above a whisper. It felt intimate and flirtatious.

"I thought all this upset you." I tried not to sound accusatory, but I could hear the tension, the hurt in my voice.

"Sam, let's forget all that. You took me by surprise, and I've been slammed at work. Have you seen the new IKEA ads? That's my group. It's been crazy. You know I support you?"

"I didn't know how you felt about me." *Did I get all this wrong?*

"It's time to celebrate. Why don't you come down for dinner tonight, and I'll plan something special?"

I couldn't because I had a final article due and an analysis for statistics, but that was okay. I didn't want to go. Josh's new attitude felt suspect, but as I said, maybe I'd misread things. Either way, I should be thrilled the storm passed.

Then this afternoon Susan Ellis called. I know, Mr. Knightley, does the drama ever stop? My heart jumped to my throat when I saw her number on my caller ID.

She wasted no time on preliminaries. "Sam, your article was first-rate, and we've received a tremendous response from it. While we'd like to see anything more you've got, Kevin and I have selected another candidate for the internship."

"May I ask why?"

"Your work is solid and has potential, but you need a track record. Get a larger body of work and you'll be ready. A smaller paper will give you the support you need."

"I understand." But I didn't. I wanted to cry. "I have six short-subject treatments about aspects of the foster care system, child rights, and youth in America that I've submitted to some smaller papers. Could I send them to you?"

She paused, then said politely, "Send me everything. I do think you've got the makings of a fine journalist."

"Thank you, Ms. Ellis. I'll e-mail them. And thanks for the opportunity. I enjoyed meeting you."

"Good luck to you, Sam. I'll let you know what I think of your new submissions. Good-bye."

It was a long shot, but I started to believe. Nothing comes easy, does it? After I hung up the phone, I quickly applied to the *Highland Park Press*, the *Evanston Review* and the *Lincoln Park Sentinel*—all good papers. I have to stay in Chicago because I agreed to house-sit for the Muirs this summer while they're abroad; I'll leave the clamoring for internships at the *Miami Herald*, the *Los Angeles Times*, The *New York Review*, and tons of other great jobs to my classmates.

I'm glad for the house-sitting excuse because, quite frankly, I don't think I could handle all those rejection letters. We're constantly told that we're the best at Medill and that the top tier is where "the best" work. But I'm not part of that elite. I'm the girl hanging by my fingernails off the back ledge.

After wallowing a bit, I donned my big-girl pants and headed north for dinner with the Muirs. Whining isn't an option around the professor. He would say, "Why does this surprise you? Get out there and do what she says—build a body of work and impress the socks off her after graduation." He'd make it sound so easy—much better to avoid the pep talk by faking equanimity.

The Muirs—and, surprise, Alex Powell—were the perfect company. Alex is in town doing advance work for his next book, set in Chicago. He's even moving here for the summer. I felt sorry for him—he clearly expected to spend time with the Muirs and was visibly shocked to find they'll be gone.

"I told you all this, son. You didn't listen." The professor laughed.

"I thought you said you were considering it. You never said you bought tickets and were leaving for two whole months." Alex sounded frantic.

The professor smiled and softened his voice. "I'm sorry if I didn't make it clear. I know you're disappointed, but I need to finish this research, Alex. Paris and a few stops in Spain are the final pieces, and I can put *The Lost Generation* to rest."

"But this summer?"

"This summer. I don't know how many years I've got left, and this is the last book I need to get out."

Alex dropped his head. "You're right; I wasn't listening . . . but don't say it's your last."

"Just my last book, son. Not my last summer with you. Bring Cole back next year and we'll have a grand time."

The room quieted. I wanted to give Alex some connection to them, so I offered up my house-sitting job. I hoped it would make him feel more secure. And it would save him from renting a place.

"Don't be ridiculous, dear. I don't want some man who doesn't know wood polish from toilet cleaner living here. He'll kill my plants, and the late charges on all the bills will drive Robert crazy."

"Mrs. Muir, I'm sure Alex is more capable than that."

"No mother would choose a son to watch her house over a daughter, Sam. You stay here." She pulled her lips in, embarrassed.

Daughter? I shoved a cookie into my mouth to cover my jaw drop. *Daughter?* What a fleeting, lovely, unimaginable thought.

Alex cut through the moment. "She's right. I don't clean unless I move, Sam, and all my bills are direct pay—never even see them. I need to be downtown anyway. Cole would never live in such a sleepy suburb." The last bit he threw to the professor.

"Sleepy suburb? I take offense at that, young man. I'll have you know—"

They carried on from there as Mrs. Muir and I escaped to the kitchen with the platter. Alex found us there an hour later, finishing off the chocolate chip cookies.

"Want a ride south, Sam?"

"Aren't you staying here? I can call a cab, or the Metra is well lit."

"You don't do that, do you? At night? Sam, I'm driving you home. I know Pops doesn't let you do that."

"He doesn't. He always takes me home. But I'm fully capable."

"It's dangerous."

"Alex." Mrs. Muir stepped in.

"Sorry." He held up his hands in surrender. "Not my business. Grab your coat. I'll behave." He kissed Mrs. Muir on her cheek. I followed suit and we headed for his car.

Alex raked his hands through his hair. "I've been a jerk all night. I didn't know they were leaving."

I suspected he wasn't talking entirely to me.

"Pops was right. I haven't been paying attention lately. Bugger . . ." Alex noticed me. "And you, I was rude to you. Mom M was right to call me on it. I'm sorry, Sam. I feel like I keep doing that to you. I'm not such a jerk all the time, I promise."

"It's no big deal."

"It's just that they talk about you all the time. I feel I know you . . . That doesn't excuse it, I'm just trying to explain it."

The car grew warm.

Alex continued, "They love me, the Muirs, and that makes me protective of them and anything important to them—now that includes you. But I shouldn't tease or criticize you. I don't know you that well."

"I'm not offended, Alex." And I wasn't. I was dwelling on *They talk about you all the time.* I took a deep breath. "What do they say about me?" I didn't think the Muirs would break my confidence, but I wondered.

"It's what they don't say. They drop your name in conversation like you're a member of the family, and you light up Pops's eyes. You can see that?" Alex smiled at me. His face was so transparent that I believed him. That's all he knew.

"No."

Alex looked at me a moment longer, letting me absorb the compliment. "You should look harder." He continued, "They've also said that you work hard, you're amazingly smart, you come for dinner weekly, you like the kids you live near, and you've got some quirky friends, namely a girl named Ashley. Hence, I feel I know and adore you too." Now he was teasing me.

" 'Accept my thanks for the compliment.' " I donned Lizzy in all her glory and hoped we could pass to a new topic.

"So I don't need to 'use my breath to cool my porridge'," he replied.

"Ugh . . . How could I have forgotten that about you? Do you know every book written?"

Part of me laughed and another part panicked. I like Alex. Heck, on some level I probably have a crush on him, or some residual hero worship—either way, he disconcerts me. I can't rely on my characters; he knows them all. And the real me? He's Alex Powell, for goodness' sake. Who am I kidding that any of this matters to him?

He chatted a bit more on the drive to Conleys' and kept it light and easy. Maybe he sensed I needed space. I got out of the car without many more words.

But of course he had the last ones. "I know what you're thinking, Sam. 'Teazing, teazing man! I will think no more about him.' I hope you won't stick to that."

This time I laughed. "Good night, Alex. 'I know my own strength and will never be embarrassed by *you* again.' "

He smiled softly at me. "You make a better Lizzy, Sam. Jane Bennet is too quiet for you."

And he left me standing in the driveway still smiling as he drove away.

He's infuriating, Mr. Knightley, but he's also a really nice man.

Now back to studying. It's been a crazy few days, but finals are next week so it's going to get worse. Then spring break starts, and Debbie and I have been invited to Ashley's house in Naples, Florida. Can you imagine the blunders I can commit there?

Sincerely,
Sam

P.S. I can't sleep. Josh dropped by.

"You're home. I've been calling for hours."

No hello? "I went to the Muirs' for dinner. I left my phone here. What's up?" I let him in the door.

"I wanted to see you. You've been so busy that I haven't had a chance to congratulate you. I'm so excited, hon—the article, the interview."

He pulled me into his arms and kissed me. Then he said, "I got you something. Come here." He crossed the room to the couch and patted the seat next to him. I followed, and he put a small, light blue box tied with a white ribbon into my hands. "Go on, open it."

I pulled off the ribbon feeling slightly detached. I remembered a similar moment, long ago, with Dan and hoped my reaction would be warmer now, more sincere. But I didn't feel it. I still don't.

Inside I found a beautiful silver necklace—a thin chain with a star pendant. And in the star's center rested a sapphire. It was extraordinary. Josh took my silence for awe. Perhaps it was.

He reached for it. "Let me put it on you. You're my star, you know." I lifted my hair as he reached around to clasp it at the back of my neck. He pressed a kiss there before I lowered my hair.

"There. It's perfect. Go look in the mirror."

I went to the bathroom, grateful for the privacy. First I looked at the necklace. It lay at just the right place, beneath the hollow at the base of my neck. Next I looked at my eyes. They did not reflect joy.

Josh called from the living room, "Hon, I gotta go. I'm meeting Logan and Drew for late-night drinks at the Aviary. Wanna come?"

I left my sanctuary, fingering the pendant. "I'd love to, but I've got some editing to do." I needed to say more. "I'm sad you have to go."

Josh looked in my eyes, then at my fingers playing with the pendant, and smiled. "I know." He led the way to the door and pulled me into his arms. "I'm glad you like it. I knew it would look spectacular on you." He kissed me again, longer this time, and with more authority. "Congratulations. You get your work done."

He left. And I'm still awake.

~ MARCH 24

Dear Mr. Knightley,

I just got home from Naples, Florida. If that isn't an entirely different planet, I'm not sure what is. Wow. It was good, but I'm glad to be home. It was exhausting keeping my jaw from constantly dropping.

We flew down last Saturday, dropped our bags at Ashley's house, and went straight to her "club" for lunch. Afterwards, lying by the pool, I decided to tell her about the article. I pulled a copy out to show her and started my story. Debbie loved adding her insights.

"So you see, Ash, it totally makes sense now why she had no clue about . . ." And off she went.

Ashley laughed and joined in, especially when we talked about my quotation habit. She's the only one with enough literary knowledge to understand what I was up to.

Then they took a tangent I never expected: you. Ashley was like Sherlock Holmes meets Nancy Drew. Do I have any clues to your identity? Do you ever contact me? Did I ask Laura any questions? Did I hire a detective? Only Ashley and Eloise, the little spoiled girl who lives at the Plaza, would think of hiring a detective. "Excuse me, I'd like a hot fudge sundae, one private investigator, two forensic analysts, and a cherry soda. 'Charge it, please, and thank you very much.' " She hypothesized for a full twenty minutes on ways I could hunt you down. Don't worry—I'm as uninterested in that as I would suspect you are.

It's ironic that as I grow comfortable being Sam, they suddenly cast me as Orphan Annie or Anne Shirley. From their perspective my childhood began to sound romantic and heroic. And you became Daddy Warbucks or Uncle Drosselmeyer. Ashley suggested that one—she's seen *The Nutcracker* on Broadway "every year for as long as I can remember." Again, only Ashley.

The cross-examination and speculation droned on and on. I wondered why I ever hid my past—they found it fascinating. After a couple hours, Debbie jumped into the pool and I noticed Ashley grow quiet. All this was bothering her more than she let on.

I reached over and poked her arm. She swung her head toward me, so sad.

"I'm sorry, Ashley. I hurt you the most. I know that."

She looked away.

"I hope you understand how scared I was. I started hiding so young, I didn't know how to stop—even when I felt safe. Please forgive me."

She looked up with a deep, shuddering breath—

a start-over breath. "You know I do. It's just that you clearly didn't think much of me or you would have trusted me."

I raised my eyebrows at her.

She slumped back in her lounge chair. "I did it again, didn't I? I made it about me."

"Kind of," I laughed. "But I understand."

"Sam? I trust you, you know. There aren't many people I trust, but you're one. I wish you felt the same about me."

"I do. You see me better than anyone. And we're a lot alike, even though our pasts are very different. I just think it's hard for us to understand each other sometimes."

"Agreed, but I'd like to."

"Me too." I smiled, leaned back, and closed my eyes.

"I won't use it against you, Sam," she whispered.

"And I won't go after you. I promise, Ashley. I'm sorry if I ever have."

"Me too."

We sat silent for a few moments. I think that was enough soul baring for both of us.

"Ohhh . . . How'd Josh take it?"

I'd just drifted to sleep when Ashley's playful voice startled me. "Why did you say it like that?"

She seemed to take his negative response as a given.

"Sam, the guy's a poser." Ashley caught

herself. "That's not a bad thing. He likes things a certain way, and I can't imagine he appreciates surprises."

She was right. Josh doesn't like surprises. Maybe it was the surprise, not the story or my past, that bothered him. The necklace confirms that. And he's very excited now.

Debbie came back, and I told them all about Valentine's Day and Josh's reaction and the necklace. Debbie said he behaved badly, but agreed the necklace is beautiful. Ashley said to cut him some slack and added that Josh is ambitious, but not mean.

I vacillated between the opinions for a while. I haven't seen him much because work's kept him busy most nights, but he's been very attentive in calls and texts—far better than usual. That's to his credit.

So I decided to cut him some slack. Second chances are good, right? I called him and flirted shamelessly, telling him I couldn't wait to see him when I got home. Very Marianne Dashwood.

The rest of the week was great. We sunned, swam, ate, laughed, and talked. The only cloud came yesterday: Mrs. Walker and Constance, Ashley's older sister, arrived.

"Ashley, Constance and I are going to Saks today. You should join us. You're looking worn. If this is what you wear every day, it needs freshening."

"Mother, I'm fine. Debbie and Sam are here. I'm not going shopping with you."

"What you wear reflects upon your family, Ashley."

"No, Mother. It reflects upon me. In Chicago, folks look at me, get to know me for me. I make my own decisions."

"If your decisions lead to sloppy clothes and shabby friends, perhaps you should reconsider."

"My friends? What are you talking about?"

"Your friends are shabby. Sam's the worst of the lot. She has no style, no presence."

"Sam's a good friend. If you only—"

Don't say it, Ashley.

Her mom, thankfully, cut her off. "Ashley, I'm not discussing this right now. Clean up and let's go. You're a mess."

Neither had seen me approach from the kitchen. I can't believe they didn't hear my heart pounding. I slowly retraced my steps and ate another bowl of corn flakes. Is that how people see me? Shabby? I thought I looked pretty pulled together. I don't have Ashley's sense of style, but I'm neat and tidy and, thanks to you, own some lovely clothes. I thought I fit in.

We hopped the plane this morning seemingly happy, but Ashley's eyes were tight and flat, and I felt deflated. I had tried to stand up straight and thank Mrs. Walker with dignity, even bravado. But my best Edmond Dantes came off limp and got waved away with a flick of her fingers.

Other than those moments, Mr. Knightley, it was an amazing trip, and I got to know Ashley and Debbie better. And they got to know me, the real me—painful and scary, yes, but also necessary and good. I refuse to let Mrs. Walker steal any of that.

Nevertheless, next time I travel to Florida, I'll visit Disney World. I need more reality. And you'll never find Mrs. Walker there.

Back home safe and sound,
Sam

P.S. Here's my spring schedule: Johnson for Civil Writes. Catchy title, huh? The sensible part of me warns I should avoid his classes. They bring down my GPA. But Johnson pushes me, and I'm getting better.

I'm also taking Investigative Journalism, Statistical Research, and Magazine Editing. Just can't stay away from those math classes.

Still no summer internship. Most of my class is placed, but I'm still here—still writing, still clawing at the ledge, and still applying for jobs . . .

~ April 1

Dear Mr. Knightley,

I've decided to drop out of school and trek with the Yucanube tribe of Guana Lampusata through the mountain pass of Indrogolia.

Josh is most supportive. We plan to be married in a Hitakutiku ceremony during the first full moon of the spring vernal equinox. Thank you so much for your support.

With deep and abiding joy,
Saman-tha

Dear Mr. Knightley,

I doubt my April Fool's letter tricked you even for a moment. I thought about striking closer to home, just: *I'm marrying Josh and he wants me to drop out of school.* But when I typed that out, it didn't feel funny.

But I do have news to report that's not a joke. I confirmed it, twice. Ms. Ellis from the *Tribune* called this morning.

"Sam, Susan Ellis here. I want to offer you the summer internship. Are you still available?"

"Yes." I played it so cool. "What happened?"

"Our candidate accepted another post. I have the spot and I admire tenacity, Sam, and good writing. The six treatments you sent were fantastic. I will run them as a series beginning next month."

"Really?" *Very articulate.*

"Really. I may be wrong about you, Sam. I thought you needed more experience, but you may simply need a launch pad. Internship starts June 15. I need your answer by tomorrow."

"I'll take it, and I'm telling you now. This isn't a joke?"

"No."

"Seriously, you're offering me an internship? At the *Chicago Tribune*?"

"Yes, Sam. I'll send you paperwork as proof,"

she laughed. "Glad you're on board. I think you'll enjoy it here."

Can you believe it? I'm so excited, but still not articulate. I hope she's right about that whole launch pad thing. What if I don't have the talent? No, I can't think that way . . . I'm going to the *Trib*!

I called Josh. "Honey, I knew you could do it." He made me feel loved and successful. We're going out tomorrow to celebrate. The *Tribune*!

I also called Kyle.

"I started all this!" he yelled. I could feel his pride. He deserves the credit, and I'm the first to admit it.

"You did, Kyle. And I can never thank you enough."

"Ditto."

"What'd I do?"

"You stayed, Sam. You never left."

"I won't."

"I know."

We both got teary so, naturally, we hung up. Kyle's doing well now—inside and out. He's calmer, not predatory and angry. He's also kinder. I think when you're fighting for your life, kindness becomes a luxury you can't afford. Seeing it in Kyle lets me know he feels safe.

And speaking of Kyle, I've got a secret. You cannot tell anyone. No one. It's so fragile that the telling might shatter it: Coach Ridley and his wife are taking foster parenting classes for Kyle.

They're in their late fifties, with two grown kids and a couple grandkids—great for Kyle, but not so great for approval from DCFS. So Coach Ridley made me promise not to tell him. As if I would. Kyle couldn't stand another "almost." Placements are rare at his age, and if this fails I say he's at Grace House for good. I don't want that for him. It's so lonely. That's what no one shares: the deep sense of aloneness that pervades a settlement home versus a family, any family.

So I'm keeping my mouth shut and my fingers crossed. I've found wishing and wanting something too badly makes it disappear. The *Tribune* better not disappear. If it sticks, I'll rethink my theory. If Coach Ridley fosters Kyle, I'll throw it out completely.

> Back to work,
> Sam

Dear George,

Do you think we should be on a first-name basis? Consider it . . .

I've got three more weeks of school and then the *Tribune*. I still can't think about it without getting giddy. I submitted my paperwork and no one has called to take it away. Life is beginning to feel real and hopeful and exciting. That's very new for me.

Now that I think and act and speak as Sam, I sometimes miss my alter egos. Occasionally I page through my books to read their more memorable lines, and then I return them to the shelf and let them be. But they're allowed to come out with Alex, and that's fun, because I'm not hiding—I'm showing off! The other day we had a battle via texting, and I lost.

Alex: Heard you got an internship at the Trib. You'll have more pub credits than me soon.
Me: I will do my best, but doing one's best does not always answer.
Alex: Nice try, Jane Eyre. You shall meet with many stumbling blocks, no doubt. But you'll persevere. :)
Me: Stumped.
Alex: Victory!

Me: Teazing, teazing man!
Alex: Gotta go, Lizzy. Bye, Sam.

It took me three hours of poring over my books before I found it in Gaskell's *North and South*. Is that too geeky to admit?

Me: North and South. Got you!
Alex: I'll say. It's 3 am. Go to sleep!
Me: So sorry. Go back to bed. Delete message . . . Off to die.
Alex: No dying. Would miss you this summer. Sleep well.

Thankfully, humiliating myself with Alex is not the only way to engage my books. I found another: Isabella and I are reading *Emma* together. We reached Box Hill yesterday and Emma insulted Miss Bates. We almost cried. I was thrilled Isabella felt the emotion of it: Emma's confusion and embarrassment, retaliation, then remorse. It was awful.

Austen's descriptions of human nature are spot-on. Isabella and I both recognize them in our friends. Like the Box Hill participants, my fellow journalists size each other up, cut each other down, and make alliances/friendships where they benefit us most. It's pretty brutal right now. Isabella told me about the girls in her class gossiping and backstabbing each other for attention—from the teachers, from the boys, from everyone. It sounded just as bad.

She also said something about Josh I couldn't place. We were sprawled on my couch chatting when she commented on my necklace.

"Thank you. Josh gave it to me." I fingered the necklace.

"I figured that. It's pretty."

"Why'd you think it was from him?"

"Josh likes the way things look. Like Mr. Elton."

We moved on, but her comment struck me. Mr. Elton is a mercenary fop. He only wants Emma, rejects Harriet, and then marries Augusta Hawkins for money and appearances. There's no substance behind Mr. Elton. But that's a side of human nature we can't deny. We want our coveted place in the sun. I keep tripping over Isabella's comment. Maybe she doesn't understand Mr. Elton? Or Josh? She's only twelve.

But speaking of *Emma* and coveted places: Ashley got her spot in New York at Sotheby's Wine Auction House. She doesn't want work in English literature. Never did. She just came to NU to get away from her mother. I'm glad she's pursuing what she actually likes—maybe she's tired of hiding too. She loves talking about wine.

We've gotten closer the past couple months. Though she appears to be an Emma, she's vulnerable too. She fears life is passing her by, fears she doesn't measure up, fears she isn't worthy. Not that she says all this, but she lets the chinks in her armor show more now.

Yesterday we saw one of Ashley's friends and a woman coming toward us. Ashley paled, turned around, and took a different path. I followed.

"What just happened?" I asked.

"I can't see him. He's been dating her for a month now."

"Will? You two are friends."

"Yes. No. I mean, I love him, Sam. I have since I was eighteen."

I stopped walking, stunned. "You mentioned him that night. The night you killed my eyebrows. You said he was a silly boy. You love him?"

"That's what makes him silly." She wasn't laughing. "He's one of Constance's college friends. He hung around my senior year. He worked at JP Morgan and used to come to dinner and stuff. He's never noticed me."

"You never told me this. How is it you're both here?"

"I knew he was coming to Kellogg. English lit got me out of New York, so why not here?"

"Seriously?"

"I know. Please don't tell, Sam. It's so pathetic. Please?"

"I'll never say a word. I promise. But, Ash, have you told him?"

"Of course not! You don't tell a guy that he's wrong about you, that you're not some flighty debutante who giggles all the time, that you're real and that you work hard. He's supposed to notice. Will's never noticed. No one notices."

"I'm sorry, Ashley."

We walked in silence. I'm sure she was pondering Will. I pondered myself, Josh, my friends, my life . . .

Changing, being real and becoming who you want to be, is hard work. Right now, I'd love a good chat with Jane Eyre. She never lost herself. Not once.

> I may need to find her,
> just for a moment,
> Sam

P.S. I'll leave it because I wrote it, but you're not a "George." It feels awkward. I'll stick with "Mr. Knightley." Don't you agree?

Dear Mr. Knightley,

Johnson gave me a C! Everyone's shocked that a C pleases me, but it does. It really does. And that was only part of my great day . . . Today was my first at the *Tribune* and it was terrifyingly extraordinary. I took the Metra early and savored every step from the Loop out to Michigan Ave. I grabbed a latté and felt very chic. But let's be honest . . . I grinned like an idiot.

When I arrived, the lobby was full of interns anxiously awaiting our orientation program. College kids get the jobs in the mail room, copy service, and the newsroom. Only two writing spots are reserved for grad students. The other writer's name is Mike and he's from Columbia's program. He doesn't say much, but he seems nice. And shy. And cute. Clark Kent?

Orientation culminated in photos and a swanky little badge that I get to clip on my waist each day and flash to the security guard. We then ate lunch in the small café at the bottom of the building, where Mike and I sat with some college girls who flirted shamelessly with him. The poor guy is going to have his hands full. He didn't mind it, but he didn't engage them either. He seemed fairly serious about his sandwich.

We then reported to our assignments. I'm with

Kevin McDermott, who runs the local interest stories and features—not hard crime, but the heavy-hitting local stuff, national stories with Chicago implications, and the downtown beat. It's perfect for me: minor investigative journalism with a bent toward human interest and larger-format writing. McDermott's also eager to promote my work and rattled a few topics he wants me to pursue. He has his own syndicated column and even offered me guest spots throughout the summer.

His cubicle is a war zone. Articles, pictures, magazines, food—everything fights for dominance. He cleared mountains of old newspapers from a chair for me to sit. I saw pictures of his "girl" (wife named Millie), their girls, and their girls' girls. He and Millie celebrate their thirty-fifth wedding anniversary tonight, so I got off easy today.

. . . Which is why I'm writing you. I'm not complaining, but it's lonely in Winnetka. The Muirs left Saturday, the Conleys are at their cottage in Michigan for the summer, Josh is in Vegas at some consumer packaging convention, Ashley sent me a text that she's working her first auction tonight, Kyle's at the movies with the Buckhorn boys, and Debbie's phone went straight to voice mail. So here I sit—all excited with news to share and no one to listen.

I have flowers, though. Josh sent roses to

celebrate my first day. The card read *I wish I could be there in person. I know it went great. Love, Josh.* They smell so good. And things are good with him too. He's been busy with work, but when we're together, it's lighter and easier. I like it. Even though we only go out once a week, if that, we seem to be having more fun together.

Speaking of fun, Alex showed up at my doorstep last night. Well, the Muirs' doorstep. He thought they were still here and was disappointed he missed them. But he rallied and stayed for dinner. I've been trying out some of Mrs. Muir's favorite recipes, and last night was spicy shrimp pasta with parsley, called Shrimp Fra Diavolo.

At Grace House, cooking was the worst chore assignment. I hated it. And when I lived with Cara, I could only afford ramen noodles. That just takes a packet and water. When I returned to Independence Cottage, I mastered cooking an entire meal in a single pot. Pasta works best. You cook the pasta, throw frozen veggies in at the last minute, drain the water, and toss a jar of sauce on top. Then eat—out of the pot. I'm embarrassed to admit I cooked and ate like that most nights. But it does illustrate what a surprise this new passion is for me. I thought my first attempt at shrimp worked well, and Alex seemed to enjoy it . . . at least he didn't get sick.

I gather Alex is here because his publisher suggested a change of scenery for his hero, Cole.

He's in a rut. Fictional characters get in ruts? Or is it the writers? Regardless, both are here to break free. Cole's here to help an interstate task force hunt a serial killer, and Alex is here to "assist"—that's exactly what he said.

"What does 'assisting' a fictional detective entail?"

"It's a boondoggle," he laughed.

I sighed. Clearly, he assumed I knew what that meant. I was about to ask when he must have caught my lost look.

"It means I get to play around Chicago, try out restaurants, go to baseball games, visit museums, and do anything I want that will help Cole solve crime and capture local flavor, and call it 'work'."

"Can I have a fictional detective too?"

"I might let you assist."

I almost pounced on that: When? Where? Why? What? How? All my instincts were firing because it sounded so fun, but I simply smiled.

We chatted all evening and covered everything: books, politics, school, weather, writing, friends, and my internship—that impressed him.

"You must be an amazing writer, Sam. I'd like to read some of your work."

"Oh no. That's too much pressure. You're Alex Powell, you know."

"That shouldn't intimidate you. I thought we were past that."

"We may never be past that." I laughed, but he didn't join me.

I wonder if I hurt his feelings. He may have thought I put the fame above the man. Does that make sense? I don't. I just meant . . . I don't know what I meant. I was careless and, heck, he *is* Alex Powell. There's no way around that.

"Then what can you tell me or I tell you so we can get past that?"

My heart raced. I wasn't ready to share, and asking him questions was only going to lead to more questions for me. So I deflected and babbled about the dishes, the day—anything inane that flitted through my brain.

"Well played," Alex said after a few moments. He laid down his dish towel and leaned against the counter. His sudden stillness filled the room.

"Hmmm?" I kept washing silverware, trying to pack both time and space with dish suds.

"Your deflections are subtle. It took me a few beats to catch on. That's hard to do."

Crap.

Alex smiled, reached over, and squeezed my shoulder. "I'd love to know about you, Sam, but I'm not going to press. Let's finish the dishes and walk to Homer's for an ice cream."

And that was it. He didn't ask any more questions about my past, only my present. But I did learn new stuff about him nonetheless.

"Why do you keep doing that?"

"What?" He glanced at me as he moved around and behind me as we crossed the street.

"You keep putting me on your right side. You did it in the kitchen too. You kept moving to my left."

Alex was silent for a moment. I thought I'd stepped too far.

"I can't think of a single person who has ever noticed that before." He stopped walking and stared at me. "I tell people, sure, but no one's noticed."

"What?"

"I can't see you if you're on my left. I was hit in the head by a baseball in high school and have no peripheral vision on that side."

"I'm sorry." I started walking again. "Are you okay? Is there stuff you can't do?"

He joined me. I moved to his right and caught his small smile. "I'm fine. I feel vulnerable at times, especially driving, but I passed the tests and I look around a lot before changing lanes. It's never been a problem. I think it's actually helped me."

"How?"

"I notice more. I focus more intently on what's in front of me. I think it's a large part of why I pursued writing. I found that details mattered more after the accident."

"I can see that."

Alex quirked an eyebrow at me.

"That came out awkward," I laughed. "Tell me more stuff that folks don't typically notice."

Alex obliged me and rattled off a random and hilarious description of himself: He likes at least two meats on every pizza; drinks only root beer if forced to drink soda; runs four days a week, unless it's raining; plays poker monthly with some hoity-toity NY elites; loves funny movies, classics like Chevy Chase's *Fletch* and *Vacation* are his favorites; can ride a unicycle; writes only five hours a day, then spends the rest reading and researching; loves eating out. And he is less than forthcoming about his current love life.

Did you hear that detail in the middle? Alex runs. He mentioned it back in Barnes and Noble last fall, but I never expected to see him again so I didn't pursue it. But now I want to know. I already crossed the line into seriously obnoxious, so I quit with my questions.

But I did have one thought: If he's anything like me, his barriers drop during runs. Run him hard enough and he might get more forthcoming about his love life. I know, that is really bad and manipulative. Still . . .

Off to plot my attack,
Sam

Dear Mr. Knightley,

I've been at work four days now and I love it. It's hard—McDermott's tough, but fair, not too far from Johnson. I edited a piece of his yesterday and he wasn't pleased.

"Moore, you changed the tone. You check my facts, you check my grammar, you can add fluff if you want, I don't care. But do not mess with the integrity of my tone. Ever. It's gone from declarative to inquisitive. Read your verbs. Fix this."

He was right. I made his work sound tentative, robbing its authority. Of course, that's the tone to which I naturally gravitate. Do you think that's my issue with Johnson? He's never said it; it would be my job to notice it. And the timidity is there, in all my work—except for the pieces about children. Those are more confident. My voice is stronger and more declarative. Maybe McDermott will let me develop some of my ideas along those lines. They feel natural for me and I come up with new angles each evening. Yes, Alex's "sleepy suburb" quip was accurate, and thinking up articles is the most excitement I see.

Josh is back in town, but he works late most nights and I don't want to wait downtown in hopes that he might have dinner with me. Lately

I feel he only calls when he's bored. I'd like to mean more to him than that.

Alex hasn't called or come up to the house either. At first I thought I hurt his feelings with my careless comments and questions. And I may have. But I also don't think Alex would visit a young woman alone. Is twenty-four very young? (Yes, birthday a couple weeks ago. Fairly unmemorable.) I'm not sure, and there's something so "old school" about Alex. I do know he wasn't pleased to find the Muirs gone. I thought he was going to decamp the front steps that first night without getting past hello. He's a lot like his hero, Cole, I think. Both could exist quite comfortably in a Jane Austen novel— except for the violence.

"Why, Emma, Mr. Weston has been stabbed in the stables and trussed up like a goose."

"Goodness, Father. Do lock the windows tonight. Prowlers are about."

"You are right, my dear. Oh . . . Goodness, Mr. Knightley, it is much too dangerous for you to walk home this evening. You may catch a chill— or your *death*."

Hey, it's no worse than *Pride and Prejudice and Zombies*.

Good night . . .
Sam

Dear Mr. Knightley,

As of today, I can say with confidence that I did not scare Alex away. He texted me this morning.

Lunch? 12:30. Billy Goat Tavern?

I giggled. Actually giggled. And immediately I replied.

Absolutely.

The Billy Goat Tavern is an old Chicago favorite under Michigan Avenue just across from Tribune Tower. I left at 12:27 and arrived right on time—no clock-watching there. The room was dark and crowded, and smelled like history and cheeseburgers. Alex found me absorbed in the framed newspaper article from 1973. The Tribune Company invited the Billy Goat (real live goat) to a Cubs game in hopes of lifting the 1945 curse and securing a win. The goat showed, and it worked—not a World Series win, but a few games that made everyone feel better.

Alex ushered me to a booth, leading me with a hand on the small of my back. I love that—it's a gentleman's touch. "Do you know what you want?"

"Cheezborger, cheezborger, cheezborger. No Pepsi . . . Coke."

He burst out laughing. "How do you know that? Do you spend your spare time watching *SNL* reruns?"

I was pleased, but confessed, "I Googled it this morning."

"Do you always research where you eat?"

"Don't you? I assume Detective Barker is meeting an informant here? Casing the joint? Pursuing a perp? Issuing an arrest?"

"Eating lunch?"

"He can do that."

It turns out that Alex has mapped out where Cole will live and eat, met with the Chicago Police Department, and developed his story line. Part of his research includes a full-scale assault on Chicago eating establishments: hence, the Billy Goat Tavern—dark, subterranean, guts and history. Anyone could meet there, pass info unseen and undetected, then fade away.

Chicago Pizza and Oven Grinder is also on his list. I almost flipped. He didn't invite me, but I'm not above begging if it comes down to it. I can't believe I haven't gotten there, but I don't want to go with my girlfriends. After Hannah's story, I feel it's a place to go with a guy. Any guy will do, no offense to Alex or Josh. Come on, it's one dinner out. Can't someone take me there?

I returned to work feeling a little sick. I had a great time, but I don't usually down two cheeseburgers for lunch. Yes, I ate two. From Alex's shocked expression, I assume that's extremely unladylike. Unlike Josh, he didn't say anything. But seriously, what's the problem? I'm hungry. I challenge either of those men to run five miles each morning and then eat like a bird. Mike and the other interns laughed at me, because first I complained about being too full, then they caught me eating an apple at three.

The interns all went out tonight, but I came home to write you. No, I didn't. I had plans with Josh, but he canceled. Remind me never to work in advertising. It sounds fun, but the hours are excruciating. So I came home to edit another article for McDermott and knock out a few ideas of my own.

I also called Ashley. I told her about Alex and now I regret it. It felt very glamorous in the telling, but now I feel small and selfish—like I betrayed a friend. Alex guards his privacy with such a *tenacious will,* and I blabbed about his life, plans, and lunch menu. Not his book title, I didn't tell that. But that's it. No more blabbing about Alex. Can I still tell you, Mr. Knightley? I must tell someone.

I didn't do all the talking, though. Ashley relayed plenty.

"He was right there in the bar, not five feet away, Sam, and I just walked away." She sounded surprised.

"Are you playing games with Will? Not a great idea, Ash."

"I'm not, Sam. I saw him there and felt tired. I'm not the kid he knew. And I won't chase someone who sees that girl rather than me. So I walked away. I'm done."

"How does it feel?"

"Oddly liberating."

"Are you seeing anyone else?"

Ashley's always got a boyfriend. Nothing ever serious, she's just never alone. And why would she be? Guys adore her.

"All done with that too—for now. Time to put old habits to bed, so to speak."

"Let them die, don't put them to bed."

"Very funny." Then she turned serious, almost tentative. "You're coming to the wedding, right?"

We've debated this for weeks. "Ash . . . you were so nice to wrangle the invitation, but this is your family's deal. Your mom and Constance won't want me there."

"Sam, you're my best friend. Mother's gone postal, and Constance is a Bridezilla. I need you in my corner."

I couldn't refuse that, Mr. Knightley. So in a few weeks I'll be kicking it up in your hometown at the Constance Walker/Bradley Douglass Wedding.

Back to work,
Sam

Dear Mr. Knightley,

Josh and I broke up tonight—at his office, of all places. It was humiliatingly awful. I went to grab him for dinner after work and found him collecting storyboards in a conference room.

Prior to walking into that room, I thought we were fine. I'd say we had fun this spring. Sure, he's been busy and we haven't spent much time together, but when we did go out, it was lighter and nicer. And it was a lie.

He's been seeing someone at work. I mean "seeing" someone—for months. I feel so stupid.

I opened the conversation with Alex. Nothing is going on, but I figured if I'm going to be friends with Alex, Josh should know. After all, I received another text two days ago.

Lunch Thursday? Spiaggia on Michigan Ave. 1 pm?

My immediate reply was:

See you then.

So if there will be lunch, there will be honesty. Turns out I haven't been able to keep my adoration of Cole Barker and Alex's writing much of a secret. Josh pounced.

"What? Cole Barker's here and you're having lunch with him?"

"You do know Cole Barker is fictional."

"Cole Barker is your perfect man, Sam, just like that Darcy or Wentworth. You don't think I'm going to be furious?"

"You know Darcy and Wentworth? How much Austen have you read?"

"None, Sam. But no one can spend two minutes with you without being bludgeoned with every ridiculous detail. And now you're hanging with one of your heroes?" He crossed the room to loom over me. "Don't tell me you're not intrigued. Will he compare? Can he live up to your impossible ideals? He can't, Sam. The writer is flesh and blood and probably an arrogant jerk, not some figment of your great imagination, not some perfect hero who will sweep you off your feet or wait around while you dally in Fantasyland!"

Speechless—that was me. I sputtered a bit while Josh collected himself. "How often do you see him?"

"Not much. Only one dinner and a lunch . . . Oh, and another lunch Thursday. We're friends, Josh. Can't I be friends with the man?"

"Sure you can—with the man. But nothing's ever simple with you." He paused. "Look, I need someone else. We've had fun, but I need more."

That's when I knew this was bigger than Alex. My stomach clenched. "What do you mean?"

"I've been seeing Lucy."

"Logan's girlfriend? Who comes out with us all the time?"

"She's not Logan's. She's mine." He let his tone linger . . . and suddenly I understood all Logan's looks, his tittering at dinner, the meaning behind his innuendo, his grabbing Lucy and squeezing her tight.

Logan wanted me to know. He wanted fireworks. He wanted to humiliate me.

"Eww . . . that's so . . . You all must have had a good laugh." I looked around the glass conference room. It felt like a fishbowl with everyone staring in and laughing at me, though in reality no one else was around.

But I knew they'd all been talking. Logan must have loved it. And Josh. One look in his eyes and I knew he loved it too: the secrets, the attention, and the game—all at my expense.

"Why didn't you dump me? Why keep me around?" My fingers, of their own accord, fiddled with the star pendant around my neck.

"There was always the chance—"

"Don't say another word."

"Sam . . ." He reached for my arm.

"Don't touch me." I got up and realized what I was doing. The pendant felt dirty and I recalled, with perfect clarity, Isabella's observation: *"Josh likes the way things look."* Then his own comment, *"They thought you were smart and pretty before, but now you've got grit,"* pounded in my brain. I was no more than Logan's ostentatious gold and silver watch, a trinket to see and be seen.

I pulled the necklace, breaking the chain and leaving a thin, red cut on the back of my neck. "I'm so blind. How could I not see? You're a Willoughby." I shook my head. "No, at least he loved Marianne. You're worse. I don't know who you are."

"What? I'm who?"

"Never mind. Good-bye, Josh." I threw the necklace across the table and walked out of there with my head high and my back straight. All Edmond Dantes. And I kept the tears at bay—until I hit the sidewalk.

How could I not have seen? Had I wanted normal that badly?

I went home and called Ashley, watched two Austen films, ate a whole pizza and an entire pint of Ben and Jerry's—and it still hurts.

In my books everything turns out well in the end. Lizzy and Emma and Elinor all had men who were worthy and loved them. Really loved them. Me, I picked a Willoughby and I'm rightfully alone.

For months I convinced myself that Josh's

paltry version of love was all I could expect—I wasn't worth something better. But I know there's more. I want the real thing. I can have that, can't I?

Because I know it exists—in books and in real life. The Muirs have it. I'm continually struck by the ways they care for each other and for me. And Hannah—I hear it when she talks about Matt. Love spills out of these people. That's what I want. Settling for anything less is a lie.

Josh was a lie.

Do you have it, Mr. Knightley? The real thing? Don't let it go if you do. That's all. I'm off to find more tissues and another pint of Chunky Monkey.

Wallowing,
Sam

Dear Mr. Knightley,

The evening began with a text.

Lobby 6pm?

Usually I get an indication of his plans, so I replied: ???? He sent a one word reply.

Groceries.

I smiled. Grocery shopping with Josh was a systematic and uninteresting affair. He grabbed the same fifteen items on every trip and got out fast. No imagination. Alex? This might be fun. Alex does so much without thinking—that didn't come out right. I mean, everything is woven into a creative process; nothing is taken for granted or thrown away.

When I reached the lobby I found him slouched on a bench, texting. His brow was completely furrowed. I hadn't noticed so many lines before.

"Give me one sec."

I sat next to him—on his right.

"Replying to slap-down from my publisher. She's nervous I'm not working."

I had wondered the same thing myself. "Are you?"

He looked straight at me. And I can't attribute that focus completely to the eye injury—Alex gets that intense.

"You have no idea, Sam. Writing is coming more fluidly now than it has in years. It's exciting and unnerving and every moment I worry it will end . . ." He paused and smiled, more to himself and some thought dancing in his head than to me. "Yes, I'm working."

"Tell me about it."

"Not yet." He tapped his phone several times before pocketing it, then reached for my arm. "I want to and I will, but not yet. Talking through stuff before I get it into the manuscript depletes its tension and magic. I have to keep it compressed or it flops."

"I get that." And I do. So much inside us is more powerful if drawn out at the right time and in the right way—like my January feature and the articles I'm writing now.

"Thanks for coming with me. Now I have an excuse to drive north to the grocery in Winnetka. It's the only one I know around here, and grocery stores can be scary places."

"They can?"

"I get Fresh Direct in New York. Haven't been in a grocery store in years."

"You've been here three weeks."

"My point exactly."

We drove north talking about nothing in

particular. I grew quiet because I know driving makes Alex nervous.

"You're not talking."

"You're concentrating."

"I'm not going to kill you, Sam. I'm not blind."

"I don't think that. I was being considerate."

He threw me a scowl.

"You want me to talk? Fine. How was your day?"

"That's better." He smiled. "Cole was good today. Got in a bit of a fight with a Chicago detective, but they'll get through it. I think he likes her."

"He needs a girlfriend."

"Does he?" His tone lifted suggestively.

Are we talking about Cole?

"Yes. Why hasn't he had one? Four books and no girl. It's odd. A relationship would help your market grow."

"My market's growing just fine." He glanced over at me and smiled. I thought he was going to hide in the banter and not answer my question, but he looked back at the road and started talking.

"Cole doesn't see women clearly. He doesn't understand what they want from him, and he fears he'll disappoint. Think about what you already know. He disappointed his dad and never got to make it right before his dad was killed. His mom blames him for that. His one brother holds it over his head, and every woman has betrayed him one way or another. I don't know that he can let a woman in. It's a risk."

"Probably one worth taking—with the right girl."

"You think?"

I thought about Josh, but there was no way this conversation was turning to my relationships. "In theory, yes. In experience, I don't know."

We pulled into the grocery store and that ended it. We both needed a change of subject. But if I'd known what was coming next, I would've launched into Josh. He might have been safer . . .

Everyone knows you begin shopping on the outside aisles of a grocery store and work your way across. Produce first. Dairy last—or however the particular circle works. Not Alex. Straight to the center and then some pinball push outward.

We started in cookies. I never go down that aisle—not enough disposable income. And I don't eat many sweets. Yet here we stood, surveying a thousand packages of cookies. He grabbed some Fig Newtons and I stood stymied by the Oreos. I almost cried. I turned quickly to walk on, but Alex noticed.

"You want to explain?" He pointed to the Oreos. "Pretty strong reaction to creamy vanilla goodness inside two crispy chocolate wafers."

"Shut up." I smiled. I wanted to share, because on some level I believe Alex is safe—slightly safe. I don't feel nervous with him as I did with

Josh, like one butterfly was always flying loose.

I ventured out and described Mrs. Chapman, my first foster mom. "My . . . aunt used to give me three Oreos each day after school. It was first grade. I sat in her lap and she read to me while we ate. Every single day." I fingered one of the packages. "I loved her, I think. I haven't thought about that in a long time."

"Where is she now?"

"She moved away the next summer." I looked at him and realized it sounded odd, never seeing or speaking to an aunt again. "And now she's gone . . ." I let it linger, hoping the natural conclusion would end the questions.

Alex reached for the package and popped it open.

"What are you doing?"

He pulled one out. "Eat."

"Alex, no. You have to buy that."

"Clearly. Put it in your mouth."

I obeyed and put the whole cookie in my mouth, but I couldn't bite it. There was something sacred about that memory—all wrapped up in an Oreo.

"Chew." He stepped toward me.

I bit down once.

"I'm going to find salsa. Catch up when you finish." He dropped the package in his cart and walked away.

I stood there slowly crunching on that silly

cookie that almost had me bawling. I concentrate so much on the pain that I suspect I miss the good: the Chapmans, a few saintly social workers, foster parents who cared, the library, Father John, Hannah, Kyle, Ashley, the Muirs, Alex . . . the list goes on. There have been people and events, even small ones that slip past my memory like a shadow, that have been good and whole and right in my life. How can I focus on those? Writing that article with Kyle started the process, and standing in that aisle tonight, eating a cookie, forced another step.

I grabbed a second package, tore it open, and ate two more. Three Oreos. When I caught up with Alex and dropped the package into his cart, he raised an eyebrow but said nothing. I like that about him. Sometimes words shouldn't be spoken.

We finished up with the oddest mix of stuff in his cart. Nothing that one could make for dinner, but seriously good snack food. Alex more closely resembles Cole Barker than I thought.

We then went to a dive called Meier's Tavern for burgers and tater tots, which made me laugh because we'd just spent over an hour at a grocery store. After that—the Muirs' house. I hopped out, thanked him, and headed for the door.

"Wait a sec." Alex got out and rummaged through the grocery bags. He handed me one package of Oreos.

"Only one?"

"You're not the only one who needs Oreos, Sam."

There was nothing to say. I reached up on my toes and kissed him on the cheek. I think I surprised him, Mr. Knightley, but I didn't wait to see his reaction. I simply waved and headed to the house.

Now I feel sick. There's a reason I don't eat sweets. No willpower. I watched some *Downton Abbey* episodes and ate the entire package— loving every bite.

> Sleep well, Mr. Knightley . . .
> Sam

Dear Mr. Knightley,

Just a quick note . . . I've got two articles due to McDermott this morning, and then I'm heading across town to conduct an interview. I'm floored that McDermott's trusting me. I'm interviewing an aide to Judge Rayburn about upcoming child welfare legislation.

"The interview is tomorrow at 11 a.m. in the Federal Building, Rayburn's suite. Get your notes organized tonight . . ." He noticed my wide eyes. "Sam, you can do this. Your voice is strong and this is your field. Trust yourself."

I took a deep breath. "Thank you."

"You're welcome. Take full notes, write it up. If you want my help, I'm here. But I suspect you'll get there on your own."

So last night I prepared my notes, and I'm ready. But—also last night—I had a conversation with Alex that won't leave me. It was brief, but special. And it was the first time he's called me.

He called around eleven. "You still up?"

"I'm outlining interview questions. What's up?"

"I'm having trouble with Cole and want to bounce something off you. You mind?"

"Not at all." I was so casual, but I can be honest with you—I have never been so flattered in my life.

"I need to push him, Sam. I need to bring Cole to the point of breaking, but I don't have somewhere safe for him once I do that. Does that make sense?"

"He'll need to heal." I thought about it for a moment. "What do you do? Where do you go?"

"I write." Alex paused. "Obviously, that won't work for Cole. You?"

"I run."

"I should've figured that out. How does that work? I run, but not like that."

"I run until I find myself. Sometimes it takes just a few miles and I know. Other times it takes ten to fifteen, even more, but I know when it happens. It's peaceful, and I feel whole and strong and nothing can touch or hurt the real me." I stopped, suddenly remembering it was Alex, not Kyle, to whom I was speaking. I felt confused.

"Can I use that, Sam? I see that working for Cole, but I don't want to take it from you."

"Please do. I'm honored."

"I like that. Sam?"

"What?"

"I write and run." He paused, and his voice dropped to a whisper. "You run and write."

I almost spoke, but he got there first. "Back to Cole now. Thanks. I can't tell you what this means to me." He hung up.

And I need to go,
Sam

Dear Mr. Knightley,

I just got back from Constance's wedding. There were over six hundred people there. Mrs. Walker said, "Everyone who's anyone is here"— so I wondered, did we bump into each other? With your own foundation, you must qualify as someone.

The ceremony was held in the Fifth Avenue Presbyterian Church, and the reception filled the Peninsula Hotel. It was spectacular . . . the quintessential fairy-tale wedding.

Mrs. Walker was at her finest and clearly relished every moment. She had on the most beautiful navy dress with diamonds and sapphires dripping all over her. And her smile was radiant. It was like she had planned and lived for this culminating shining evening, and it answered all her dreams. Maybe she had and maybe it did. At one point I wondered if she was trying to outshine the bride, but who competes with her own daughter? And on her wedding day?

Ashley was the maid of honor in a beige/gold-toned dress. She looked like a glass of champagne from her blond hair to her dyed shoes. Each bridesmaid wore the same dress, but carried different flowers. The other five girls held small bouquets full of strong colors. Ashley held Peruvian lilies and Constance held a tight bouquet of white lilies. I love lilies. They are the most perfect flowers—so strong, yet infinitely detailed and delicate. I once looked them up at the library, and all that information flooded back during the wedding. I wondered if the florist was oblivious or possessed a sharp sense of humor.

Ashley's bouquet: Peruvian lilies—the symbol of friendship and devotion.

Constance's bouquet: White lilies—chastity and virtue. No comment.

Bradley's boutonniere: A single bold white stargazer lily—sympathy.

Mr. Walker's boutonniere: A lone pink star-gazer—wealth and prosperity.

One must admit—that's funny. And while they are most often associated with funerals, the beauty and innocence lilies represent felt perfect for the wedding. And the fragrance floated through the entire church, for a small bouquet was tied to the end of every fourth pew. It was exquisite.

I arrived Friday and went straight to the rehearsal dinner. Ashley looked shredded. I gather Mrs. Walker had provided her with a date of "suitable income and good family," and Ashley was ticked. Mrs. Walker didn't offer me the same service and seated me as ninth at a table for eight. I got the message, but I was there for Ashley so I let it slide off.

The next day was chaos: hair appointments, makeup, brunch with all the women invited (at least three hundred of us), then photographs. I trailed Ashley for support. She knew the other bridesmaids, but clearly wasn't good friends with them. They all reminded me of Constance in her more vapid moments. Their conversations and concerns never dipped below the packaging.

But they all looked great in that champagne color, and I'll give them this—not one of them said a mean or catty thing about the wedding. They were insipid, but not unkind. What could one criticize? Constance glowed and Bradley looked equally thrilled. Mrs. Walker looked tense at first entering the church on Saturday, but soon relaxed under the warm glow of adoration and praise.

And Ashley found Owen, her very suitable date, another young lady with whom to dance. So all went well, and everyone seemed pleased. Ashley and I ended the evening sitting at our table, admiring the whole affair and toasting that we weren't in the limelight.

"I ate my weight in appetizers tonight."

Ashley threw me a glance. "Not hard to do." She returned her gaze to the dance floor.

"I see that Will's here," I said.

Ashley followed my stare. I expected her to light up, but she only nodded.

"I saw him earlier. He called last week."

"He called you?"

"He's called a few times. That was the first one I answered. I wanted to be done, Sam—odd that he's calling now. He looks nice tonight, doesn't he?"

"He always does." I paused and decided to ask. "Is he a good guy, Ash?" I didn't want someone playing with her emotions. I envisioned Josh and Logan.

"He is. That's why I adored him for so long. He's one of the good guys." I couldn't tell if she sounded disappointed or resigned, but this wasn't the place to dig, so I let it go.

We sipped our champagne and watched the world dip and twirl around us. Constance changed from her bridal gown into a lovely pale pink suit, and the happy couple left in a shower of rose petals and sparklers. They're off now on a "European tour." I couldn't help but think of Amy March from *Little Women*. Constance isn't so different from Amy: she loves beautiful things and is quite tenacious about acquiring them. But I think, like Amy, she truly loves her family and her new husband. She gave Ashley the sweetest hug as she fled to the limo. They both had tears in their eyes.

I left Ashley at brunch this morning and headed

for the airport. She had a huge smile and super-bright eyes, and seemed happier than I've seen her in a long time. Maybe this moving forward is working for her. She's doing what she loves, living in her own rented apartment, and generally stepping out on her own. I noticed her mother left her alone more this weekend too. She seemed to respect Ash more, and didn't talk down to her or across her. She reserved that for me, but that was okay. Everyone needs an outlet.

So the summer progresses, and I have exactly one month left at the *Tribune*. I already dread the last day, because I'm moving forward too. I hop off the Metra every morning with the biggest grin on my face, take a deep breath, and know I'm stepping into my best dream. I never imagined this. Even Josh seems a distant memory.

I also upped my running and think I'll try the Chicago Marathon again. It's been a couple years and I'd like to give it a go. Besides, with all the food Alex feeds me, I need the exercise. We get together most days now, and tomorrow we head to the café at the Art Institute. I've no idea what horror he plans for Cole inside those walls, but I want to peek around the galleries before lunch.

I laughed at Kyle this evening because he's running more too, but not for sheer enjoyment. Coach Ridley told him about passing the foster parenting classes. They're now awaiting judicial approval, and Kyle is beside himself with anticipation. The poor kid runs each day to calm his nerves. A ruling should have come weeks ago, but there was a hang-up, so Kyle waits— and runs.

I'm off for a run too,
Sam

Dear Mr. Knightley,
The text

Coffee? Lunch? Day? Start at Starbucks on Wells and North. 10 am?

awaited me when I came home from my run this morning.

Hmmm . . . Old Town on a Saturday and a whole day? This was new and intriguing . . . I texted back:

Just got this. See you at 10:15.

I showered, threw on a pair of khaki shorts, cute ballet slippers, and a white short-sleeved blouse. The Muirs left me their cars, so I got to Lincoln Park quickly and felt dressed for anything—except Alex's plans.

"You're not wearing running shoes." Alex bounced around the Starbucks—too much espresso.

"You said nothing about running," I laughed. "I've already run ten this morning."

"You ran?" Sad, puppy-dog eyes.

"I can run more. What's up?"

"I thought we'd start the day at the zoo and

wander Lincoln Park, eat lunch, then go for a run later this afternoon and catch a movie."

It sounded perfect—no quick lunch, but an entire day with a good friend.

"Great. I'll drive back up and get my gear. I'll be—"

"No!" He grabbed my hand to pull me in line. "You need your vanilla latté, then we'll go. Shoes will take care of themselves."

I grinned and submitted. He was like me with a new book—but jacked up on caffeine.

After paying for my coffee and another for him, we wandered the entire neighborhood and the zoo. I stood for a long time at the elephants, and he made me stay equally long at the penguins—cute but cold little guys. We didn't talk much, and the silence hung like a silk curtain, light and lovely. He was eager to share the day and I was equally delighted—both in the activities and the company. Alex is easy to talk to. He doesn't press and he's beginning to share. We both are.

He's also really handsome. Women look at him and I don't think they recognize him; they just think he's cute. What's even better? He doesn't notice. Again, it's not the whole left eye thing—I believe Alex chooses to focus on what's in front of him. The rest just floats by. It's flattering, though daunting at times, to be in that zone.

I refuse to dissect our relationship, but old

habits die hard. Are we friends? Semi-family via the Muirs? I can't tell. I assume there's nothing more than friendship on Alex's side. He never gets "that look" or holds my hand. Sure, he grabs it occasionally, but that's for speed or directional corrections. I also get a guiding hand at the small of my back sometimes, but again, it's a directional thing. And it's gentlemanly. Alex is that.

After a sidewalk lunch at Gemini Bistro, Alex directed us to Fleet Feet. I was in the door before I caught on to the man and his mission: "What size shoe do you wear?"

"Nine. Why? Hey, you aren't buying me shoes. I'll buy them. Or I can just go get mine."

"No, this is my idea. I'm buying the shoes." He looked very serious.

"I'll buy the shorts."

"Shorts?"

"Alex, I'm wearing walking shorts and a blouse. I'm going to need more than shoes."

"I hadn't noticed that."

"Thanks. I'll have you know I thought about this outfit." I feigned indignation.

"Sam, I didn't mean that. You're beautiful." He stopped and looked at me—really looked at me. I tucked the compliment and the look away for safekeeping.

We wandered the store and I found everything I needed. Alex insisted on paying, and since he was being stubborn and makes far more money than I do, I let him. We then hoofed it to the Belden Stratford to change.

If you've never been to Chicago, I think the Belden Stratford is the equivalent of renting an apartment at the Plaza in New York. (No, I haven't seen it. I've read *Eloise*.) Gorgeous, I would guess; a fortune, I guarantee. Alex's apartment is there, near the top floor with a gorgeous view of the lake. We changed quickly and were off.

The day was perfect—mild, gentle breeze off the lake, and every moment felt charged with sunlight. Alex felt it too. The guy couldn't stop smiling. It was an infectious good feeling.

You can always talk more deeply when running because it feels safe. You can't directly look at the person next to you. And you can't hide much in so few clothes and so much sweat. Exhaustion also addles your inhibitions.

"How is Cole?" I was really asking about him, and he knew it.

"He's better, Sam. I think that's what my publisher knew—he needed to be pushed, but I was scared to do it. To push him means pushing me. That's hard."

Alex then asked me about my relationship with Josh. At our first lunch I told him I had a boyfriend but didn't add much detail, and I've never provided an update. It's embarrassing. I still feel stupid. But I was completely honest. I told Alex everything.

". . . So that's the end of my first real boyfriend. You know, we barely spent any time together all spring. That should have been a sign. I mean, don't you want to be with your girlfriend?" *Subtle probe*.

"I haven't had one in so long, I can't remember."

I threw him a scowl, suspecting he was deflecting or lying.

"I'm not kidding, Sam. But, yes, I'd want to be with her every moment I could. And when separated, I'd probably think about her constantly."

"Then I wasn't the one for Josh. He wanted 'something' from me all right, but not me. I'm pleased I came out as well as I did."

"What do you mean?"

" 'He imposed on me, but he didn't injure me.' "

"Is that Emma or Sam talking?"

"You are so good," I laughed. "It's both of us. Josh didn't touch my heart. My ego and expectations, yes, but not my heart, not my soul. I walked away whole. I liked the idea of a boyfriend more than I ever liked Josh . . . Maybe boyfriends are better in books."

Now Alex threw me a scowl.

"No, seriously, most of my notions come from books, not reality." *Did I admit that?*

"Why is that?"

I had ventured as far as I could. I didn't want to lie, but I also couldn't break down, and possibly ruin, this moment and this friendship.

"My childhood wasn't easy. I buried myself in books. I guess I'm a recovering book addict."

"I wish you wouldn't do that."

"What?"

"Deflect. Make light of something painful. And I know, by your tone and your expression right now, that it is."

I watched the road. "Alex, sometimes the real answers are too hard."

"To share with a friend?"

"Is that what we are?" *Did I ask that?*

"We may be many things, Sam, but we are at least that."

"Good to know. What else will we do today, friend?" I lightened my voice in hopes the subject change wouldn't appear too abrupt.

Alex pushed two strides ahead. I surged to keep up. "Sam, I'm irritated with you right now. I want to stop running. I want to take you by the shoulders, shake you, and tell you that I care. I don't want you to deflect with me, and I certainly don't want you to change the subject when we start to get real." He glanced at me, but I refused to pull my head or my gaze from the road.

"But clearly you're not ready for that. Maybe neither of us is. So I'm going to run even faster out of sheer frustration." And he picked up the pace another notch.

I was speechless. I can't tell you what I thought because I couldn't think. Another four miles and I was exhausted. We ended up laughing, because neither of us backed down, and somehow we ended okay.

Alex didn't press me again as we headed back to the Belden Stratford to change our clothes. I was still pondering his comment—and still am. I think more was said than what he actually said. But it's like smoke; I can't catch it.

We ended our perfect day with pizza, ice cream, and a walk around Old Town—then back to the professor's car, still safely parked on North Avenue. I drove home singing. Now I should sleep. Needless to say, after eighteen miles, I'm exhausted. But, Mr. Knightley . . . Alex cares. I'm not sure what that means and I promise not to dwell on it . . . too much.

Sweet dreams,
Sam

Dear Mr. Knightley,

Cara was taken to the Cook County Hospital emergency room yesterday with broken bones and internal bleeding. She actually gave Father John's name and number as next of kin—and he called me.

Oddly, I was looking at an old picture of us at that very moment. I found one last week and have been using it as a bookmark, hoping it would help me figure out my next step with Cara. I had apologized, but still felt we weren't done. Closure? Forgiveness? Something more flickered out there.

So I grabbed my bag, asked McDermott if I could leave an hour early, and headed the few blocks to the hospital. Father John was alone in the waiting room. He stood when he noticed me and pulled me into a hug. He whispered, "She'll be fine, Sam."

"What happened?" I stepped back and looked into his sad, tired eyes.

"Ric pushed her down the stairs. She's got a concussion, two broken ribs, some internal bleeding, a shattered wrist, and bruising. She's pretty beat up." He looked like he was going to cry, but I was angry.

"Where's Ric now?" I wasn't a six-year-old anymore, and I wanted a fight.

Father John pulled me back into his arms. "Let's focus on Cara now, Sam. She's safe. Both of you are safe." He took my hand and led me to a chair in the corner.

Then I noticed that we weren't alone in the waiting room. It was packed: mothers with crying babies, teenagers hanging over chairs like old coats, older men chatting in quiet voices.

We reached our seats, but he didn't let go of my hand. He started patting it like he was soothing a small child. "She had surgery to set her bones, but she's scared. And she's broken more than physically."

The nurse came and led us to Cara's room. She looked small and fragile, with the *blip beep blip* of her monitors making the only noise. Father John took her hand and whispered a prayer. I stood by the door and watched. As he crossed the room to leave, Cara glanced at the door and noticed me.

"Hi, Cara," I whispered.

"I'll visit tomorrow, Cara. You rest tonight and chat with Sam. God bless you, my dear." Father John left us.

I crossed the room and stood next to her. "I'm sorry, Cara. Can I help? Somehow?" I waved my hands around the room, the monitor again the only noise.

She turned to me, tears running down her face. "Why are you here, Sam?"

"I'm here because this is where I should be. I never gave you enough credit, Cara, and I left you when I should have helped."

"It happens." She laughed, small and bitter. "No one ever sticks around."

"I'm changing that, Cara. I'm sticking around for anyone who means anything to me. It's tough, but I'm learning to do it."

"Do I count in that group?"

"Sure. Why not?" That's who I want to be—a friend who sticks—sticks to Kyle, to Ashley, to the Muirs, to Alex. I want to be someone to count on—someone with permanence.

"You won't last," Cara cried.

I tentatively reached out and stroked her hair. The gesture felt too personal, but it's the most comforting feeling in the world when you're sad or hurt. Mrs. Chapman used to do that.

"I thought Ric would last," Cara said. "I thought he would marry me."

Poor Cara still reminded me of Lydia Bennet. Lydia thought Wickham would marry her too, and it "did not much signify when."

"Did he push you to make you leave?"

"He's hated me for months." She shook her head back and forth. "I can't tell you. I can't tell you."

"You don't need to. Stop. Don't tell me anything."

I chatted with Cara until the nurse kicked me out. As the Metra sped me home, a new memory flashed with each bump of the tracks. I saw the differences in Cara's life and mine. I saw the similarities. I saw Josh and Ric, my Willoughby, her horrific Wickham. The window dressing may change, but as Austen shows us: human nature remains the same.

I visited Cara again after work today and snuck her some ice cream. As I got ready to leave, I decided to give her some advice—not that she ever listened to me before.

"Here it comes," Cara groaned.

"What?"

"You've got that 'I'm-going-to-solve-your-problems' look."

"How do you know that?"

"You always thought I was too dumb, but I listened, Sam. And I know that look."

"Oh." I remembered some of the ways I had dismissed her in high school. "Since you know it's coming, here it is . . . You need to go back."

Cara blanched. "He'll kill me."

"Not to him. To Grace House."

"Forget that, Sam."

"You'll live in Independence Cottage—no Dr. Wieland if you don't want to talk, no social workers, no meds if you don't need them. It's a safe clean place to live while you get your GED and some business classes."

This is her Medill—her one shot to make a new dream. I wanted her to see that, and I tried to convince her by sharing all the good things that have happened to me: Grace House, Kyle, Roosevelt University, Medill, and the *Tribune*. I left out Ernst & Young.

I also told her about my letter from Hannah, whom Cara knew from our days in Charing Cottage, describing her lovely beach wedding in Maine. I contrasted that with Constance's glamorous ceremony in New York. I wanted Cara to see a bigger world in a whole variety of colors.

"Sounds great, Sam. You've done a lot, but nothing changes."

"What do you mean?"

"Sammy-girl, lots to do, but nothing to feel." Cara whispered the words with a singsong lilt. And my nickname came out just loud enough to pierce my heart.

"That's too far." I grabbed my bag as a deep, painful, red blur flashed before my eyes. "Do what you want, Cara. We're done."

"Don't leave." She rushed the words out. I heard desperation in her voice, and that's the only thing that made me stop.

I turned, more furious than I've been in my entire life. The nickname had ignited a fire, rather than a fear, in me.

"Do you want to go there, Cara? Do you? Because I'm not hiding anymore, and if you want to fight . . ." I paused and waited for her to look me in the eyes. "I will decimate you." With each word I stepped closer, until I stood above her.

Cara blanched. "I only said it to hurt you. See if I still could. I'm sorry. Please?" She took a shuddering breath, cringed with the pain, and looked to the ceiling.

I stepped back, closed my eyes, and took a deep breath myself. "I'll stay." I dropped my bag. "But it was too far, Cara. Don't do that again—ever."

"I know." She held my eyes for a moment before concentrating on her blanket. "I used to get so jealous of you and be glad when you shut down and went away into your head. It made me feel strong. I want to feel strong again."

I understood, so I stayed. But I didn't sit, and it wasn't comfortable. We skirted around our feelings and protected our secrets for a few minutes before I realized we were done. I reminded Cara about Grace House one more time and left, leaving my anger with her. No sense in carrying even that home.

Maybe Cara and I will be more someday, but right now I feel closure and peace. I hope I helped her too. Maybe she'll take my advice and return to Grace House. It will change her life and, as I'm learning, change isn't always bad.

It's been quite a couple days and I'm ready for

some lighter fare—which starts tomorrow night—with Alex. I didn't tell him where I've been these past two days. *Coward.* He texted a few times, and I simply replied that I was busy with work.

I want to share, but think of the can of worms I'll open if I mention Cara—too many worms. Here's the exchange from earlier:

Alex: Where are you? 2 days too long! Don't say you're busy or I'll march to Trib Tower and demand your release!
Me: Don't get me fired. Free now and like being missed. Such nice compliments will get you anything.

Too flirty? I still can't define our relationship, and I press every now and then to see what he'll do. Despite his criticisms about deflecting, Alex does it better than I do.

Alex: Need a date for dinner @ Chicago Pizza and Oven Grinder. Lobby 6pm tomorrow?
Me: Can't wait.

So there it is. Still no clue about our relationship, but I get to go to Chicago Pizza and Oven Grinder. FINALLY! That's worthy of caps, don't you think? I've probably built it up in my mind, but I'm so excited. I need to text Hannah.

Oh . . . I gotta go. The timer buzzed. I tried a new recipe, Forty-Clove Garlic Chicken. It sounded wonderful and smells even better; but now I wonder how long I will stink. Will forty cloves of garlic wear off by tomorrow night?

Have a good evening,
Mr. Knightley . . .
Sam

Dear Mr. Knightley,

I know it wasn't a date—not a real date—but I couldn't help myself. I brought a change of clothes to work so I'd be in a cute floral skirt and wedge heels for tonight's dinner. Chicago Pizza and Oven Grinder deserved that. And it was worth it. What a night!

The small waiting area was packed when we arrived. The host studied our faces, just like I'd heard, and declared, "One hour." I wondered if that was determined on real time or a cuteness scale. Maybe that's why Josh never wanted to go. Unnecessarily mean, I know.

The wait didn't bother us. I wanted to absorb the room and the experience, and suspected an hour might not be long enough—but something caught my attention. Two couples nudged each other, looked toward us, and started whispering. Alex noticed too. He turned slightly to his right, gently maneuvering me in front of him.

"You're putting them in your blind spot," I giggled. I do that a lot lately—very unnerving.

"They're talking about me, but they're not quite sure."

My eyes trailed over to them.

"Don't look." There was a flicker of panic in his voice.

"I won't." And I didn't.

"I must seem so strange to you, like I'm afraid of my own shadow. But I don't like meeting other people's expectations. I never measure up."

"They have expectations?" My vision flicked to the couples. They were still tittering about us.

"Don't be naive. Everyone has expectations."

Alex was clearly upset—and it surprised me. Usually he's so composed, almost cavalier. But tonight he was jumpy, all his nerves exposed to the moment.

I looked him straight in the eyes. "Focus on me. My only expectation is to enjoy a wonderful evening."

"I need an Oreo," he quipped.

"Glad you're back." I almost called him on the deflection. He's done it to me enough times, but I sensed he needed some space.

Once we sat down, I told Alex about Hannah's proposal and how I've wanted to come here for over a year.

"Why didn't you say something? Or why not just come?"

"I don't know. I remember her saying that the booths were so private you felt alone in a crowded room."

Alex quirked his eyebrow.

"I'll kill you if you start singing." He held his hands up, and I continued. "It sounded so special that I just wanted to land here, not orchestrate it. And here I am."

"Here you are." He settled into the booth. "Are you disappointed?"

"Not at all." I settled in too. "Now tell me your deepest secrets. We're alone." I said it flippantly, then couldn't believe it. After that scene earlier? Besides, that street runs two ways. I paled, but for once Alex didn't notice—he was two shades paler himself.

I rushed on. "I'm kidding. I would like to ask one thing, though." I paused, wondering if even this was too personal right then. "How'd you come to know the Muirs so well?"

"They took me in—adopted me in a way." He stopped, and I thought that was the end.

I waited.

"I didn't go home Thanksgiving my freshman year. Christmas either. Pops was my English lit professor, and he invited me to stay with them for both holidays. I'd already spent countless hours in his office discussing books and writing. I thought I was so smart. Really I was an angry, lonely kid."

"Why didn't you go home?"

"Dad told me not to bother, and I couldn't afford it on my own." Alex looked at the table. "He refused to pay any part of school if I didn't stay in state, and I got that—state schools are cheaper. But it wasn't about the money—it was about control. He thought I was a dreamer. A waste. Still does."

"He can't. Look what you've done."

"It's not what he wanted. Dad's happy, though. My brother toed the line. He lives a few blocks from my parents, takes his family over for Sunday dinner, and works in Dad's tax firm."

"And you?"

"I'm okay—now. Pops has helped me. He's taught me what a father can be and what a son can be. I'll keep trying with my dad, but it's hard." Alex looked up at me.

I nodded. That's all I know about parents—it's hard.

"Your sisters?"

"I'm closer to them. Jenni lives in Texas and Suzanne in California. They don't get in the middle, but they don't shun me either. But it's all hidden, all in secret. Even my mom won't call unless Dad's out of the house."

"I'm sorry, Alex." I needed to offer him something in return. But how much? "My parents died a few years ago. The Muirs accepting me like they have is a miracle for me."

Alex stared at me a moment, and I could see his jaw flex. "I'm so sorry. Why didn't you say anything?" He paused and leaned forward. "I feel a little selfish complaining about my perfectly healthy—if dysfunctional—family."

"I like it. Not the dysfunctional part. I mean I

like hearing about them. About you. I don't like to talk about my parents. In fact, very few people know even that much."

"I'm honored. Will you tell me more?"

I held my breath. I didn't want to deflect, and I refused to hide, but I lacked courage. "Can I tell you about them another time? It's not an easy subject for me. But someday I would like you to know."

He smiled, slow and long. "When you're ready, I'll listen." He held my eyes. "What shall we eat?"

"Everything."

The food was delicious. The pizzas are cooked in bowls with the dough draped over the top. The waiter then flips it over onto your plate and pulls out the ceramic bowl, and the cheese, which was at the bottom, is now on top and spreads over the sauce.

As we ate, my mind wandered back to my parents. Usually thinking about them fills me with fear and, more recently, anger. Not tonight. Tonight I remembered something Father John said when he told me my father had died.

"He was sick, Sam."

"I'll say."

"No, I mean he had clinical mental illness." Father John took my hands and held them, drawing me into his words. "I read his file, Sam. He suffered terrible abuse, and only in prison did he get counseling and medication. There's no indication that on the outside he got any help at all."

"He went to college, Father John. He was some drugged-out genius and dropped out. That's what my mother once said."

"That's not entirely true. But she was right about his being smart. He was off the charts in some respects and not hitting even minimal markers in others. It's hard to say how the brain works. I think the abuse broke an already fragile brain."

"What are you saying? He was out of his mind?" I spat the words out.

"Yes." Father John squeezed my hands to gain my attention. "I am not excusing him, Sam. I'm saying that he may not have known what he did or why he did it. He was terribly sick."

"I don't care."

"Not now, but someday you might. And when that day comes, I wanted you to know the truth. He caused tremendous pain, Sam, but he was also in tremendous pain."

I sat in that safe, high-backed booth eating pizza while all this played through my memory. And I accepted it. I let it flow over and through me in a way I had never allowed before. I don't know how I feel about my father now, but tonight the memories took on a different tone. The black/red fear I associate with him faded. There are shades of yellow and even more temperate colors like blue swirling in the scene.

Alex was quiet too. Maybe his own thoughts swirled about him—I don't know. I simply know it was comfortable and wonderful. I felt safe not striving for words and smiles and laughs and sighs—all those things Ashley and Debbie threw out at that Halloween party—to intrigue him and show my interest. I felt sure that no matter how quiet or contemplative I became—Alex would call me again.

Sincerely,
Sam

~ August 12

Dear Mr. Knightley,

The professor had a heart attack. At least that's what I think happened. Mrs. Muir called it "atrial fibrillation." He had chest pains and shortness of breath and passed out. I call that a heart attack.

"He's going to be fine, dear. I wanted to call so you wouldn't worry."

"Does Alex know?"

"Yes, dear, I called him. Robert has had episodes before, and this one wasn't as bad as others. The doctors here have examined him thoroughly and given him new medication."

I leaned against the counter. There was nothing I could say. I know this was about them, but I could only think of myself. Horribly selfish. But I felt like a fool for wishing, for letting them in, for wanting them to be mine.

"Sam?"

"I'm here."

"He wants to talk to you. Just a moment."

"Mrs. Muir, he should rest, please don't—" I didn't want to hear the professor's voice. I wanted them to fade away. I wanted to finish washing the dishes, keep their garden, pay their bills, and in a month—pack my bags.

"Sam?" The professor's voice was soft and breathy.

"I'm here. Are you okay?" I wiped my hand across my eyes, leaving a trail of suds.

"Did I scare you?"

"I think you scared everyone."

"I'm sure I did, but I bet I got you . . . I bet I got you good, Sam."

"Why do you say that?"

"Oh, Sam, I see so much in you. We're alike, like father and daughter. And I think you feel . . ." His voice grew soft and drifted away.

The line fell silent, and I panicked. "Professor? Professor?"

"Sam?" It was Mrs. Muir. "He's asleep, dear. He's been so anxious to talk to you, and I think now that he's heard your voice, he can rest."

"My voice?"

"Don't you know how much you mean to him?" She paused. "Sam, God was good to us today. Don't forget that. Robert will be fine, and we'll be home soon."

"I don't know . . ." Tears trickled down my checks. "This doesn't sound good."

"Oh, darling. You should see the look of peace on Robert's face right now. We were right next to a police officer when he had the episode, and he's been given a wonderful report. We are blessed."

I wanted to believe her, to have her faith and confidence. I felt my heart trip forward—almost to hope.

They're going to stay in Paris a few days longer so the professor can rest before continuing to Spain. And if he gets too tired, they'll stop completely and wander in the "pink light" of Paris. I didn't get that. Is the light really pink there?

I hung up the phone, and fear crept back into me. I felt small and alone. I called Alex. It was the first time I'd initiated contact—a huge mistake and not my finest moment. I didn't even say hi.

"You knew. You knew and you didn't tell me? Don't you think I care? I know they mean more to you, but I'm staying in their house. I'm not a nobody, Alex. How could you do that to me?"

"Nice to hear from you, Sam."

"Don't give me that."

"Give you what? Mom M called me twenty minutes ago. I didn't call you because you were her next call. Calls one and two, Sam. I don't think you could've found out any faster."

"Well . . ." My anger lost its steam. "Still . . ."

"Still what?"

"I don't know." I put on a new coat of mad. "You should fly over."

"I'm not flying to France."

"He should mean more to you than that, Alex. I—" *What would I do?* That moment surprised me. What would I do for the professor? Almost anything . . .

"Sam, stop. This has happened before. Pops is fine, and I'm not going to insult him by acting like it's worse than it is. He wouldn't want that."

" 'I beg your pardon. Excuse my interference. It was kindly meant.' " I cringed.

"Caroline Bingley? Really?" Alex paused. "You think I insulted you? Is that it?"

"It's nothing."

"I didn't." Alex's voice got gentle, and that upset me even more. "Is that what you do when—"

"I'm hanging up." I felt so embarrassed and exposed.

"Sam, don't—"

I didn't hear another word. I can't believe I did that to Alex. What must he think of me?

> I need to finish the dishes,
> Sam

Later . . .

I won't be able to sleep until I update you.

As I finished the dishes, I sobbed. I can't explain why. I've known the Muirs a shorter time than some of my shortest foster placements.

But they could slip away. The professor could die. I could die. Everything changes, you know. Each and every moment things change. I was beginning to think that change could be good, but I was wrong. I know I'm twenty-four and I don't need a mom and a dad, but I wanted them.

That's a lie too—I need them. I hoped the Muirs could be mine and nothing would take them away from me. And the heart attack broke *my* heart.

Then the doorbell rang. I scrubbed my eyes with a dish towel as I raced to answer it. Alex was the last person I expected to find.

"What are you doing here?" So much for making a good impression—ever.

"I thought you could use a hug." Alex stepped into the doorway and held me for the longest time. It wasn't romantic. It was strong and comforting and exactly what I needed. I held him tight around his waist, sniffed into his shirt, and rested.

When I started breathing normally, he stepped back. There was a very embarrassing wet mark on his shoulder, but he kindly didn't note it.

"I'm so sorry." I started swiping at it with my dish towel. "I was so rude to you."

"It's okay. It was a shock. And I'm sorry if I appeared blasé. I'm not, you know. I love Pops very much."

"I know you do. You're not blasé about anything that I can tell."

" 'Accept my thanks for the compliment.' "

"No Lizzy. I can't believe I did that to you." I almost started to cry again, for completely different reasons.

Alex smiled and held up his hands in a gesture

of surrender. "No more quotations." He tilted his head out the open front door. "It's a gorgeous night, Sam. Let's take a walk."

We walked to the lake and then stopped at Homer's for ice cream on the way back. I was so tired from the stress and sobbing that I don't think I was good company, but Alex didn't seem to mind. He told me more about his relationship with the professor.

"We'd go down to the Boys and Girls Club every Saturday and play basketball and stuff. Pops would sit on the side and read to anyone who'd listen. I played ball."

"On Saturday mornings? Not what I'd expect."

Alex laughed. "I know. Pops made me do it. I was so angry when I got to NU. It was me against the world. Pops was trying to show me it wasn't, and that I wasn't alone feeling that way."

His whole face lit up. "You should've seen it, Sam. It was a blast—a bunch of angry kids and scary thugs coming together to play ball. That gang leader in *Redemption*, Crit? He's based on a guy from there. Scariest dude I ever met, but a good ballplayer and honorable on the court. Never left a guy on the ground without offering him a hand—weirdest thing."

I smiled, thinking of Kyle. Someday—if I get the courage—I'll introduce them. They'd really like each other.

"Why don't you find something similar in New York?"

"I've tried. Once they learn my name, I never get past the development directors. They want my name and my money—and that's important too, I'm not knocking it—but they don't want me."

"You should try again. You could make a difference, Alex, and you clearly loved it. Think of the new characters you might find."

"True." We walked without saying more for a while. He simply stayed beside me.

It was good. And I didn't make it that way. Alex did. He also told me about the professor's previous episodes, his medications, and what he does to take care of himself. It was good to hear. Not only because it didn't sound so tragic after all, but because Alex made me feel like my knowing mattered.

And this is where I must stop, Mr. Knightley. Writing helps me process things, but these emotions are too much, too foreign. And I'm too tired. I'm so glad the professor will be well. But more . . . I can't consider that right now.

~ AUGUST 22

Dear Mr. Knightley,

Summer is over. My internship ended two days ago. I wrote sixteen articles under a joint byline and seven under my own name. I edited seventeen of McDermott's pieces, and by the end he trusted my voice and my judgment. He was a great mentor and I think he liked working with me. He hugged me as I left the building and said, "You did good, kid."

I'm sad that it's over. I didn't knock the ball out of the park—Mike actually won an award for one of his fifteen solo articles—but I did good, solid work and I'm proud of it. Ms. Ellis asked me to apply for a full-time job after graduation. I didn't get an offer, but she didn't say good riddance either.

But now Alex is gone too, and I'm sad all over again. We spent the past two days in a frantic effort to see all that remained of Chicago: another Cubs game, Navy Pier, one museum, six different restaurants, a last run along the lake . . . He jotted notes and I took pictures, building details for the book as we walked along. I think he may even use a few of my quips and quotes—and he hinted about giving Cole a girlfriend.

"What happened with that detective Cole hated?"

"I never said he 'hated' her."

"He should."

"Why?"

"Conflict drives emotion, Alex. If he hates her at the beginning, he can love her at the end."

"You are so set on him getting a girlfriend. Don't you think once he finds someone, he'll be all in? He's a pretty intense guy. What if she doesn't feel the same? Best not to rush it."

I pondered this. "Don't avoid it, though. That's a cop-out."

He laughed. "Love stories are too easy. They're trite. Cole doesn't need that."

"Then don't make her light and easy—make her tough, and real, and flawed. I'd like to read about that, because if it's difficult, but beautiful, then I'll believe it can be real. And you can draw that out. Complexity will give Cole time."

Alex stopped and stared at me. "Okay, I'm sold. You sure you want to be a journalist?"

"For now. Gotta use all this training. But I'd like to write a children's book someday—a book of fun stories that go completely wrong, but end well with the kids tucked into bed safe and happy."

"That I'll read."

And that was how these two days felt too—safe and happy. I was so desperate to hang on that I asked if I could take him to the airport tomorrow.

"You'd have to get up at three thirty. I'll take a cab."

"It's no big deal. I'll go back to bed after." My face flushed. I must have sounded pathetic.

Alex touched my chin and turned me toward him. "Have dinner with me tonight instead?"

"It's your last night. What about your friends? Jim . . . or that other guy?"

"I'd like to spend it with you. I'll pick you up at six?"

"Sure."

I hopped the train north to go home and change. I could barely breathe for how pleased I was to spend his last evening with him. *What to wear? What to wear?* That one thought consumed the half-hour train ride.

After scrounging around, I settled on a fitted black sundress with a cream shawl. I also wore a pair of high wedge sandals that I could never wear with Josh. I love Alex's height. When he arrived, I walked steadily to his car and didn't feel like a tree. In fact, I felt quite pretty.

He took me to Topolobampo on Clark Street and requested the chef's five-course tasting menu.

It started with *Sabana de Jitomates*, tomatoes in sherry dressing. The tomatoes were so sweet against the pungent sherry that you could feel the sensation at your lips and again at the back of your mouth. My favorite course after that was the *Borrego al Pisilla*, lamb infused with black garlic. And last came dessert—in a class by itself. *Pastel de Chocolate, Helado de Menta*. It's a fancy Spanish way to say devil's food cake, glazed with chocolate crème and served with mint ice cream. I think that's when I closed my eyes and sighed. (If you're wondering how I remembered all this so well—I asked to keep the menu. I'm sappy.)

Over the past several weeks Alex and I have met almost daily for coffee, lunch, dinner, runs, shopping trips, grocery trips, movies . . . But tonight he let me see more.

We'd been talking about our history with friendships, and for the first time he mentioned a woman named Simone. It was casual—too casual—and the hair on my arms stood up.

"Tell me more about Simone?" I tried to sound indifferent. I was scared he'd laugh it aside, when I could tell it was important.

But he sat back in his chair, and I could tell he drifted in time. Maybe all good writers do that: they don't remember, they see. Alex can weave a story or describe a scene so distinctly that you feel you're there. He went back and I followed.

"Simone . . . I haven't thought about her in a while. There was a time when she was all I thought about." He paused and focused on some spot beyond me. "We met my last fall at Columbia. I was writing *Redemption* and Simone was working at Jarad-Patel, the hottest gallery in the meat-packing district. She was gorgeous—tall, raven-haired, half French. She knew she had allure, knew she could wrap us all around her finger. But I thought I was different. I was just young and stupid." He glanced at me and grimaced. "How old do you think I am?"

"Maybe thirty?"

"I'll be thirty in a few months. That's a lot older than you."

"Mmm . . . five years, Alex. That's quite a gap."

He gave a self-deprecating smile. "A lot's happened in those years, Sam."

What did this woman do to him? I took another bite of the cake and leaned forward. I couldn't tell if eager attention or dessert-induced distraction would get me back into the story, so I landed in the middle.

"After only a few months together, I asked her to marry me. She put me off with kisses and a bit of French, telling me that we shouldn't rush and that she loved me. And rather than pull away, Simone drew me tighter. But she wouldn't accept my proposal.

"It became a dance—one she choreographed. At first I wondered if she might be right, maybe I was rushing—wanting stability and assurance from her because I couldn't find it in my career or anywhere. I don't know." Alex sighed and stayed silent a moment.

"So I spent the next year chasing her, while working in a coffee shop, editing *Redemption*, and outlining *Three Days Found*. I turned down 'real' writing jobs, and that infuriated Simone. But I felt Cole Barker could make it, and the coffee shop gig paid me enough to survive and gave me the time and freedom to write." He grabbed a bite of cake from me with a smile.

"HarperCollins then bought *Redemption* and gave it the biggest marketing campaign in its history for a new author. The publicity assured the book's success before anyone ever read a word." He glanced at me again—gauging my reaction? I wasn't sure. I took another bite and nodded slowly.

It was enough, and he continued. "Fortunately for me, the public loved it. Word of mouth took off, and *Redemption* leapt to the top and stayed. Cole Barker was an American hero, and I got movie offers and a contract to make him a series. It was unbelievable. And Simone wanted a ring. At first I was thrilled—it all worked. My book was a hit, and the most beautiful woman in the world loved me. Then it felt wrong, and I couldn't understand why.

"That's when I met Ben. He's that pastor Cole meets in *Salvation Bound*. I hated him at first because he made me see how much I was getting wrong in my life. *Three Days Found* was due at Harper, but I couldn't finish it. Couldn't write a word.

"And I couldn't envision life with Simone. I could see us at a party—we were always at parties and openings—and maybe even at the wedding ceremony, but I couldn't picture the day after that or the day after that. We never stayed in, never rented a movie, never cooked dinner or talked deeply . . . We were never simply together."

I nodded. Alex's eyes showed an intense amount of longing. I hadn't seen this vulnerability in him all summer. I wanted to hug him, but that definitely would have ended his story. And, unlike when he offered me comfort after the professor's heart attack, this wasn't that moment. He was somewhere else—with someone else.

Alex continued. "But how to communicate that? Simone loved to go out, and after *Redemption* sold, she quit her job and was relentless. When I protested, she pouted, then quit speaking to me. And when she finally looked at the book, she was livid. I hadn't put my picture on the cover." He smiled, small and flat.

I remembered my question the first day we met. Here was the answer.

"The end came when I asked my agent to negotiate an extension on *Three Days Found*. I saw a new direction for Cole. I wanted him to have more integrity, more strength, more vulnerability even, and I knew those changes were within him and within me. I wanted this new series to be good, really good." He rubbed the back of his neck as if trying to release not only tension, but words.

I nodded. "You did that. What did Simone think?"

"She believed that asking for an extension constituted failure. To punish me, she started going out with friends I didn't know and ignoring my calls. Our wedding was weeks away. And I got physically sick."

Alex looked back at me and paused. He studied me for a moment, and I realized that for the first time in his telling, he was with me—not trapped in his memories with Simone. I smiled with sympathy—I certainly understand losing oneself to the point of being sick. If I'd had the courage, I would've confided in him. I would have told him all my past, my fears, my longings, my every-thing.

Then I would've kissed him—then and there. Something lit in me, and I realized how much Alex means to me. I wanted him to know me— the real me. And I wanted to give him new memories. It startled me so much I shuddered. Alex raised an eyebrow, and I raised mine in reply. *No way I'm telling you what I'm thinking.*

He shook his head slightly as if clearing a thought and then he continued. "A couple weeks before the wedding, I sat Simone down and told her that things had to change. We could work it out, but I needed to know if she loved me—without the books, without anything else. And I wanted her to hear about what mattered

317

to me and about how I wanted us to live."

Alex looked so sad. And I understood why Mrs. Muir gets up from the table and makes tea or pours milk whenever the professor and I talk seriously. I wanted that distraction too. Not for me; I wanted it for Alex. He needed space to work through this, but I couldn't give him any at our small table. So I simply pushed the cake plate to him. He took a bite and went back to his memories.

"Simone's disgust was palpable. She calmly laid down the ring and walked out the door. I would have preferred her screams. The calm showed a contempt for me that I didn't know existed. I couldn't believe that was the end. I called, she wouldn't answer. I went to her apartment, and her doorman wouldn't let me in. After a few days, I unraveled our wedding. My mom offered to help, but Dad wouldn't let her—said it was my mess. So I called every guest, every supplier, everyone.

"And on our canceled wedding day, I received a hand-delivered envelope: Simone was engaged. She'd landed some Russian guy and actually sent me an invitation to her wedding." He leaned forward and poked at the last bite of cake. "And that is the story of my one engagement and my last real girlfriend."

"Whoa. I'm so sorry, Alex." I sat for a moment absorbing it. You had to give the girl credit—she knew precisely how to trap him, then destroy him, and that takes skill—disgusting, calculated skill. I tried to think up a similar character, but couldn't find one to match—even Edmond Dantes, my paragon of precise ruthlessness, pulled back at the end and found a way to let go and forgive.

"You've dated since then . . . that's . . . what? Four years ago?"

"Three years and seven months ago. But no, I haven't. Not really. I've dated a couple women here and there, but I don't know what they want or see now." He sat back as if exhausted, and smiled that lopsided, self-deprecating thing he throws out. "Trust was never my strong suit, and now they see only Cole. They expect me to solve crimes, quote poetry, and play polo. All before drinks."

"Cole plays polo?"

"He should. He'd be good at it."

"How long do you plan to live this way?"

Alex laughed. "Typical straightforward news-woman. Not long, I think. My publisher was right. This change was good. I feel better than I've felt in years. Probably all this food and the running."

"You're welcome."

"Seriously, I do feel better. And I'm not get-ting any younger."

I smirked.

"I mean, I'd love to be married someday. I'd at

least like to start dating the right woman . . . I'd love to be a father someday—" He started, like he had surprised himself or me. "That must seem so staid to you."

"It's not staid. It's a great dream, and it'll come true for you. You just have to let it."

"You're sweet."

"It's true. You got injured, not ruined. You're okay, and you deserve better. You simply have to believe it. I see the way women look at you. Not Cole, Alex, you."

He hiked his eyebrow again, questioning more directly this time. I refused to elaborate.

We had a quiet drive to the Muirs' house. The fact that this was the end suffocated me. I didn't say much because I didn't want to appear grasping and foolish, as I had earlier about the airport ride. And I felt like a fraud. Alex shared a lot of himself tonight, and I never possessed that courage. How much of me have I shown him?

He pulled into the driveway and walked me to the door like a perfect gentleman. He took my hand as I started up the steps.

"Sam?" He gently pulled me back. "I've loved our time together. Thank you for everything. You brought out the best in me this summer. I haven't seen that guy in a long time."

"My pleasure. He's a good guy," I whispered. My throat felt tight. There was so much I wanted to say as the moment slipped by.

"Good night, sweet Samantha. Good-bye."

There was something in his voice. A sad tone I didn't like. *Is this good-bye? Forever good-bye?*

He took my face in his hands and leaned down. At about two inches away, he stopped and looked into my eyes for eternity—only a few seconds really, but it felt that long. And with a small soft smile, he closed the gap and touched my lips for the breadth of a second. Then he left—no words, no last look. A forever good-bye.

So there ends the best summer of my life, Mr. Knightley. The *Tribune* internship is over, and that was thrilling enough, but Alex was more so. He brought out the best in me too. Even though I was never honest about my past, I was myself. Tonight was the end, though. I get that. He made no promises, no gestures, nothing. And he announced that he's ready to move on with his life. I'm somehow the closing of the old, the end to one of his books—the soft final denouement.

And now I hurt. Alex was like those dreams I told you about—the ones that disappear if I hold them too tight. I know I said I'd pitch that theory when Coach Ridley got Kyle, but forget it . . . I'm Elinor or Charlotte, and for those two reality always wins. Actually, forget Elinor—she got her man in the end. I'm Charlotte, and some odious Mr. Collins will be the best I'll ever get.

Sincerely,
Sam

Dear Mr. Knightley,

Classes began yesterday. I'm ending my time here with Government Policy Reporting, Advanced Public Affairs Reporting, Web Technologies, and Advanced Nonfiction Long Narrative. Debbie says my schedule is suicidal and she's right; it's tough. But I figure that's why I came. There's more I need to learn, and I have no distractions. That sounds more pessimistic than I mean it. Let's just say, little keeps me from a strong finish. Kyle is good. Josh and Alex are gone. And everyone else is too busy hunting down jobs.

Running and the Muirs keep me going. I decided to attack the Chicago Marathon again this year. It's a month away and I have only two long runs left before taper begins. Kyle is eager to run with me this weekend, but I can barely spare time from work to knock out twenty miles, much less add the commute time to and from Grace House. He didn't question or pester me—which makes me think he knows the truth: I'm retreating. I can feel it—not into books, but into my work. Nothing feels bright and shiny any-more.

Except the Muirs. I head up there about twice a week now and am met with good food, better hugs, and solid advice. The professor loves to review my work and has a remarkable ability to critique without being critical. It's a gift I appreciate. He mentioned Alex the other night. I feigned indifference.

"He believes this next book may be his best."

"Does he?"

"I'm proud of him, Sam. He's had a tough road and I've worried these past couple years, but he sounds stronger now."

"Hmm . . ." I pretended to read.

"I'm glad you spent some time with him this summer. Always good when the kids get along." The professor chuckled.

And despite myself, I smiled. Alex was right —the Muirs love their "kids."

We went back to our reading—at least the professor did. I didn't read another word all night. I sat there with *Unbroken* carefully placed in front of me, feeling exactly the opposite.

Time to run,

Sam

Dear Mr. Knightley,

The Ridleys adopted Kyle! No foster parenting —straight adoption! Isn't it wonderful? The requirements for adoption are more lenient than for foster parenting. Go figure. So as the delays kept mounting to foster Kyle, they jumped over them. Adopted, Kyle's adopted!

I've never heard him so excited. They invited me to the family dinner and party—and what an evening it was. And what an extraordinary family Kyle now has. My eyes are weary and weepy, but you need to know . . .

It was still light when I got off the 'L,' which was important to me. It's not a safe neighborhood, and I was nervous. But I Googled the address, and the Ridleys live two blocks from the train stop. A cab made no sense. It was time for bravery. As I got off at Division, I headed west. Three blocks later I hadn't passed the Ridleys' house. I almost bolted when a group of teenage boys approached.

"So, pretty thang, where you goin'?" The smallest one blocked my path.

I stepped into my best Edmond Dantes— thirteen years in prison teaches you to fight—and said, "I'm looking for the Ridley house at 1360, but I can't find it. You can help me or I can head to the police station two blocks down. Shouldn't take me more than a few seconds to run."

At the Ridley name, all three boys blanched and pointed. "Coach? He's that house." And they backed away.

I guess no one messes with Coach Ridley. But I didn't see it. When I arrived, he couldn't have been more mild and kind. His wife was lovely too. They welcomed me like I was Kyle's sister, as did their two kids and their grandkids.

"We did it, Sam. We got our boy. Can you believe it? Can you believe he's home?" Coach hugged me.

"I'm thrilled, Coach. I can't tell you what this means for kids like us. Kyle's whole world will change." Tears pooled in my eyes, and Coach pulled me close for another hug.

"You've got a family now too. You remember that."

I smiled, and Kyle beamed all night. I thought he was going to shoot from his seat during grace. I've never seen a grin so wide.

Coach Ridley stood at the head of the table and prayed like nothing I've ever heard.

"God, you gave us your Son, and now you've given us ours. We are so humbled and rocked to our very core to be blessed with this boy. Keep him close to you, Lord. Keep our eyes wide open when any danger approaches, any fears invade, or any enemy comes to steal the peace, the love, and the grace you've granted us. You are our God, and we are your children. Never let us forget. Amen."

His voice bellowed over the table with such confidence that I knew—I knew no one can mess with this family. Bad things may come. But these people are God's.

We ate, played charades, and laughed. It was a true home filled with true love. When it was time to go, I thanked them and headed to the door.

"Sam, how'd you get here tonight?" Mrs. Ridley asked.

"I took the 'L.' It's only a few blocks, Mrs. Ridley. I'll be fine." I was slightly panicked, but I'm also tired of fear.

"Carl, Sam took the train here," she called into the next room.

Coach was beside me so fast, I jumped. I can't move that fast.

"I take it all the time, sir. Really, I'm fine."

"You are not. Once you're on, you may be fine; but you shouldn't walk around alone at night. You must tell us before you come visit so we can meet you at the stop." He called back into the living room, "Kyle, come on, son, we need to walk Sam to the train."

Kyle popped up with a "Yes, sir" and followed us out the door. I see why the boys trembled when I mentioned Coach Ridley. His very essence demands integrity. Kyle's in good hands.

As the train pulled up, Coach turned to me. "Thanks for coming, Sam, and come often. You're family now."

I couldn't stop the tears from pooling, then falling. I nodded, hugged them both, and boarded my train. As it pulled away, I saw Coach put his arm around Kyle's shoulder. And I cried.

Everything I ever dreamed for Kyle is happening. My idea of "normal" was mere window dressing compared to this. Kyle's got the real deal: a family who will stand by him and guide and love him for the rest of his life. You can tell there's no halfway with the Ridleys.

And Kyle will need that strong, singular devotion because it's going to be hard for him. I thought writing our story was tough, but Kyle will need more courage now. He's changed so much in these last few months, but fears still plague him. He must lay them down, surrender his heart, and learn to trust others completely—I think that's what having a family, having true love, really takes. I can't quite process that. Surrender is foreign to me.

I'm proud of him—so proud, so happy, and so sleepy.

I'll write more soon,
Sam

Dear Mr. Knightley,

Classes are going well. Running is going well. The marathon is next Sunday. This week's rest will give me more study time for midterms. Forget going out, forget fun . . . The job hunt has charged the air and no one is even nice anymore. I've stayed away from the nationwide fray by limiting my applications to the Chicago area. Kyle and the Muirs are here, and I see no reason to leave the only town I've ever known. But it's an aggressive fight for the local jobs too.

On a bright note, Susan Ellis called yesterday to encourage me to apply at the *Tribune*. I know seven classmates applying there. Debbie's one of them, and everyone concedes she's best. So, while I was flattered Ms. Ellis called, I doubt my chances. I called Mike to see if she'd called him with the same encouragement, and she hadn't—she'd offered him a job, two rungs up the ladder. Jealously surged for a few minutes before reason prevailed. I'm not in Debbie's league and I'm not in Mike's. I stopped pouting, submitted the application, and then searched for some more township papers to which I can apply.

I told Johnson, thinking he'd be pleased, but he wasn't. He didn't know I was Chicago-centric and demanded I send applications and writing samples to the *New York Times*, the *New Yorker*, and a host of other long-narrative papers and magazines. Now I must expand my scope—because Johnson agreed to mentor my final project, and I can't afford to tick him off.

I dread all that rejection, but I dread a job offer from New York more. Alex is there. He's gone from my life now—no calls, no texts, nothing. I'd hate for him to ever think I chased him. If this is what he wants—silence and rejection—I'll honor it. I'll send some New York applications to satisfy Johnson, but that's as far as I'll take it.

Enough about the job hunt. It's all anyone talks about, and it's wearing.

I skipped Governmental Policy yesterday to clear my head and went to Kyle's first cross-country meet. Kyle ran like the wind and won. He's only a sophomore and already the team's star. And he smiles. Kyle smiles and laughs and possesses that teenage sassiness you only get when you feel secure. I love it.

And my walks to and from his house and the 'L' are quite an adventure now. Yesterday I arrived half an hour early, and the same three boys who harassed me last month were loitering on the platform. I almost stayed on the train when I spotted them, but jumped off at the last minute before my courage fled completely.

"Ma'am, you goin' to see Coach?"

"I am."

"It's not real safe. Coach told us to keep an eye out for you. We'll walk you there."

"Thank you." We chatted along the way, and I found they aren't scared of Coach Ridley at all. These boys love him and want to please him. Kyle, being his son, is practically a demigod now.

It's odd, isn't it? As Kyle joins a family, I leave one. I thought I'd plow through grad school like I did college, but I made friends here. I found a life here. And I made other friends along the way. The Muirs and Alex will stay in my heart forever. But the rest of my friends are breaking apart as we hunt down that next chapter. I liked this one. And now it's ending. I'm so sick of endings, Mr. Knightley.

> Enough wallowing and
> much work to do,
> Sam

~ OCTOBER 13

Dear Mr. Knightley,

It's over. Not completely. I have to recover and, as I limped to classes today, that may be the hardest part.

The Chicago Marathon was yesterday—in pouring rain and, at some points, 30 mph winds. The course is mapped in a series of loops, so about a quarter of it was directly into the wind. Unbelievable. I hoped they would cancel it, but with forty thousand runners paying about $175 per entry, it takes a lot to shut that engine down. We ran.

At the start, trash bags flew everywhere. Runners often poke holes in the tops of huge black garbage bags and use them as disposable ponchos. It always cracks me up—we foster kids traditionally use trash bags for a much different purpose. Anyway, bags flew in my face and wrapped around my feet. I slipped several times and can't believe people didn't fall all around me.

The first twenty miles were typical: five to settle in and the next fifteen in my groove. Muscles ached in different places than usual because my shoes were soaked and lugged extra water, but it was okay. The wind and rain kept me from obsessing about the miles, and I had fans to cheer me: Kyle yelled at mile 12, Hannah and her husband, Matt, held a ridiculous sign at mile 15 that read SAM—ARATHON! RUN, SAM, RUN and the Muirs waved their hearts out at mile 19.

Debbie and Ashley were at mile 22, but I missed them. My mind was elsewhere . . .

Mile 22 to the end is always tricky—you break down mentally and physically. This time it happened earlier. Maybe it was all the wind and water, but at mile 20 the race took on an eerie tone, especially along Lake Shore Drive. Thoughts pounded my brain in rhythm to Lake Michigan's waves crashing and surging next to us. I couldn't push them away or direct them.

In the past I've usually run scenes from my favorite books in my head—especially *Jane Eyre*, because I love her courage, her decisions, and her voice. I love her stamina. But yesterday Jane failed me. Lizzy failed me. Emma failed me. At mile 21 I had no control over my thoughts, and my past ballooned in my brain: my dad and mom, Father John, the holdup at the White Hen, Cara, Hannah, Kyle . . .

But none of it hurt. I felt distant and safe for much of it. That surprised and relieved me because I had no defense had it felt otherwise.

Then came Alex—all we said this summer, all we shared, all I wanted to share. The truth about how deeply he affected me. Panic washed over me, and I couldn't shut it down. It's hard to explain what little control you hold over your body and thoughts at this point in a marathon. Sure, you can stop running, but even that takes cognitive effort and, if you're not totally broken, it doesn't occur to you. I kept going. Step. Step. Step. The memory of another day, and another run, with Alex flitted through my mind.

"You're going to find a great guy, Sam."

"I doubt it. There's a lot about me that'd scare any guy off. I wonder if I'm cut out for a healthy relationship." I tripped so close to laying it all out for him that morning.

Alex ran a few steps. "You are. All it takes is honesty."

I glanced over at him. He held that same furrowed expression he made whenever bothered or irritated.

"There's a lot about me that'd scare you . . . or any other woman, off too."

"What?"

"Forget it." He fell silent. A few more steps, and he continued, "I don't like to disappoint people. I let things go on too long and get too complicated because I fear the way they'll look at me when it's all done."

"Your father?"

"He's one, and maybe that's where it started, but it doesn't stop there. I let people down, then run like a coward before it hits the fan—friends, acquaintances, and colleagues. I feel safer at a distance."

Alex turned his head away, and we ran another couple miles before either of us spoke again. We ended up chatting about a lot of stuff that day. Stuff that didn't matter much, but the stuff that—as the professor likes to believe—builds a strong friendship. We understood each other.

But on this day, in the pounding rain, that conversation meant something different, something more. Was he alluding to Simone? Partly. But at mile 23 I surmised that Alex told me something else that day—that he would never be mine. *Is that what I had hoped? Did I want that? Do I?*

Yes. Yes. I believed it could happen. Step. *Yes.* Step. I moved through two miles of loss before I tried to focus on the Muirs. *They won't leave me.* Step. Step. Step. *They won't abandon me.* Step. *They call me their daughter.* Step. *They love me . . .*

No go. My mind drifted back to Alex, no matter how much I wanted it to rest elsewhere—any-where. *Alex left.* Step. *You weren't enough.* Step. *"Sam failed to connect."* Step. *"Sam has failed again."* Step. Step. Step. The panic shortened my breaths—not good at that point—and I started seeing stars. I wobbled, and an older man grabbed my upper arm.

"You good?"

"No."

"You've got less than a mile. Repeat after me, 'I'm okay. I'm okay.' The phrase is the length of three strides. Perfect cadence to fill your head. Say it."

"I'm okay. I'm okay." I pushed out a weak smile. "Thanks."

"No problem." He pushed ahead a little, and I tucked behind him. The 3:45 pacer had announced at the race's start that the wind would cost us over thirty seconds a mile. He had encouraged us to stick with the group because drafting would ease the load. I'd stuck for most of the race, but lost the pack at mile 20 when my mind wandered. I hadn't noticed.

"Stick right there and we'll make it," the man called back to me.

"Thanks." I tucked closer. "I'm okay. I'm okay."

The man ran me in and gave me a hug after the finish. He didn't seem surprised when I burst into tears.

"You did great."

"I didn't, but thank you."

"You did. It's my eighteenth marathon, and I've seen a lot out here. Each one is a unique and dangerous experience."

We pushed through the chute to receive our medals. I lost him. Instead I found Ashley and Debbie.

"You didn't wave!"

"I didn't see you."

"We didn't think so. Your face was horrible. Were you crying?"

"I don't remember."

I didn't elaborate. Alex still filled my thoughts. I hoped he would leave soon. To distract myself, I concentrated on food. I ate a banana, an energy bar, and a bagel from the food tent, sucked down three chocolate milks, then found Ashley and Debbie again. They kindly drove me home and left me alone at my apartment. I shook so badly with the cold that I wanted only a hot shower and soup. I wasn't very coherent. Alex still filled my mind.

He left when the Muirs arrived, and I finally felt at peace. Sore, unable to bend my knees, but at peace. They brought me a full meal of chicken, stuffing, vegetables, and potatoes. And two pints of ice cream.

"We won't stay, dear. You need to rest." Mrs. Muir fluffed the pillows and blankets, making a nest for me on the couch.

"I'm so glad you came."

"How could we not? You were wonderful today. What an accomplishment." She glowed.

"I was eight minutes off my backup plan."

"In that wind! You should be thrilled. Don't diminish this, Sam. I'm so proud of you." The professor pulled me gently into a hug.

After they left, I curled up on my couch, watched a couple *Sherlock* episodes, and ate every bite of food they'd brought—including both pints of Dulce de Leche.

Today, I limp . . .

Sam

Dear Mr. Knightley,

When the Muirs returned from Europe this summer, Mrs. Muir brought out fabric swatches and asked me to pick my favorites. She didn't tell me why, but now I know.

We were baking cookies yesterday when she asked me to grab a book from her bedroom. I returned. "It's not there. Could it be somewhere else?"

"Check the guest room. I wandered through there yesterday."

I walked down the hall, opened the door, and stopped. It's gorgeous: pale green walls and filmy white-and-green draperies. The bed is covered in a soft floral pattern of whites, greens, and pale orange—lilies, of course.

"It's yours, Sam. It's everything you picked out, right?" She sounded tentative as she stood right behind me.

"Mine? My room? Here?"

"Your room, my dear, here." She hugged me tight.

I was speechless. And that was only the beginning.

Last night the professor and I built a fire and played Trivial Pursuit Book Lover's Edition. He won, as usual. And while he was basking in the glow of victory, Mrs. Muir asked my opinions about orphans and bonding with second families. They've read all my writing and know that my interest has gone beyond personal experience. My research this summer has made me something of an expert. So I gave her my standard professional answers.

And then she blurted out, "Don't you want parents? A mother? Even grown up, isn't that a good thing?"

"I expect so. Everyone wants to be loved. And I certainly didn't get that from my mom and dad." I looked at her sharply as I realized that she wasn't talking about them. She was talking about herself. I held my breath.

She looked to the professor, tense, and he nodded almost imperceptibly in reply as he spoke. "We know you're all grown up, Sam, but we feel so blessed to know you. We'd like to make it permanent. Would you consider becoming our daughter? Officially? On paper?"

He got nervous then and started rapid-firing his words, much like I do. "Think on it . . . We understand if you're not interested . . . Big decision . . . You will always be welcome here . . . We love you."

I must have looked bug-eyed, for Mrs. Muir put her hand on the professor's arm.

"We aren't asking anything of you. We simply want to love you forever, and thought making it 'official' might be fun and give you a tangible sense of family." She stood there silently and waited.

Looking at her, one might think she seemed peaceful. Her expression was bland, not even expectant, but I saw a familiar look in her eyes. I call it the "trial," and it's related to fear. Someone is deciding and weighing your worth: Do you pass? Are you enough? Do you measure up? Are you acceptable?

I know that look, and I hated myself for putting such uncertainty into her mind. How could she not measure up?

I stopped thinking and fretting and simply hugged Mrs. Muir first, erasing her doubts. Then I reached for the professor to join us. They were thrilled—and I am too, but I feel slightly detached. Did Kyle feel this way? Or am I that much more cynical? Alex came to mind, and I mentally stepped back even further. I hate that his memory did that. Will I ever stop protecting myself, and simply love?

We had laughter and cake. Mrs. Muir had baked a cake yesterday morning with a big bold *Welcome Home* scrolled across the top. I didn't ask what she would have done had I refused. Everything felt too fragile for jokes. It didn't sound funny in my mind anyway.

Remember Icarus, the boy who flew too close to the sun? The wax on his beautiful wings melted, and he plunged to his death in the sea. This may sound harsh and random to you, but it hits close to home for me. It's how I think about big dreams. I'm not being trite or flippant when I say they slip away. I'm serious. Now here's another I need to hold close and pray won't disappear.

Yes . . . I wrote "pray." It's not a word I've used before and not one I write lightly. But I can't listen to Father John, the Muirs and the Ridleys, and once-upon-a-time Alex, and not believe that there is something to it. How can I not believe that there is a God who exists and loves, when the people before me are infused with that love and pour it out daily? I still can't grasp that it's for me, but what if it is? The professor says it's okay to pray even if I'm not sure.

There's so much I'm not sure about these days. And these big dreams still frighten me. I recognize that they don't always slip away. Kyle is with the Ridleys and thriving. And the Muirs seem to be here for the long haul. But my parents didn't stick, no foster family stuck, I failed every attempt to stand on my own, the *Tribune* didn't offer me a job after my internship, I'm not brilliant at Medill, Alex left, Josh never loved me . . . I sound silly, but these were the elements of my "normal" life, my dreams, and I gave each my all.

I try to stick to the people I now love. And I press, push, and pursue my work. But I still don't measure up. What if I'm not what the Muirs want? What if they tire of the burden? Everyone else always has.

There you have it. Much more than you need to know and much less than what fills my heart and head. See why surrender and love remain so foreign? There is a lot in the way. How can I reach them? I've never made it to anything before.

The professor outlined the "adoption," and it's so easy. There will be no social workers, classes, hearings, or waiting involved. There's some paperwork to fill out, and a judge needs to sign it. The professor said I could add their last name to mine if I want. Samantha Moore Muir. It's certainly better than the name I've got.

Have I ever told you about my name? That's one story I never share . . . Mom left me in an alley at five days old, and someone turned me into the Ninth District Fire Station in Rogers Park, specifically to Captain Sam Moore. When the social worker from DCFS came to take me, she wrote Samantha Moore on the paperwork.

I don't know if she meant it as a joke or a tribute to the captain, but the name stuck. DCFS found Mom and returned me to her a month later. She got a slap on the wrist, passed some parenting courses, worked some community service hours, and took me home. She never bothered to change my name.

Years later Father John stumbled across these ancient records and drove me by the alley and the fire station. A bunch of fire fighters stood outside cleaning their rig, and I asked if Captain Moore was still around. He blanched when I introduced myself. He said he was sorry I still carried his name—I guess he caught what that meant. I never contacted him again.

I think I've told you this before, Mr. Knightley, but a name is a powerful thing. I don't know that I could have shared so much with you if you were a Mr. Elton or a Frank Churchill. They weren't honorable men. George Knightley was. So I trusted you on that association alone—at first.

Since then, you have never violated that trust: you paid for graduate school, you allowed Laura to contact me when needed, you clearly read my letters, and you never wrote back, except the two times I demanded it. You have never stretched the terms of our agreement. And you send thoughtful gifts. Okay, the last is not a trust issue, but I do like the gifts. Thank you, Mr. Knightley. As I count big dreams that slipped away, I need to remember that you stuck.

Now I'm completely sidetracked—which illustrates my point: a name is a powerful thing. "Sam Moore" is not a name that I mind changing.

343

I won't tell the Muirs that or the story of Captain Sam Moore. It reaches a place too deep. I'll simply request a name change at the office and surprise them. So mark your calendar. December 10 is the date. And, Mr. Knightley, please keep your fingers crossed that it all lasts until then.

Sincerely,
Samantha Moore Muir
(It looks good, doesn't it?)

~ DECEMBER 10

Dear Mr. Knightley,

Thank you for the spectacular bouquet of lilies. The note was the perfect touch. So simple. *Best wishes, G. Knightley*. That's what is traditionally said to a bride. And I felt like that today—new and loved. In fact, I've felt that way all week.

The Conley kids delivered drawings and gifts to my apartment on three different days, Mrs. Conley gave me a gorgeous heavy crystal vase to mark the occasion and hold her huge bouquet of flowers, and Debbie and Ashley gave me little treats all week—mostly joke baby cards and rattles that read *Welcome Baby*. I could go on . . . Father John, Kyle, Hannah, the Ridleys, even Cara . . . Everyone has shown such excitement about this. Alex sent something too—a huge box of chocolates with a card: *Congratulations, Sam. Welcome to the family. I'm glad I'll always be a part of your world. It makes me smile. God bless you . . . Alex.*

I would have liked something more personal, but I won't let him distract me right now.

Back to the day . . . The Muirs pulled into the Conleys' driveway at nine o'clock this morning. Debbie and Ashley had arrived moments before with coffees in hand, so we piled into the car and headed downtown. Mrs. Muir could hardly speak.

345

"Mrs. Muir, thank you for inviting us." That was Ashley.

"Yes, dear."

"Mrs. Muir, can we bring anything to dinner tonight?" That was Debbie.

"Yes, dear."

"Mrs. Muir, Sam said you'll adopt me too." Ashley again.

"Yes, dear." She fidgeted with her fingers and counted cars. The traffic clearly upset her.

"Now, Frances, you know that Paul will wait. He can't proceed without us. Try to enjoy the moment," the professor said. He then winked into the rearview mirror. "It's her first baby girl. She's a bit nervous."

Mrs. Muir swatted him.

When we arrived, Kyle was waiting in the lobby. Coach Ridley had let him skip, and I can't tell you what it meant to have him there. I grabbed him into a hug so tight he choked and whispered, "Chill, Sam."

Judge Montgomery's office was comforting and just what you'd expect: wood paneling, covered in books (the old leather/legal kind), and a faint pipe tobacco smell. He's an old friend of the professor's, so there was much back-slapping and manly hugging.

He then looked at me, and his eyes got soft and round. "You have found a lovely daughter, Robert. And I understand she has a brain like yours and Franny's." He then reached across and hugged Mrs. Muir. "You look beautiful, Frances. Now let's get this under way."

He read from some forms, and we all signed. He then asked about my name, and I said I wanted to add Muir. Mrs. Muir got tears in her eyes and the professor beamed.

"Wise choice, my dear. I know you will treasure the name and the family."

I then signed my new name: *Samantha Moore Muir.*

It was much scarier than I imagined—it was like physically handing my heart to someone. It aches even though no one hurt it. The Muirs only offered to love it. Does that make sense? It doesn't to me, but that's how it feels.

Afterwards we went to lunch at Fonterra Grill, right next to Topolobampo. Of course my mind drifted to Alex. I wonder about him more often than I'd like. Other than the card and chocolates, which arrived yesterday, I haven't heard from him since he left. Not a single text, e-mail, call—nothing. If I didn't feel like I missed something at the end, I would call him. Part of me wants to demand an explanation and tell him how deeply he has hurt me. I almost trusted him . . .

That's a lie. I did trust him. While I didn't let him in completely, it was only a matter of time. I believed he was worthy. At the very least, we were friends—even he said that—and I don't understand this silence. But I won't trespass. And I won't beg. If Alex's farewell was final, so be it. I'll forget him soon. In a few months this won't feel so dark.

The Muirs hear from him, though. The professor mentioned how excited he was when they told him about the adoption and how disappointed he was to miss the day. And upon arriving at their house this afternoon, we found the most spectacular bouquet of flowers in the hallway.

Dear Mom M and Pops, I am so thankful for this day and wish I could be there to celebrate. Delighted Sam is joining the family. Please give her a hug and know that I love you all deeply. Love, Alex

Maybe I was wrong about him. Maybe he is blasé. He wouldn't fly to Paris. He wouldn't come here. He makes his own schedule and he certainly makes enough money. Do we mean so little to him? The Muirs think of him as a son. And I . . . What do I think of him?

I'm confused. Under duress or torture, I might say I loved him. But I don't want to feel that way—not now, not him. It's the whole Icarus thing. This summer I knew reaching for Alex Powell was too high, but I let myself enjoy him and our time together, and look what happened. Sure, he opened up and at the end said he loved

348

spending time with me. He even said I was beautiful occasionally, but other than that last night, he never touched me or kissed me or made any attempt to be more than a friend.

As I replay the summer in my mind, I think I should have caught on. He maintained a careful distance. He said it himself, and I recalled it during the marathon: "I don't like to disappoint people. I let things go on too long and get too complicated because I fear the way they'll look at me when it's all done." Now I'm all done. I will give him no more of my time, my heart— any part of me. And I doubt I'll read his next book, even if it is the "best one yet."

Putting the confusing Mr. Powell aside, today was something delicate and delicious, and I'll hold it forever. I have a family now, a real family in my heart and officially on paper. Thank you. Thank you for all this, Mr. Knightley. It started with your generosity and Father John's insistence on Medill. I'm sorry I resisted.

Love,
Samantha Muir

P.S. I forgot to tell you about something else quite extraordinary. I came over last week with my final project's rough draft for the professor's review. He launched into the Industrial Revolution, the invention of the automobile, World

Wars I and II, FDR, the Fifties, the Sixties, Woodstock, birth control, salary equalization—I don't think he drew breath for forty-five minutes—and landed at Hemingway (he always lands there), children, and our foster care system. I have no idea how he got there, but he did.

By the end Mrs. Muir and I were stifling laughter because he didn't need an audience and wasn't even aware of our presence—he was pontificating. Then he woke from his delirium, rounded on me, and demanded, "So what type of daughter are you? Are we equal? Will you call me Professor forever? Am I to be Robert?"

He stood, gesticulating like we were three hundred students in a lecture hall. His motions were too grand for his small study—his "tell" for nerves.

I stood up and announced, "You will be Dad!"

I shocked us both, Mr. Knightley. I wondered if I'd crossed a line as he stared at me. Time stopped. His eyes got teary and soft, and he opened his arms. I stepped into them, and he whispered, "My girl."

Then Mrs. Muir joined in. "Me too. I get to be Mom, right?"

The professor answered, winking at me, "Of course you do, my dear, and it's about time."

It felt awkward at first. My memories linked to those names aren't good, but I simply forged ahead. "Mom" and "Dad," on the other hand, felt comfortable by salad.

~ DECEMBER 21

Dear Mr. Knightley,

I'm at the Muirs' right now and our Christmas production is under way: tree trimming, cookie baking, gift organizing, movie watching, and song singing. They're off to a cocktail party, but I begged off to write you. And I will sign this missive with my new silver pen, thank you very much. It's a lovely gift, Mr. Knightley. I appreciate it a great deal.

Exams ended, and Christmas break has started. I will return to Medill for graduation in January, but all my classwork is done. I don't have a job yet—that remains the last sign that I really was the one clinging off the back ledge. Everyone else I know has an offer. But I made it. And for some reason, I'm not worried about my job prospects. I truly believe I will be okay.

Do you ever feel like there are plans for you? Not ones you make, but plans for good that will come about if you trust and remain patient? It's a strange feeling, but it has crept upon me lately and I can't shake it. I told Mrs. Muir about it, and you won't believe what she found: " 'For I know the plans I have for you,' declares the Lord, 'plans to prosper you and not to harm you, plans to give you hope and a future.' " I didn't make that up. It's a direct quote from the

Bible—Jeremiah 29:11. It describes my feeling precisely —there are plans, good plans just out of reach. And I wait, feeling hopeful and peaceful, not desperate and tense. That's brand-new. The Muirs keep praying for me, and there's power in that too. So I won't fret about the job, but I will work. I owe my future and your generosity my best effort.

I finished my annual reading of Dickens's *A Christmas Carol* today. The tradition started several years ago, because I felt so aligned with Scrooge. I understood his fear, confusion, and longing as each ghost took him through his life and he was reminded of the pain he endured, then caused. I let go of people and relationships to protect myself too, and then I detached so completely that I lost the ability to connect. I still remember my first day at Medill when I met Debbie, and she looked at me like I was from another planet, before she and her friends left the table.

I've changed. I laid down those characters and I faced my ghosts, but unlike Scrooge, my transformation builds slowly. That's the one thing that still bothers me about that story. How was Scrooge's transformation so complete and joyful? How did he lay down so much so quickly? Did he ever slip back? We are led to believe he changed forever. He found freedom.

I haven't found it—freedom remains elusive.

And there's something more Scrooge possessed that I don't. Joy. The professor says it has to do with surrendering my heart, my plans, and my will. I think that first requires a softening of the heart—a "cease-fire" on fighting inside. I do feel that, so maybe I am beginning to understand.

Speaking of elusive, I got an e-mail from Alex yesterday. For a man so eloquent in person and even more so in print, he can be an uncommunicative jerk.

Coming to Chicago for final research. Have dinner with me Christmas Eve? Wait and hope, Alex.

A confusing note. I haven't heard from him in months, other than that vague good-wishes-on-your-adoption note—and now a dinner invitation? And "Wait and hope"? Those were my winning words in that literary game we played the first day we met, Edmond Dantes's final written words to Maximillian. They are instructions to young lovers, instructions for life. The irony that those words articulate my feelings for the future has not escaped me—but that has nothing to do with Alex.

Nevertheless I accepted his invitation—the malicious fury it ignited proved too tempting. I honestly feel as angry now as I did in Cara's hospital room. I wonder if I could "decimate"

Alex with words too—might be worth a try. When I told the Muirs about the invitation—not the fury—they insisted I invite him to join us for our church's midnight service. Alex agreed.

Now I must go. There are cookies in the oven, and I promised not to burn them again. Thanks for the pen, Mr. Knightley, and Merry Christmas.

Love,
Sam

Dear Mr. Knightley,

I'm sick. I feel like I've been this way forever. Have you ever been so sick for so long that you think you'll never recover? That's me. I had a nice Christmas with the Muirs. Alex came to town for Christmas Eve. We went to dinner, but he left before church. That was my fault.

We'd gone to dinner at Café Matou downtown. He seemed nervous, and I was angry. I wanted to hurt him—make him pay for playing it safe, for trying not to "disappoint" me by withdrawing. Petty and peevish of me, I know. And I got it all wrong.

"I'm sorry I didn't call this fall." Alex looked so sincere. He was trying to connect, but I wanted no part of it.

"Or write. Or text."

"You're right. I dropped the ball."

"It's not a big deal, Alex. You had your book to finish, and I graduate next month. Besides, I still have to find a job. No worries. We've both been busy."

"I tried to forget you."

"Excuse me?" I meant it to sound like a question, but it swam in sarcasm.

He rubbed his forehead. "I thought up a million reasons to stay away, but I love you and you make me feel so alive. We understand each other. But then I worried about honesty. There's so much about me you don't know. Things that may make you hate me. And while I love that we can talk, really talk, I wondered how honest you've been with me. We owe each other that." He stared at me. "Don't you think that we're worth that?"

"I'm not following you." I'd caught his "I love you," but the rest of his garbled speech was vaguely reminiscent of Mr. Darcy's first declaration to Elizabeth—the one in which he claims to love her and then proceeds to insult her.

"I thought if I kept away, I might feel less. And you'd forget me. You'd find someone without the baggage we both carry. You didn't need to know about all the mess in my life. The mess I've created. It could stay secret. I could be done." He leaned forward. "I thought I'd be okay. There are a lot of women in New York, right? You said so yourself. I just have to let it happen. And the same holds true for you, Sam. Tons of men could love you. Who wouldn't?"

"Excuse me?" *Are you for real? You can't think this sounds good.*

He raked his hands through his hair. He'd let it grow this fall, and it reached beyond his fingertips. "But I can't do it, Sam. There isn't anyone else. There's only you. It's been only you for a long time now." He looked at me expectantly, like this final point cleared everything up.

"Meaning . . . ?"

"Marry me? . . . I'm asking you to marry me. Will you marry me?"

Alex spread his hands across the table, his eyes eager and begging. I wanted to stop time. *Marry him?* I closed my eyes for a moment, wondering what it would be like—Alex Powell's wife. Someone he loves. Getting to rake my hands through that hair every day. I wanted to rest in that moment.

My eyes flew open. *He said he loved me, but had been trying to forget me? He looked for someone else? What happens when he tries that again? Does he actually think this won't infuriate me?*

"Are you serious?"

"Proposing marriage? Yes. I'm sorry. I'm doing this all wrong. It's just that I'm nervous. There's so much you need to know, Sam. But I'll tell you. I won't keep anything from you. And this fall was no good without you."

I think Alex babbled on, but I didn't hear him. I was still lost in "I tried to forget you" and, my favorite, "There are a lot of women in New York." A few seconds of these gems bouncing in my brain and I couldn't help myself . . .

I will be ashamed to my dying day for what I did next. Not for saying no. That was right. But for how I said it. I wanted it to be from me. I wanted to stand on my own two feet and say what I felt. I wanted to say that I was mad at him—furious—and deserved more than this pathetic explanation and certainly more than his insulting pseudo-Darcy proposal. What was he thinking? I had a right to be angry, and I had a right to be heard. I lost both by hiding in the most despicable way I could.

"I think I should be thankful to you, Alex, but I don't feel it. I don't want your love and, clearly, offering it isn't what you want either. I'm sorry if this hurts, but I'm sure you'll recover quickly."

"Sam . . . don't do that."

I was paraphrasing, not quoting, but he knew.

"It's no worse than what you just did. You told me you never meant to love me, tried to forget me, even sought others to replace me. Were you playing our game, Alex? Because if you weren't, you missed the mark."

"I didn't mean it like that. I was just . . ." He reached for my hand, but I pulled it back. "Please. Talk to me." His eyes glistened.

I didn't know I had any power over Alex. His silence this fall led me to believe I held none, but he was clearly upset. He shook his head as if trying to push the moment away. I should have stopped. I didn't.

" 'You're the last man in the world whom I could ever be prevailed on to marry.' " I finished with a direct quote, just to drive the nail deep. One single tear ran down my cheek before I could stop it. I swiped at it and hoped he hadn't noticed. He reached for me again. I looked away.

"I'll get the check." He sounded so disappointed. "If all you can offer is a hackneyed refusal stolen from Elizabeth Bennet, we have nothing more to say." He captured my gaze until I pulled away. "We were more than that, Sam. We saw each other—really saw each other from the first moment we met. There was none of this between us. It was our game because we never needed it as a weapon. And I wasn't playing tonight." He got the check, and we left in silence.

At the Muirs' walk he turned to me. "I can't stay and see Mom M and Pops tonight. Tell them I had to go."

I nodded and walked past him, but then he called me back.

"Sam, is this really how you want us to end? Why won't you trust me?"

My heart was broken, but I was still angry. Maybe it was pride, but mostly fear. "I did trust you, and look what it got me: a long, silent fall and an insulting proposal. Don't look so sad, Alex. You'll forget me soon—again."

"Forget you? If you only knew . . ."

I looked at him. Part of me wanted to grab him and share everything. Tell him that he was already an indelible part of me. Tell him I loved him—that I felt alive and whole and excited when he was near, and that, when we were together, the world glowed shiny and bright and I could be brave. And tell him I hated him—that the fall was gray and grim and felt like drudgery without him, but that he had abandoned me, and now my happiness would never be tied up with him because I would never make that mistake again. I clenched my jaw and shook my head. It was all I could do.

Alex's face hardened. " 'And this is your opinion of me. This is the estimation in which you hold me. I thank you for explaining it so fully. My faults, according to this calculation, are heavy indeed! But perhaps' "—he stepped toward me—" 'these offenses might have been over-looked, had not your pride been hurt by my honest confession of the scruples that had long prevented my forming any serious design. These bitter accusations might have been suppressed, had I with greater policy concealed my struggles.' " He watched me absorb every word, every nuance. Then he walked away.

As I replay the evening in my head, I don't think he meant to sound like Mr. Darcy—until the end. I think he was scared. But why? I'm not the one who ran. He had nothing to fear from me. I never asked anything of him. I may have hoped for more, but I didn't expect it.

But he wasn't scared at the end. He was angry —as angry as I'd ever seen him. No paraphrasing for Alex. He always did play the game better.

He called the Muirs on Christmas morning and said he had to fly back to New York immediately. They were disappointed, but didn't question me. I caught a cold that day and have been sick ever since.

Mrs. Muir says I'm working too hard and not eating well. She's right. I love that she cares, but right now I want to stay in my quiet apartment, shut the whole world out, and fade away.

Graduation is tomorrow. Everyone is partying, then leaving. And I'm actually missed. I did it. I made friends who care, who want my company and who like me. Debbie made me soup; Ashley keeps delivering gossip magazines and chocolate; and lots of folks call, invite me to parties, and wish me well. It feels good to be included, but I'm still missing out. I'm stuck at home, feverish, green, and stuffy. And I ache so badly, Mr. Knightley. I hurt all over. I think I'll cry.

Your pathetic reporter,
Sam

~ JANUARY 15

Dear Mr. Knightley,

I need you—one last time . . .

Graduation was last week. I couldn't go, as my fever still hovered around 103. Debbie delivered my diploma afterward, so I have proof—and a job. I can start at the *Evanston Review* next month, or I can take the one-month trial Susan Ellis offered me yesterday. I have three days to decide: a steady but low-paying job or working for free for a month in hopes of an offer at the *Tribune*. I make it sound grim, but it isn't. The *Trib* job is good and I'm considering it, but by personality, I'm risk-averse. A one-month "trial" might end me. That said, when my rental agreement here is over at the end of the month, I'm moving in with the Muirs until I get on my feet. So I could take a month "trial" with no pay. I'll let you know. But none of that matters. I'm filling space to avoid the real issue . . .

The Muirs called this morning. Alex had called them moments earlier to tell them he'd been hit by a cab a few days ago. He's actually still in the hospital, Mr. Knightley. Of course, the Muirs hopped on the first flight they could get to New York. I gather Alex's parents aren't going out, and the professor believes he shouldn't be alone right now.

Mrs. Muir called again from the airport. My reaction when she'd first called had unnerved her. "Are you better, dear?"

I wasn't.

"Sam? He's going to be fine . . . Sam, are you there? . . . Sam, speak to me."

"He can't be hurt, Mom. He can't . . . ," I mumbled. Tears got my phone all wet again. I felt wrecked and still very much alone.

"He's going to be fine. Will you?"

"He's hurt. I hurt him." I started to hyperventilate.

"Sam, I told you, a car hit him and he's been sick. You had nothing to do with this." An announcer cut across her voice. "We need to board the plane. I'll text you when we land." She didn't hang up. "Sam?"

"I'm here."

"You need to pray. Whether you believe or not, I want you to pray. Pray for Alex, and pray for yourself, dear."

"Why?" I was too numb to think.

"Sometimes the action begets belief, and you need that now. In the end, it's all that matters. Alex has it and he'll be fine."

"But—"

"No buts, darling. God is in this. I'm not diminishing Alex's injuries, but I am asking you to trust that God is in this and that he's got you too, Sam." She let the words sink into me. "I need to go, darling." She hung up.

I know she's right. God is with Alex. I know he's with the Muirs. I believe that. I even believe, through the mist in my brain, that he's with me. But I also know I've lied. That's what I couldn't tell her during either conversation this morning. I lied to myself and to Alex—so many times— and I layered those lies with vicious, hurtful words. I don't want Alex out of my life—he's already smack in the center. He's mine and, despite the mess I've created, I'm his. Now I sound like Emma. Maybe that's my first clue this is all wrong . . .

But I love Alex completely—the broken, the quirky, the strong, and the serious sides of him. It's a powerful emotion—one that electrifies and terrifies me—and it's the most real thing I've felt in a long time. I called Ashley, who came over immediately.

"Lizzy Bennet? You actually used her words to refuse him?" She couldn't laugh. It sounded as horrid as it felt.

"Yes. I'm so ashamed," I sobbed. "And now he's hurt . . ."

"You do know she marries Darcy in the end?"

"Not funny, Ash. This isn't a book."

"That's the first honest thing you've said."

"Huh?"

"Come on, Sam. You didn't reject Alex because he ticked you off. You rejected him so he couldn't hurt you. You had to be the last one standing. All alone."

"That's not fair. I'm not alone. I've got you, I've got the Muirs, I've got friends. I laid down those characters. I've laid myself bare for months. Do you understand how hard that is?"

"More than most." Her small frown confirmed her words. It's unbelievable that I ever dismissed Ashley; she's more like me than anyone I've known. We came at loneliness from opposite ends of the world, but we both found it.

Ashley continued, "You accept those relationships on your own terms. We can't hurt you. Not really. I don't have access to those places deep within you. And if I did reach one and I harmed you . . . you'd walk away justified and never look back."

My jaw dropped. It didn't faze her.

"Don't give me that face. I'd do the same to you, and we both know it. And the Muirs? You let them in, but it isn't the same. Parental love is safer than romantic love."

Again I looked shocked, and she backtracked.

"I don't mean your real parents; they caused wounds I'll never understand. But the Muirs aren't going to hurt you deep in your heart. They won't betray you, and you know that. Letting them in is not dangerous. You can remain whole."

She scooted toward me on the couch and took my hands. I sensed something bad was coming.

You see it in the movies. The adult takes the kid's hands before telling her that the puppy died. I closed my eyes.

"Alex? He could wreck you. You've loved him since the first moment you saw him. Josh's betrayal could never touch what Alex could do to you."

"You're not helping." I started crying again, that slow kind when tears course down your cheeks because you've been hit by something so painful and so long lasting that sobbing lacks the stamina to endure it.

"You're not a coward, Sam. You never were. Tell Alex your fears. Tell him your past. All of it." She paused. "Did he ever read your first *Tribune* article?"

"I don't think so. He never mentioned it."

"Why didn't you show it to him? I never understood that."

"Josh—"

"Josh was a jerk. Don't put him in the same conversation with Alex."

"Josh made me feel like *less*—first my past was shameful, then he held it up for display with that horrid necklace. And I didn't see it, Ash. You did. You tried to tell me. Even Isabella knew—and she's twelve! How could I *not* doubt myself? I don't know the first thing about love or relation-ships. I didn't want Alex to make me feel like that."

"You made yourself feel that way. Josh didn't do that. And Alex wouldn't."

The professor's words flooded my brain: *"Never let something so unworthy define you."* That's what I did. I believed the lie that Josh could define me. Nice revelation, but not helpful at that moment. I had still screwed up with Alex.

"What do I do now?"

"You're going to tell him the truth. If he rejects you, then it's honest and you're done. You walk away whole. If he doesn't, then it's real, and that honesty will begin an amazing relationship. I know it." She paused and leaned back next to me.

"You can't spend your life hiding, Sam—not in books, not in work, and not from love. This isn't you. You're the most courageous woman I know. You *must* fix this."

"Do I call him? Write him?"

"Are you kidding me? Sam, you can't be this clueless!"

"I am." I sniffled more.

"Do I have to do everything? Get me your computer."

"Why?"

"You're taking the first flight to New York. Grab your credit card."

So I'm booked on the 7:35 a.m. flight to LaGuardia tomorrow. I am packed and ready for action.

That's a complete lie. I'm scared witless. But I'm so tired of fear—all forms, all kinds. I want to be free. I want to be Scrooge. I want to lay it all down in one moment and feel joy—weight-less, bubbling joy. I don't want to be first—

That's it, Mr. Knightley! I'm so stupid, so blind. That's how Scrooge did it. He realized that others were more important than he was. Scrooge laid it all down because he didn't need to be first. He finally saw more outside of himself. All those years he hoarded vapor—meaningless security—to protect himself. And he destroyed others in deep and crushing ways. He finally recognized the cost, and that others paid it. Then he saw it clearly . . . And they came first.

I've been so busy protecting myself that I didn't see it. I don't need protecting. I'm safe, aren't I? And even if I weren't—I am not defined by that fear. Just because I like the color yellow doesn't make these walls any more or less yellow. They simply are yellow. And I'm still standing. I don't need Alex to tell me that. I don't need running to show me that. Others don't need to pay the price as I push and pull to simply confirm what is. I'm okay.

Maybe that's the first step to surrender. Maybe that's my first step toward the joy the Muirs talk about all the time. Self-protection keeps you from love, Mr. Knightley—all love. I am so sad at how I've kept them at a distance—the Muirs,

Alex, Father John, Kyle, Hannah . . . anyone and everyone who has ever stood by me. I played God in our relationships. I determined their value and their worth by how much I let them in, by how much I let them determine my worth. I'm not God. And I don't need to work so hard any-more . . .

I love Alex—plain and simple. I love Alex, and I want him to come before me. I don't care what it costs. Giving him the truth and fixing the hurts I've caused is more important than anything I think, feel, own, expect . . . No matter what happens between us, I can free us from these lies. I can be honest.

So, Mr. Knightley, here is the part where I need you. I figured this one out before I realized all this other stuff—and it still feels right, so I'm going to press on.

We need to meet. We need to meet so I can say thank you and good-bye. Ashley talked about my "hiding places" this morning. You're one of them. I found sanctuary in these letters, but no more. If I'm going to truly love my new parents, my new friends, and especially Alex, I need to be real. I need to be present.

I want to do this properly, though. I want to be brave and show you the respect you deserve. I want to thank you in person. Father John gave me your foundation's e-mail for this letter. It was like squeezing a state secret out of him, but you need this tomorrow. And it doesn't violate our agree-ment, Mr. Knightley. That ended with graduation. I am asking you to do this as a friend, as someone I have come to trust and rely upon. So please, Mr. Knightley, e-mail me when and where we can meet. Please let me say good-bye properly.

And, Mr. Knightley, forget my theory about Icarus. If you don't sail high, with the risk of crashing and burning, do you really live? Can you love? I doubt it. I'm ready to fly.

Love,
Sam

~ New York

Sam stepped out of the cab. New York Presbyterian Hospital loomed in front of her, darkened by shadow. The street was packed and noisy, but she heard nothing. She couldn't drag her eyes from the building. With all the people bustling in and out, only two men mattered—two men in all of New York. First Alex. Then Mr. Knightley. She pulled her phone out of her pocket. No e-mail.

Start with Alex. One step at a time.

The noise of the cab pulling away penetrated her fog.

I can do this. Just be honest.

"Ms. Moore?"

"Yes?" Sam turned toward the door, searching.

A petite woman stepped forward from under the awning. She had straight blond hair, cut neatly below the chin, and looked chic in her black slacks and crisp black wool coat. She smiled and stretched out her hand. "I'm Laura Temper. Mr. Knightley asked me to meet you and escort you upstairs."

"He's *here?*" Sam put her hand to her throat.

"Yes."

"Oh . . . I . . ." She shook her head and pulled her shoulders back in an effort to gain courage. "I'm pleased to meet you, Laura. Thank you for all you've done for me these past couple years." Sam thrust out her hand, willing her voice to sound approachable and friendly. But she couldn't separate her mind from her mission. "Did he . . . ? Did Mr. Knightley show you my letters?"

"He did not." Laura turned and gestured toward the revolving door. "Shall we?"

Sam followed.

The older woman's heels made staccato taps on the stone floor. She offered no conversation, and Sam's thoughts skittered in cadence with the *click, click, click.*

Did Mr. Knightley meet Alex? What's been said? I feel sick. I should've eaten . . .

The ride to the sixth floor was over too quickly. The elevator opened onto a small lobby, and straight ahead Sam saw the Muirs standing in close, tense conversation. The professor was visibly upset.

"Darling!" Frances noticed her first. She pulled Sam into a tight hug. "I texted you earlier that Alex is going to be fine. Why are you so pale?"

"Where is he?"

"Room 607, about five doors down on the right." She moved her hands to Sam's cheeks, forcing her to focus. "He's fine, Sam. Breathe."

Sam let out the breath she'd been holding and offered a small, flat smile. "Forgot about that."

"It helps, dear. Now go see Alex." She turned

to Laura. "Thanks for waiting for her, Laura."

Sam turned back, startled. "Wait—you know each other? How?"

No one spoke, but Frances nodded.

"Then . . . have you met Mr. Knightley? Is he with Alex?"

Frances paused and glanced at her husband. "He's in there too."

Sam didn't hear another word as she walked away. The hall tunneled before her eyes, its edges blurring. *It doesn't matter that they've met. It changes nothing.* She reminded herself of all she'd laid down and how far she'd come. *Stay focused.*

She stopped outside Room 607. Now was the time for courage and conviction—not fear. She rounded the corner, and tears sprang to her eyes. Alex lay in a hospital bed, attached to more tubes and monitors than she could count. He was propped up on pillows, with purple and blue bruises across his face, pain etched in his eyes, and deeper lines across and around his mouth than she remembered. But he was awake—awake and staring straight at her.

"You're here." He smiled and grimaced with the effort.

Sam hesitated and looked around the room. "You're alone?"

"I am."

"But Mom said Mr. Knightley was in here."

"I know."

"Know what? You know him?"

Alex scooted over in his bed, stifling a wince, and patted the empty spot next to him. "Come sit, Sam." He held out his hand.

Sam looked around the room, perplexed. "Alex?"

"I'm so sorry. I'm scared."

"Why? Why are you scared?" Her heart shifted and broke the tiniest bit. Alex's feelings meant more than her fears. Wasn't that what this journey was about? She sat gently and reached over to brush a tear from the corner of his eye.

"I never meant to hurt you." His voice was barely a whisper.

"You didn't. I hurt you."

Alex closed his eyes. "No, you didn't. I always knew. You unfolded your heart in every letter . . ." He hesitated. "Every letter to me."

"To . . . you?"

"Forgive me . . . ," Alex whispered. He opened his eyes and stared at her with such longing that for a moment Sam lost herself in the confusion. Only for a heartbeat—

"You?" She recoiled, and before she knew it she was across the room. The hit came to her heart, not her head—it couldn't be true.

"Sam, come back."

She swiped at her eyes. "This whole time? Mr. Knightley?" The truth settled, full of details and emotions—full of the letters she had written.

"Alex?" Her voice broke, and the tears started.

"Don't cry, Sam. Please. Come sit down. I can't reach you over there."

She covered her face with her hands and stepped backward until she bumped the wall. She held one last thread of hope—it couldn't be true.

"No, this way . . ."

Without removing her hands, Sam stood still.

"Let me explain."

She shook her head, her face still hidden.

"Then listen from right there." Alex cleared his throat. "Grace House solicited my foundation years ago. You started out as just another grant. But when I read your college writing, I wanted to know you. Father John thought you needed to be drawn out, and I thought letters would be a good way to achieve that. I never expected more." Alex delivered the speech all in one breath, then stopped and inhaled.

"But you came to campus. I slammed into you." Her voice sounded sharp in her own ears. She moved her hands down—just enough to see him over her fingertips.

"You did." Alex smiled softly. "You barreled out of that lecture hall and into my life. I came to campus to catch a glimpse of you, not to meet you." He paused. "I didn't plan it. You could say 'I was in the middle before I knew I had begun.' "

"Not funny. Quoting Darcy will not get you out of this. First that proposal and now this . . . You asked me to marry you. Was I going to stumble across my letters someday? How long were you going to let me write? Forever? Were you—"

"Sam, stop. I wanted to tell you. I was going to, I promise."

"But you didn't. Not until I pushed you into meeting me. Not until . . . you read my lette—in the e-mail! How could you do this to me?" She fluttered her hands, trying to encompass the enormity of the pain and exposure.

Alex leaned forward and stretched out his hand. "I'm sorry I didn't tell you. I tried so many times, and I tried not to cross that line. To keep a distance until you knew the truth. I screwed up."

"You crossed that line every day. With every letter. Kyle, you know about Kyle . . . my appendix, my classes . . . why I run . . . my parents, Josh . . . you know all about him." Sam gasped. "You're another Josh."

"Don't say that. I love you. Every bit of you. I'm not a Josh." Alex's voice became hoarse and raspy. "Please forgive me."

"I . . . I can't. You're not who I thought you were." Sam dropped her hands and watched Alex's eyes travel with them. His gaze rested on her fists, clenched at her sides. Neither spoke. And then she did the only thing she could—she turned and walked out the door.

As she rounded the corner, she heard Alex gulp in a wrecked breath. It sounded like a sob, but she refused to consider it. She reached the hall before her legs gave way, and she grabbed the wall for support. She looked toward the lobby and remembered the Muirs waited there. She couldn't handle their questions. Not now. She slid down the wall and held her head in her hands. *How could he?*

Her legs ached. Eventually the thoughts stopped firing and only a soft gray color remained in her mind. She slid further down and sat, truly believing she could rest there and never move again. She closed her eyes and knocked the back of her head against the wall. The thump felt good.

She felt someone sit next to her, but she didn't open her eyes.

"I thought I'd find you out here." The professor. Dad.

"You know?"

"He told us everything last night. I've never been so angry in my life. I don't know what he was thinking. The cowardice, the deceit . . ."

"I can't forgive him."

"You don't have to. You can walk away."

"Walk away?" Sam's eyes popped open.

"You trusted Mr. Knightley. Alex betrayed that trust. He played false." The anger in his voice startled her. She knew how deeply he loved Alex.

Sam closed her eyes and imagined life without Alex, and then she pictured Alex's life without the Muirs. She saw herself walking away. *No Alex*. Then her heart squeezed tight. *No Alex? And the Muirs?* Life without the Muirs would kill him. Was that what she wanted to do to him?

The professor cut through her thoughts. "I guarantee this whole thing terrified Alex. What a mess. I haven't seen him so invested, not even in—"

"He was scared, Dad. You said it yourself, and even I see that." Sam thumped her head against the wall again, letting weariness wash over her.

"That doesn't excuse him."

"It doesn't, but *you* can't walk away."

"I won't," the professor whispered and bumped her shoulder.

She opened her eyes to find him watching her.

"I love him like he's my own son." He paused and bumped her shoulder again. "But you *are* my daughter, dear Samantha, and I stand with you. I will do whatever is needed to protect you. You can walk away and never see Alex again if that is your wish."

Sam felt a single tear fall as she absorbed the depth of his commitment and love for her. She sat for a moment. "I don't know."

He smiled, soft and knowing. "What don't you know?"

"Part of me wants to walk. I'll admit it." Sam

swiped at fresh tears. "But, Dad, that's not who I want to be, always running away. This summer meant more than that. Alex and I . . . we became friends. No, we were more than that. We understood each other. I let him in, Dad." Sam paused. "I thought when he walked away this fall that I'd misunderstood, but I hadn't."

The professor took her hand and squeezed it, but he said nothing.

"But now it's all wrong. Was I a game to him?" Sam's voice cracked.

"No, darling, no. You musn't think that." The professor nudged his arm around her and held her tight. "It wasn't a game at all. From what Alex told us last night, you mean everything to him. Besides, he's never been good at games." He chuckled lightly. "Think about this . . . remember when you asked us not to tell Alex about your past?"

Sam nodded.

"We never did. But he's known all along, and rather than go away, he pressed closer." He paused and let his words sink in. "He did it all wrong, Sam. We both know that, but it wasn't a game. As you just said, the boy was scared. Can you understand fear like that?"

"What do I do?"

"That's between you and Alex . . . but I agree with your instincts. Don't run away. Walk away, if that's what you decide, after all is said and done, but wait for that moment. You'll feel it when it comes and then, perhaps, you can leave with no regrets." He sighed and shifted his weight. "My dear, my knees are killing me. Help me stand?"

Sam smiled and pulled him up, and he tugged her into a deep hug.

"You're known and loved, my dear girl. You always were."

Sam nodded and held on tight. His words sifted deep within her. She was known and loved and had been all along . . . by Alex too. He had seen her heart from the beginning, and rather than walk away—Alex sought her, pursued her, and fell in love with her. Her heart softened.

Then she recalled how he went about it . . .

She felt her jaw grow tight and noticed the professor watching her. He chuckled.

"I'm going to find your mother. She's a nervous wreck. But I think you have some talking to do here." He nodded toward Alex's door and walked down the hall.

Sam looked through the doorway. Alex held his fists pushed into his eyes and his chest rose in an exaggerated fashion, as if he too was finding it difficult to draw air. Sam remembered his words—*I let people down, then run like a coward before it hits the fan*—and Ashley's indictment from the day before—*You rejected him so he couldn't hurt you. You had to be the last one standing. All alone.*

So much mess, so much pain—the professor was right. There was talking to do.

Sam stepped into the room. "How many ribs are broken?"

"I thought you'd left. I thought you hated me . . . What?"

"What's broken? What hurts?"

"Three ribs, they took my spleen . . . I don't know. Why?"

"I want you to hurt really badly right now . . . Because you've hurt me. You need to share in that."

"I can't hurt any worse." Alex studied her. "But I won't run, Sam. No matter what, I'll take it. I'll stick."

"Don't do that."

"What?"

"I wrote that to Mr. Knightley . . . You don't get to use my words. They weren't meant for you . . . Look what you've done, Alex. You've messed this all up." She took one step forward. "I'm mad . . . so mad I can't see straight. But you know that because you know exactly how I think, how I feel things—because I've armed you. I gave all that to Mr. Knightley, and now you've got it."

She paused to organize her feelings. It felt crucial to say how she felt, not to hide, but to stand. "I'm angry, and worse, I'm hurt. I feel betrayed."

"I know, and you're right." Alex looked out the window. "I should've written you back last year. Remember when you asked? Right after your time with Kyle?"

Sam cringed.

"I could've ended this. I was a coward. We both know that. But you needed Mr. Knightley. I couldn't take him from you. I wanted you to need me."

"You never gave me the choice."

"If I could take it back, I would. You must know that . . . I know you said I can't quote Mr. Darcy, but that is exactly how it was for me. 'I cannot fix on the hour, or the spot, or the look, or the words, which laid the foundation. It is too long ago. I was in the middle before I knew I had begun.' And that's how it felt, Sam. I can't recall a moment in which I didn't love you. But I made a mistake. I thought I could walk that line and know you as both Knightley and me—we could remain separate. And then it was too late.

"It happened so fast. You were at the Muirs' for dinner. And then you were in my life and they kept talking about you, keeping you in front of me. And your letters . . . I am so sorry. I never should have come to Chicago. I should've stayed away, but I wanted to be near you. I wanted you to feel the same—about me. But I was too scared.

Too scared to tell you the truth. Too scared to lose you. And now . . ."

Alex reached toward her, and Sam involuntarily took a step forward. She caught herself and stopped.

Tears gathered in Alex's eyes and ran down his cheeks. "Forgive me, Sam. Deep down, please know I'd rather die than hurt you. Please . . ."

"Stop, Alex. Stop crying." Despite the pain, Sam realized she felt strong. She felt whole. She also remembered why she had come—to put Alex first. Had that changed?

"Please give me another chance." The vulnerability in his voice and the softening in her heart brought her another step forward. "I'm in this for keeps. Whatever it takes to make this right, to make you stay, to make you safe. Just don't leave. We belong together."

"I don't know who *we* are," Sam whispered.

"We're Alex and Sam. And we're a mess. That's partly why we're so perfect for each other." Their eyes caught, and Alex smiled. "How else can two such dysfunctional people fall in love?"

Sam laughed through her tears. There was truth in his statement. "I never said I loved you."

Alex quirked his eyebrow.

"Fine. I told Mr. Knightley, you jerk." She let out an exasperated sigh.

"Come here." Alex patted the bed next to him. "Why?"

"I can't reach you over there."

"That's awfully close."

"I'm not the enemy." Alex's broader smile compelled her to take the last few steps. She sat on the edge of his bed and stared at her lap. She saw his hand reach as if to touch her fingers, then it withdrew.

"I want us to get to know each other. No more lies and no more letters." He reached for her fingers. "All I want is to be with you—completely, passionately, and forever." Alex moved one hand up to her face and brushed a tear resting under her eye, but he didn't let her go. "We can't start over, and I don't want to. All of this is a part of us. Good, bad, and ugly, Sam, this is our story."

"Don't put it in a book."

Alex laughed softly. "I promise. But I want to hear about everything from you, as me. I want to meet Kyle, and Father John, and Ashley."

"You want it all, don't you?" Sam's voice wavered.

"Yes. I want all of you, and I'll work every day to earn your trust and your forgiveness."

They sat in silence and, after a few moments, she felt peace steal over her.

"I'd like to go running."

"I wish I could join you. Ten miles and we could work this out."

"It'd only take six."

"What do you mean?" The hope dancing in Alex's voice made Sam smile.

"I mean I can forgive you . . . and I do, Alex. Part of me understands all this. I hid for years, and I hurt people. But now I don't know how to let go of this feeling, this hurt. Six miles and I could sort it out. But on my own . . . here . . . ?" She glanced around the room, fluttering her hands.

Alex sighed. "You're not on your own." He grasped her hands and pulled her closer. "I'm right here." He paused, then whispered, "May I kiss you?"

"Why?"

"Because I love you." As she nodded, Alex moved his hands to the sides of her face and gently pulled her toward him. He kissed her softly, with reverence. "Forever, Sam. I'll love you forever."

Sam bit her bottom lip. Questioning the kiss? Savoring it? Maybe both. She felt her eyes drift shut. *I'm okay. I feel . . . I feel . . . joy.* The lightness surprised her. It wasn't nearly as difficult as she imagined it to be. She could breathe. Alex caught her expression.

"What?"

"I love you too, Alex."

Alex smiled and pulled her across his chest, stifling a small gasp of pain. Undeterred, he settled her there and she fit perfectly. He kissed her again, this time unable to keep his love and his passion quite so contained.

A thought drifted through Sam's head . . . *Only daring to hope for a little respite of suffering;—she was now in an exquisite flutter of happiness* . . . and she smiled. Finally, she knew what it felt like to be Emma.

Moments passed before Alex held Sam a few inches away, unwilling to let her go any farther. "What did that kiss say?" he whispered.

Sam almost reacted, but the softness in his voice stopped her. He wanted to know. And while she suspected this was going to be a twist to the game they played, it felt too soon, too raw. "You're quoting my letters again."

"I'm sorry." Alex hesitated. "I just want you to know how much I . . ."

"It said nothing." Sam watched his face drop, and relished the new and exciting—and flirtatious—power she held. Power, she conceded, that shouldn't be abused. "It was a 'completely, perfectly, and incandescently happy' moment," she said.

"Ah . . . you're cheating. That was from the movie, my darling Mrs. Darcy."

"Yes, it was." This time Sam reached for Alex.

~ Reading Group Guide

1. Sam found a safe haven in her books, but Hannah accused Sam of hiding in her books. Knowing Sam's past, her retreat may seem justified. What do you think? Do you ever hide? Are there places you naturally gravitate toward when you feel afraid, hurt, or vulnerable?

2. Father John believed that the best thing for Sam would be to find her way around the "real world and its people." Do you agree?

3. Did Father John take away Sam's right to choose by selecting journalism for her graduate studies? Was it her right to choose or was it a gift to accept or reject as offered?

4. How hard is it to recognize a "Josh"—a Wickham, a Willoughby, a Henry Crawford? Why do we let these real-life characters impose on us? Injure us? Is there a difference in the two?

5. Sam said that Kyle would need "more courage to learn to surrender" than he'd needed to survive his abusive childhood or

write about it. What does *surrender* mean? Do you agree with Sam?

6. Alex told Sam that he doesn't like to disappoint people. Is that a failing or a virtue? How would Alex answer?

7. Sam wrote that the Muirs dropped "hope and hints like bread crumbs" regarding their faith. What does that mean? Do you think this was the right approach for the Muirs to take to introduce love and Christ to Sam? Could Sam have heard or understood a more overt approach? What stands in your way when hearing and absorbing such messages?

8. Was Mr. Knightley right to continue in his anonymity? If not, at what point did it go too far? Is it justifiable to withhold the truth from someone when you believe it's in that person's best interest?

9. Sam stated that Austen was brilliant partly because she so accurately reflected human nature and "human nature doesn't change." Do you believe that? Can our natures change? If so, what might change them?

10. So many characters change in this story: Sam, Alex, Kyle, Ashley. This suggests the notion

that we are all constantly changing, defining, and redefining ourselves. Do you believe that? If so, at what point, does it end?

11. At the end of the story, the professor told Sam she could walk away, that she had the right. Did his advice surprise you? Why? Why did he give her that advice? Was he unfair toward Alex?

12. In the beginning of the story, Sam declared that she does not forgive but in the end she forgave Alex. What changed for her? What barriers to forgiveness do you struggle with?

~ Q & A WITH KATHERINE REAY

Are there many similarities between you and Sam?

That's a tough one because I think so many struggles are universal. I hoped to show an aspect of that through Ashley and Sam's friendship. I can certainly relate to feelings of uncertainty, insecurity, and the search for what I believe and to whom I belong. That said, Sam and I do not share a similar history and any mistakes in the logistics of her childhood are my own. I spoke to so many people and read quite a lot, but I know there is much I couldn't capture.

Is there anything autobiographical in the story?

Very little, but I did attend Northwestern and I have run a marathon—and I earned my black belt in tae kwon do a few years ago. Hmm . . . I may have to redefine "very little." There is another incident that cracks me up: The scene when Sam corrects Alex and Professor Muir on their Shakespeare is from my life. I am sure many of you recall a similar moment in the wonderful 1995 movie *Clueless* but, as my husband can attest, it happened to me first—on the night I met my future in-laws. I was so nervous that I said nothing until I opened my mouth and set their *Othello* straight. Humiliated, I then closed my mouth for the rest of the evening.

What was your inspiration for writing Sam's story?

In 2009, I was seriously injured and, while most people receive flowers in the hospital, my friends brought me books. I left my three-day stay with over thirty titles—and a bit of time on my hands for recovery. Yet, despite all these new stories, I wanted to spend time with old favorites, including *Daddy Long Legs* by Jean Webster. The idea grew from there. As for Sam's hiding behind characters, I do not do that, but I have been known to belt out song lyrics when someone conversationally uses a phrase. It's highly embarrassing for my kids, but don't let them fool you . . . They do it too.

What is the story behind Sam's faith? You bring many themes into the book, primarily forgiveness.

Forgiveness is paramount. We can think of it writ large in terms of our relationship with God and Christ or more tangibly in terms of our daily interactions with friends, family, and ourselves. It's an ever-developing aspect of our faith and I did not feel led to finish Sam's journey in this regard. She forgave Alex, but there is still much more for her to lay down. Great people surround her though, so I'm not worried.

I mentioned that the book came from a time of recovery. It also came from a wonderful time of prayer. And while I wouldn't want to be in such physical pain again, I feel blessed that it happened because of all I learned from it and all that came from that entire experience—including this story and the extraordinary opportunity to write another.

What's next?

Right now I am working on a manuscript with another fascinating young woman. She is bold and possesses a sharp sense of humor, which was not available to Sam. I loved writing Sam's story and I'm thoroughly enjoying this one as well. The process is very different because there were no expectations while I wrote *Dear Mr. Knightley*. I hoped people would someday read and love it, but I certainly had no guarantee it would make it off my computer. That's been a gift for me. But this next story has a deadline and, if someone liked *Dear Mr. Knightley* and honors me by picking up the next book, I want to give them my very best.

~ Sam's Reading List

If asked about her favorite books, Sam would reply "all Jane Austen." She loved Austen's "safe, ordered, and confined" world. Granted, Austen heroines might dispute Sam's assertion: Charlotte Lucas certainly didn't feel safe—otherwise she would have passed by Mr. Collins without a second thought. But everything is relative . . .

Pride and Prejudice: Who wouldn't want to embody the indomitable Elizabeth Bennet with her quick wit and "fine eyes"? And who doesn't love beautiful, demure Jane Bennet? And Lydia? It is perhaps not prudent to follow in her steps, but such obtuse, brash boldness is probably fun on occasion. One can readily understand Sam's longing to spend time within the Bennet family.

Emma: Sam hardly dared to dream of what life might be like in Emma's warm bubble of adoration and love. Certainly many other Highbury residents didn't feel so secure. In fact, most didn't. But Emma? She "cannot really change for the better."

Sense and Sensibility: Austen's most obvious juxtaposition of two opposite ways of thinking, feeling, and living. Thankfully,

Sam grew right alongside Elinor and Marianne. And, after fleeing Josh, she too gravitated to a nicely moderate center.

Alongside Jane Austen, Sam would place *Jane Eyre* as a dear favorite. And how could these two *not* be fast friends? Yet, in Jane, Sam found more than a friend. She found the guide she desperately needed. Sure, Miss Eyre got swept away for a moment—and what a scene it is!—but on the whole she was a young woman with her feet firmly planted on the ground.

Sam also adored Edmond Dantes in *The Count of Monte Cristo*. His is the story of a young man robbed of everything of meaning—by his best friend no less—and left to die in a horrid prison. But wait. He escapes, he finds a treasure beyond measure, he devises a ruthless, elegant, and sophisticated plan for revenge . . . So satisfying. It's easy to see why Sam found him appealing. But thank you, Dumas, for underpinning your adventure with strong threads of faith, hope, reconciliation, and forgiveness. Sam needed those too.

There are so many others, but I'll just run through a few, otherwise we could be here for pages.

The Scarlet Pimpernel by Baroness Orczy: It's easy for anyone to delight in Percy

Blakeney, the true master of disguise and a dashingly handsome hero.

Anne of Green Gables by L. M. Montgomery: If you're an orphan, Anne is a good friend. She's spunky, fun, ready to get you into mischief, and determined to keep you safe on Prince Edward Island. However, Anne always wanted to be a writer and poor Sam would be horrified if she knew you'd read her letters.

A Christmas Carol by Charles Dickens: I don't think Sam set out to love Ebenezer Scrooge, but I think she now considers him a dear friend. Alex certainly does and thanks Dickens for his tale.

North and South by Elizabeth Gaskell: Margaret Hale and John Thornton are a couple different in every way but so clearly meant to be together. Sam says it was the "one last go at all that matters" that appealed to her; I think it was John Thornton.

Sam started with *The Voyage of the Dawn Treader* by C. S. Lewis but is now working her way through *The Chronicles of Narnia*. She can't read them fast enough. Peter, Susan, Edmund, and Lucy enthrall her, but Eustace will always be most near and dear to her heart—as will the glorious lion, Aslan, who saved him.

And I must add . . . Please never let Sam know

her letters were published. She may have a psychotic break like poor Miss Havisham from *Great Expectations* and we will find her seeking solace in her banquet of books forever . . .

Thank you . . .

KBR

~ ACKNOWLEDGMENTS

A friend once called God's love "extravagant." I've always loved that description—and if I ever forget, I will look back at this book, this journey, and all the people who came along beside me . . . and I will remember.

First I owe a debt of gratitude to Austen, Brontë, Webster, Dickens, Dumas . . . The list goes on. This is a book about loving books, and they wrote some of the best. Their words and worlds gave Sam—and give all of us—safe places to grow.

Then, I want to thank Lee Hough, who believed in this story from moment one and has guided me as both a friend and a mentor.

I stand amazed at the skill, poise, dedication, and acumen displayed daily by Daisy Hutton, Becky Monds, Katie Bond, and Ruthie Dean—I thank you, trust you, and cannot imagine a better home. Natalie Hanemann, LB Norton, and Jodi Hughes—thank you for your wonderful editing. Kristen Vasgaard, I'm still in love with this beautiful cover . . . And to the Sales Team—thank you for getting this book out into the world. There are many others at Thomas Nelson who have contributed to this endeavor—I sincerely thank you all.

I also want to acknowledge Sandra Byrd,

Linda Kokemor, Suzie Townsend, and Bob Haslam for your insights and time. Without you and many others, who helped push the story and me forward, it would still be only in my heart and on my computer.

Closer to home—Thanks, Team Reay. Mason, you never doubted for a moment, even when all the great ideas seemed to come from your brain, not mine. And Elizabeth, my sister, your never-ending enthusiasm and willingness to read each of my many drafts keeps me smiling. My "sisters" in Austin—thank you for making the miles seem negligible. And, Pam, I hope the story—especially that one character—makes you laugh. I love you all.

And . . . Thanks so much to *you* for reading *Dear Mr. Knightley*!

~ ABOUT THE AUTHOR

Katherine Reay has enjoyed a lifelong affair with the works of Jane Austen and her contemporaries. After earning degrees in history and marketing from Northwestern University, she worked in not-for-profit development before returning to school to earn her MTS. Her writing has been published in *Focus on the Family* and *The Upper Room*. Katherine currently lives with her husband and three children in Seattle. *Dear Mr. Knightley* is her first novel.

Center Point Large Print
600 Brooks Road / PO Box 1
Thorndike ME 04986-0001 USA

(207) 568-3717

US & Canada:
1 800 929-9108
www.centerpointlargeprint.com